# BLIND TRUST

By Adam Zorzi

Limitless Publishing, LLC
Kailua, HI 96734
www.limitlesspublishing.com

Formatting: Limitless Publishing

ISBN-13: 978-1-64034-048-0
ISBN-10: 1-64034-048-3

# Dedication

*Ai fantasmi di Richmond*

# CHAPTER ONE

**March**

"One patient was killed and more than a half dozen suffered smoke inhalation injuries when a two-alarm fire broke out at Commonwealth Psychiatric Hospital in Petersburg, Virginia early this morning. The fire, which started at approximately four o'clock, was confined to one section of the main hospital ward. No statements from the Petersburg Fire Chief or the Virginia Department of Behavioral Health and Developmental Services, which oversees Commonwealth Psychiatric Hospital, have been made.

"However, in an exclusive interview with a staff member who asked not to be identified, this station has learned that the fire started in a patient's room. The patient has not been identified, but the staff member indicated that a male had been restrained and placed in seclusion due to his multiple violent outbursts as well as his threats to harm staff and other patients."

LouLou recognized the TV reporter as the guy who'd interviewed her about her latest album. Music and fires. What a beat. He obviously couldn't access the hospital grounds, so he stood at the gated entrance with a 3D map projected on the TV screen.

"As you can see, the hospital is a sprawling campus. The forensic hospital, which is the only one in the state, is housed in a secure freestanding building. It's where defendants who are awaiting competency hearings reside along with all of Virginia's violent persons found Not Guilty by Reason of Insanity, or NGRI."

Mug shots of patients who had spent time there scrolled across the screen while the reporter continued. "The most famous patient was Lorena Bobbitt, who cut off her cheating husband's penis while he slept. The newest resident is a thirty-year-old woman and mother of two children who shot and killed her Iraq war veteran husband when he came home from work as a civilian computer programmer.

"Commonwealth Psychiatric Hospital has come under increased scrutiny by mental health advocates. I interviewed advocate Marion Navarro of the Virginians for Better Mental Health Society, who told me any patient in seclusion is required by law to be under twenty-four-hour surveillance. She questioned how a restrained patient could acquire material to light a fire while in seclusion or start a fire without immediate intervention if he'd been under the required surveillance. She also told this reporter that state Reductions in Force had eliminated more than twenty-seven percent of clinical jobs at the hospital over the past two years. The jobs lost were in security and nursing."

Footage of a woman in a white beret and black parka speaking at a rally outside the Virginia House of Representatives rolled. The woman said, "Cuts at Commonwealth Psychiatric Hospital are a disgrace. What do our legislators have to say? That jobs have been added to the hospital. That's right. The hospital hired people in high paying computer and administrative positions at the expense of those caring for patients. Clearly, the state cares more about paper pushers than people." Loud applause cut off the rest of her remarks.

In one quick cut, the reporter's face again filled the screen. "As most of our viewers know, Commonwealth Psychiatric Hospital, formerly known as Commonwealth Lunatic Asylum, was established in 1869 as an institution for African-Americans of unsound mind. It was opened to all races in 1967. The hospital has a long history of suspected hauntings and paranormal sightings. The oldest section of the hospital is on the National Register of Historic Places.

Back to you..."

***

LouLou knew about the fire before she saw the news. She'd spent the night in Petersburg with a fireman called to the scene.

"Gotta go." The guy shook her awake. He hustled to pull on his clothes and get out of the apartment. "Two alarm at Commonwealth Psychiatric."

LouLou sat up. Braced on her elbows, she asked, "Can I stay here?" She didn't want to haul herself to a new place or sleep in her car for what was left of the night.

He looked at her for a split second and said, "Yeah. Make sure you lock the door behind you. Be out by ten." He left.

LouLou slid back under the sheet and scratchy blanket, rolled herself in the middle of the lumpy double bed hoping to find a comfortable position, and exhaled. She was grateful he'd decided she didn't look like she'd take off with the family jewels and could stay.

Not that there was much here. It looked like what it was—a furnished apartment in a community known as a refuge for the newly separated, divorced, and displaced. She hadn't seen a single personal item beyond a toothbrush between the front door and bedroom. His most valuable possession was probably the remote to the flat screen TV hanging on the living room wall. Even that was rented as part of the furnishings.

He was right to be skeptical. He couldn't know she wasn't the type to root around the drawers and cabinets after a one-night stand in search of cash, evidence of other women, or his cell phone number. LouLou wanted a place to crash after her DJ gig, then to shower and dress in fresh clothes before getting back on the road to Richmond.

She closed her eyes. Sleep would elude her. He'd left the fire department scanner on, so she heard the details as they emerged through dawn. A patient in seclusion burned to death in bed. Such unimaginable horror made her shake. She curled on her side and tightly wrapped the blanket around herself. She rocked back and forth. Back and forth. The motion soothed her. She was safe.

Patients at the state's only psychiatric hospital weren't safe. Security monitoring hadn't helped that poor guy who'd burned to death in bed. Surely, this was an isolated incident. Nothing like that had ever happened when she'd been a patient. She had to stay vigilant about taking her meds. She couldn't go back there. She wouldn't survive another stay.

# CHAPTER TWO

LouLou smiled as she pulled into the parking lot beside her loft building. Home. There was Roy with his bald head, dressed neatly in a white shirt, black pants, and a crisp white apron that hid the paunch on his otherwise slim frame, standing on the sidewalk waiting for her. He and his wife Sara owned the deli/patisserie/bodega where LouLou ate most of her meals. They watched over her as though she were their oldest daughter even though they weren't that much older than her. LouLou hadn't told him what time she'd be home so he'd probably been pacing the sidewalk this morning on the lookout for her since just before six o'clock, when the deli opened. He'd either left Sara or Caesar, his assistant manager, in charge while he'd waited for her.

LouLou had barely turned off the ignition and stepped out of the car before he was beside her. "Welcome back to the world's greatest DJ. Here, let me give you a hand," Roy said as he grabbed her duffel bag and tote from the back of her black compact Honda SUV. "You look and smell like hell, no disrespect."

"Does that mean no hug?"

Roy softly kissed her cheek. "The hug can wait."

"Whew, that was a long tour. Hot. I'd no idea temperatures reached the eighties north of Florida in January and February." She carefully stacked equipment cases in an order known only to her and strapped them on a wheelie. No one touched her gear.

Roy moved ahead to her building, held the door open for her, and rang for the industrial elevator. LouLou quickly caught up.

"Roy, don't send your kids to college in the south," LouLou advised during the short ride. "Way too much partying. I expected twenty-somethings at my shows, but I had a lot of college kids, even in the middle of the week. Most of my sets didn't start before ten o'clock. Those kids should've been studying in their dorms or sleeping. I didn't party during college."

"LouLou, you didn't go to college."

"Did so. Two semesters at Virginia Commonwealth University. Art, music, and dance. There wasn't anything else to take after that." The elevator stopped. Roy opened the gated door and used his key to open the steel door to her loft.

"Right." He nodded. "No point taking anything that might lead to a degree."

LouLou brushed past him with a smile and started to unload the equipment boxes and place the contents into custom-fitted shelves in an alcove in her otherwise undivided loft. The brick wall next to them was filled floor to ceiling with vinyl records.

After putting her cases away, LouLou stood to face him and stretched her back. "How about some breakfast?"

Roy stepped back to appraise her. "Not until you shower, wash your hair, and put on some clean clothes. Breakfast will be waiting for you. Right now, you're bad for business."

She blew him a kiss. "House special? You won't run out of anything?"

"All the sacred ingredients await you." He walked across the gleaming wood floors to the industrial door. "When are you going to get some furniture for this place? Seventy-five hundred square feet of nothing."

"I've got furniture." She pointed to a Steinway ebony concert grand piano, a sleek bed with platform lights and speakers, and a designer, striped sectional sofa that once had been photographed for an interiors magazine in her parents' villa in Ibiza.

"It'd kill you to have a table and chairs?"

She silenced his fretting about furniture by closing the door.

# CHAPTER THREE

Although LouLou had refused her mother's generous offer to decorate the entire loft, the one luxury LouLou had accepted was a snazzy steam shower with a bench seat and multiple jets. She punched the pre-set pad that gently sprayed warm water on her from all angles. Dirt and fatigue sloughed off her body and down the drain. Her hair was matted in a few places and really needed conditioner. She couldn't see with shampoo in her eyes, so she blindly felt along the cool, marble wall for the ledge that held toiletries. The tall curvy bottle felt like her conditioner.

She rinsed her hair, applied conditioner, and hummed while it set. So soothing. She'd decided to skip the shower at last night's accommodations before getting on the road. She was unnerved by the news about the fire at Commonwealth Psych and tired from the drive and being away from home for two months. Who knew whether the guy even had clean towels? This. This was home. She almost nodded off to sleep, she was so relaxed. She forced herself to rinse her hair and cream her body before reluctantly getting out of the shower.

She put on a paisley mini dress and burgundy suede boots and checked herself in the mirror. Pretty good. Her cornflower blue eyes stood out like they belonged to someone else. She was ordinary otherwise. Straight blonde hair, medium height, slim build, JLo ass. She grabbed a stack of vinyl next to her duffel and headed downstairs and around the corner to the deli/patisserie/bodega called Roy's. She and Sara had a bet as to whether Roy would ever determine exactly what his establishment was and tell them what to call it. The bet was still going after five years.

"A new woman," pronounced Roy as he placed a vegetarian omelet, buttery croissant, and a large cup of black coffee with steamed milk in front of her. A bowl of blueberries sat on the side.

She took the first bite, closed her eyes, and swallowed. "This was what kept me going those last miles from Petersburg."

"Virginia State on your tour?"

She shook her head. Her mouth was full. She swallowed, took a deep sip of coffee, and said, "Club. An old friend has an underground blues club in Petersburg. People come from all over. A lot of musicians seek it out after playing Washington, Richmond, or Virginia Beach. Great audience. They understood me. Played a lot of my new stuff and they loved it. Cecil was really supportive. Made me feel like a star."

"Good way to end the tour." He refilled her coffee. "Were you spinning when the fire at the hospital happened?"

She shook her head. "Done by three o'clock. I think the fire was about an hour later. What's the deal?"

"According to TV news, and we know that's iffy, some poor guy in his thirties, tentatively identified as an ex-Marine with PTSD, was restrained and secluded for being too much to handle. Supposedly monitored 24/7. Somehow, he managed to light the bed on fire and being in restraints, couldn't escape. Crisp." Roy shook his head. "Can't believe that goes on in the United States in the twenty-first century."

"Wonder how he managed the fire," LouLou mused. "They're pretty hard core about searching for weapons. Hard to cheek a cigarette and matches or a lighter. One or the other, but not both. I hate to think he didn't intend to smoke. That he intended to set a fire." She shivered again.

Roy and Sara were among the few people who knew LouLou had been a patient at Commonwealth Psychiatric Hospital three times. Diagnosed with schizophrenia in her teens, she got into trouble if she went off her meds.

"Was anybody else hurt?" she asked.

"Not that I saw on TV. Smoke inhalation by a nurse and an aide. Nothing about patients."

"Doesn't mean it didn't happen. I know, I know. I'm a cynic. I'm just wondering about Big. I hope he's okay."

"Big?"

"Obviously, a big, tall guy. He must be there for life. Sweetest guy in the world. Knows everything about that place. Sits in the same corner of a beat-up leather couch in the common room every day. I used to wonder if he had a room. He's there every morning when it opens and every night when it closes. Always wears the same outfit. Jeans, white cotton tee, and red suspenders."

"And he was nice to you? Looked out for you?" Roy probed.

"Always." She looked to her right as if she could see the hospital in the distance.

"That's good enough for me. I hope he wasn't hurt." Roy made two mocha lattes, capped them, and handed them to the delivery guy. "Where are you headed next?"

"I just got back." LouLou laughed. When she did, it sounded like the music inside her. "A month off. Then Tokyo, Beijing, and Bangkok with stops in between. Back here. Fall in Scandinavia."

She sighed and put her elbows on the counter. She turned again in the direction of the hospital. "I never want to go back there."

***

Cloudless blue sky. This was one of those rare days in Richmond's spring when the sun was out, the air was warm, and no precipitation fell. Rain, sleet, and snow were always possibilities in early spring. She walked to her favorite—actually, the only—music store left in the city aptly named Vinyl. Everyone downloaded anything they wanted, but she loved the feel and smell of vinyl. She walked down a flight of steps to the store.

Music history. Album covers that were works of

art. Bright yellows. Moody black and whites. Sensual sepia. Smooth brown or stiff white sleeves that held records so they wouldn't be scratched. Autographed first presses. Liner notes and lyrics. The smell was clean and fresh. No dust or musty odor for these fine records.

"Skylar," she called. "You here?"

The owner, who was in his seventies but never seemed to age, often left the register unattended while he sat in one of the two listening booths, lost in whatever music he'd chosen. Could be anything from Haydn to Lady Gaga, but she knew the blues held his heart.

Robert, the black Siamese-mix cat named for blues legend Robert Lee Johnson, slept on the counter. LouLou kissed the top of Robert's head and rubbed the long body he stretched out for her. He loved massages, and he didn't mind who performed them. When Robert was satisfied, he turned his back to her to indicate she could move along. LouLou walked around the aisles to Skylar's booth and knocked on the door.

"LouLou." Skylar put down his headphones and bounced out to give her a bear-sized hug. "How was the Bodacious Southern Tour?"

She looked at his tanned face, long grizzly hair, and properly trimmed beard His eyes were so bleary she thought he must be stoned all the time.

"Good. No huge audiences, but they were appreciative. Columbia, Wilmington, Durham. A couple of good festivals. Asheville was the best. People seemed to understand my mixes. Beautiful weather except for some surprisingly hot days. I don't think it got below sixty anywhere. I had no idea places could be so balmy in the winter except south Florida. Don't people miss the seasons?"

"The only one they care about is hurricane season." Skylar grimaced. "Any problems?"

"Not really. One night some drunk frat boys in togas tried to crash my booth. Security was right on it. I didn't know frats really did that. I'm for a good time and all, but that just seemed so…"

"Lame?" said a slim man in his thirties who must have been browsing, unnoticed at the back of the store.

She and Skylar exchanged looks. This guy was drop dead handsome. Lean. Sandy brown hair. Friendly brown eyes. A nice smile.

"Lame," she said. "That's exactly the word I was looking for. Thanks. I'm LouLou."

He put out his hand. "Gregg. Nice to meet you, LouLou." The feel of his hand sent waves of calm throughout LouLou's body. His touch made her feel safe.

"I'm Skylar. I own this place. Haven't seen you before. Welcome." Skylar and Gregg shook hands. "My partner Robert's up front."

Gregg motioned around the store. "This is heaven. I've never seen anything like it."

Skylar beamed. This was his child Gregg was talking about. "Look around. I've got some business to handle up front with LouLou."

Usually Skylar danced behind the counter while LouLou opened her bag of treasures she found on her travels. Now, he danced twice as fast with the possibility of new stock and a new customer.

"What've you got?" Skylar asked.

LouLou slowly took records out of her tote. "Some good stuff. Some online sale stuff. One treasure."

Skylar wiggled his fingers, the gesture saying, "Come on. Come on."

She handed him the good stuff—five LPs from Howlin' Wolf, Madonna, Sea Level, The Allman Joys, and Harry Belafonte. Skylar looked at each one as though he might kiss it. LouLou knew the possibility of damaging them prevented him from doing so.

"No smudges," she said. "No scratches. All up to Skylar standards."

She had about ten rarities, but not collectibles, that he would sell online. Herman's Hermits, The Animals, Pink Floyd, and Yoko Ono. He pawed over them, muttering, "Good, good, not bad, good, interesting," while she hid the two prizes behind her back.

"Drum roll, please," she said. "Close your eyes and I'll hold up the first one. Keep them closed. No peeking."

He did as she directed and then opened his eyes again. "Wait. I thought you said you had one. What do you mean the first one?"

"Patience." LouLou scolded. "As you were."

Skylar stood about as a still as a three-year-old waiting for presents on his birthday. LouLou pulled the album from behind her back and held it in front of her at chest level. "Open your eyes."

"Sweet Baby James, it's mint condition The Beatles' *Christmas Album* from 1971. LouLou, this is solid gold. I can't believe it. I can sell it to any one of three regulars right now. Bless you."

"I have one more," she reminded him.

"Oh, this is enough, LouLou. This makes my year."

"Should I hold onto it then?" she teased. "It can wait. It's been around for fifty years. What's another decade?"

"Ah, LouLou, don't tease an old guy. It's not healthy for me."

"Maybe you should take just a tiny look. Close your eyes and I'll show it to you."

He did. LouLou whipped out the prized album and held it in front of her, touching it only on the sides with her palms. "Open your eyes, Skylar."

With an agility she didn't know he had, Skylar scrambled over the counter, kissed her on the mouth, picked her up and twirled her around until he was dizzy. Robert leapt off the counter in a show of disgust at this unusual display of emotions.

"I've got to sit down, LouLou. You can't do this to me." He put his hands on the counter for support. He closed his eyes while he recalled the stats. "The *Elvis Christmas Album*. Pressed on red vinyl. RCA. 1957. Catalog LOC-1035." He paused to catch his breath. "Red. Vinyl. Cherry Red. This is the stuff I dream about."

"TMI, Skylar."

"I don't know what to say. I…" Skylar was speechless.

"Say you'll take them all, including Cher," said LouLou sternly. Otherwise, she'd cry along with him. She'd never seen him so happy. She'd never seen anyone so happy.

"Yes, yes, I want them all. I'll trade the store for them."

"Nice try, Skylar. I'm looking for Judy Collins and Olivier Messiaen. Maybe Cuban."

Skylar wiped off his glasses with a shirttail and headed to the classical section. He pointed. "Messiaen. Under-rated. What Cuban there is would be in International next to Movie Music." He started toward the back of the store with his treasure. "Browse away," he called as he went into his office.

LouLou could have sworn she heard sobs from him behind his office door. She quickly found what she was looking for and moved on to Judy Collins.

"You really made him happy. How did you do it?" Gregg asked.

She kept her head down as she quickly rifled the stacks. "I do a lot of poking around vintage stores, tag sales, and liquidation stock on my travels. I've got a pretty good idea of what he wants."

"Cool." He hesitated. "I can't believe this store. It's overwhelming. There are tons of Joni Mitchell albums. She's a goddess."

"Please don't say Dylan's a god," LouLou interrupted and looked at Gregg.

"Oh no, he's a nasal, whiny, really bad rapper."

LouLou burst out laughing. "That's the best description I've heard of him. Spot on. I'm not wild about Joni Mitchell, but she writes well. I'm in a Judy Collins groove right now. Ethereal." She kept flipping through the bin until she spied the album she wanted. "Got it."

He kept looking at her, but it didn't make her

uncomfortable. More like he was trying to memorize her features for a painting.

"Happy hunting," she said and turned to leave.

"I'd like to get these records. Do you think he'll be out soon?" he asked. Skylar could be intimidating on a good day. In the throes of ecstasy, he might scare off his new customer.

LouLou winked at Gregg and yelled toward the back of the store, "I'm leaving. Get your butt out here to write up Gregg's sales. Put them on my account."

"Later," she said to Gregg. She hurried out. She knew he was going to ask for her number, and she didn't want that. No way. Why had she winked at him? What a stupid thing to do when she knew she couldn't have him. LouLou could fall for a guy like him. That was something she could never allow herself to do.

# CHAPTER FOUR

Of all seven continents and countless luxury hotels, resorts, and private homes she'd visited, Bella Davis considered Hamilton, Bermuda to be one of her favorite places. There was nothing more soothing than sitting in the courtyard of the old Princess Hotel, resting her bare feet on the stone bulkhead, and watching boats slowly glide through the calm waters of the channel to the port while sipping a Pimm's Cup. Directly across from where she sat was a hillside of British Colonial style houses painted in pastel colors. Her late husband referred to it as a hill of dots—something akin to the artist Rauschenberg's combines. Yellow villas popped amid the pink, sky blue and sea foam houses, all of which had wooden shudders with complementary colors. Bermuda lacked the glamour of the European Riviera and the crowds of Caribbean islands. It was old-fashioned and quiet. Bella liked that. When she wanted solitude, Bella went to Bermuda.

Not that she rested. As a ghost, Bella never tired,

never rested, and never slept. She cleared her mind and thought of nothing. She went to that blank space where she didn't exist for a few hours or days. Doctors would call it a coma, but she could wake herself.

She'd had a difficult two years. Maybe longer. She really didn't follow earthly time all that closely. It wasn't important to her unless she had a specific appointment.

She was staying at the Princess Hotel in one of the rooms that hadn't been renovated. It was small, at the rear side of the hotel, and only had one window that overlooked a small, wooden pier where locals docked two small skiffs. The room soothed her. No one ever entered to clean or even check it. She certainly didn't do anything that would require maid service. She had no need for towels, room service, or fresh bed linens.

Bella remained invisible when she rested her mind. Visibility required concentration. She couldn't help but see other ghosts, including two pirates who couldn't have been more than twelve years-old, but they didn't interact. Occasionally, she mingled with hotel guests or walked the short distance from the hotel to Hamilton's main shopping street. She chose busy days, when cruise ships were in port, to select clothing for her stay and go back after hours to steal them. Anything she hadn't worn, she'd put back before she left. She didn't need much—a swimsuit and cover-up, two sundresses, and sandals. She always needed a purse or tote. As a treat, she snapped up sunglasses in either white or black.

Bella chose clothes that flattered her toned body and skin. She'd died in early September. Her summer tan hadn't faded. She knew she was exceptionally beautiful. Shoulder length blonde hair, enormous iridescent blue eyes, a smile that melted men, and a great body. She was forever thirty-one—not a bad age for a ghost who sometimes sought men to manipulate to advance her plans.

This morning, she sat on the patio overlooking the harbor, pretending to drink coffee while reading the local newspaper. Cricket news was the lead item. She noticed the couple who'd been sitting at the table next to hers had left a copy of *The Washington Post* behind. She picked it up and glanced through the international and national sections. An article in the metro news startled her and caused her to knock over her china coffee cup. It clattered to the brick patio and shattered. Still, she waved the busboy away so she could read.

Fire. There'd been a two-alarm fire at Commonwealth Psychiatric Hospital in Petersburg, Virginia where her beloved Daniel was a patient. The article merely mentioned that the decedent was male. Other people had suffered smoke inhalation. People. What did that mean? Patients? Doctors? Staff? Daniel couldn't have died. She'd have felt him leave this realm.

She read further and then skimmed. Advocacy organization findings. Deplorable conditions, dangerous understaffing, and lack of security. Bella had to leave. She had to make sure Daniel was safe. Her only reason to live as a ghost was to wait for

Daniel to join her for eternity. He could only die on her terms. Bella had to save Daniel from Commonwealth Psychiatric Hospital.

# CHAPTER FIVE

Schizophrenia. That scary word LouLou had first heard when she was sixteen consumed her life. She'd given it the nickname "Sick" in an attempt to separate who she knew to be the real LouLou from who she became and what she did when the disease took over her mind and body. LouLou spent every day battling Sick. She had routines, medications that had to be taken at exactly the right time by mouth or injection, and a memorized list of Dos and Don'ts. With the help of her parents and the specialists they'd found, LouLou had made peace with the fact that her life wouldn't be normal compared to her high school friends. In time, she learned to follow her psychiatrist Dr. Youzny's motto of "What's normal?" His point was everyone had limitations or secrets of some kind.

LouLou's Sick wasn't secret. She and her parents had decided there was no reason to hide it. Her high school classmates knew. She wasn't going to strive for the highest grades, the most honors, or the most active social life. Her passion for music, dance, and art were re-directed from traditional paths. She wasn't going to be a concert pianist or a painter.

Her medications changed as she aged. Some of them were taken on such a strict schedule that even attending classes every day was impossible. She needed rest, if not sleep. Taking breaks throughout the day were mandatory.

As she grew into her twenties, LouLou learned to let her creativity flow in different ways. She painted and drew. She took dance classes of all types for fun, not perfection. She continued to play the piano and practice, but without the determination she once had. Where she once felt competitive, she now felt calm. LouLou found solace in music. When she sat at the piano her mind thought about phrasing, key signatures, and the tens of thousands of notes in just one sonata. She needed to play like she needed Dr. Youzny's meds.

LouLou surprised herself when she'd become a sought-after DJ who had great moves as well as a great ear. She'd started playing parties for fun. She selected the music, switched gears according to the crowd, and danced however she pleased. Gradually, she found herself more and more in demand. Her career just happened, but she maintained it on her terms. As a freelancer, she made her schedule and took time when she needed it. She was as happy as Sick would let her be.

Resting after a two-month tour was necessary. Her trip to Vinyl to drop off Skylar's treasure was the only errand she allowed herself. The first week back from tour, LouLou lounged, read, and took short walks in nearby parks. She wanted to see her parents in Washington, DC, but needed to wait at least ten days before making the drive. In the meantime, she and her parents spoke by phone. She had dinner with Roy, Sara, and their three kids at their home near her loft. When she didn't, Sara brought her healthy meals and stayed to chat. Mostly, LouLou slept. Toward the end of the week, she and Sara went for haircuts, manicures, and pedicures.

After the ninth day, she made it to DC, where she was pampered, cherished, and most of all, loved. Her mother's sleek grey cat Orchid looked at her disdainfully, as though LouLou was of a lesser species. Her dad's mutt Tux loved her and slept at the foot of her bed.

LouLou regaled her parents with the best anecdotes from her tour. They caught her up on news of family and friends. The girl who had been her closest friend in high school before Sick, Quincy Matthews, had been in town for a weekend earlier in the month. LouLou's mom had run into her at a charity luncheon. Quincy was now a partner in the white shoe law firm where she'd started her career.

"Good for her," LouLou said. "She was destined for that. I liked her a lot. I don't blame her for not spending a lot of time with me after Sick. She focused on her grades. She simply had to get into Harvard, and she did."

"She asked about you. I told her about your tour, but I don't think she knew what a DJ/emcee was. She's a nice young woman, but not well-rounded. She sends her regards."

LouLou's mother took her shoe-shopping and out to tea. The night before she left DC, LouLou and her mother sat in a pair of comfortable blue arm chairs in LouLou's room and looked at international fashion magazines. Having lived in Paris until she was fifteen, LouLou loved clothes and trends. She and her mother followed designers' runway shows and were always pleased to find someone new. LouLou turned a page and saw a color-blocked mini-dress that would be perfect for a first date with Gregg. What was she thinking? She'd met the man once. Still, she knew she wanted to see him again.

"Mom, I think I've met someone. Someone who could be special. It scares me."

Her mom took off her glasses and looked at LouLou's face. "What's he like?"

"Cool. Handsome. Interested in music from the 1970s."

Orchid, who must have noticed a magazine-free lap, jumped to sit with LouLou's mom. "He sounds like someone you'd like."

"No, Mom. I mean, I felt an instant connection with him, like two old souls meeting, as sappy as that sounds. It wasn't lust. It was something bigger."

"Where'd you meet him?"

"At Vinyl. I stopped to take some records to Skylar, and this guy named Gregg was there. At first, Skylar was pleased to meet him, but after he saw the cherry red vinyl Elvis Christmas album, Skylar couldn't think of anything else. I think he went in his office and cried, he was so happy. That left me alone with Gregg. Robert was sound asleep on the counter. I talked as little as possible and breezed out of there. I knew if I'd stayed, he'd have asked for my number."

"*Hmm.*" Her mother stroked Orchid. "This was his first time at Vinyl. Was he visiting Richmond? Had he just moved there?"

"I don't know. He was almost as emotional as Skylar. He was awed by the sight of so many albums, especially by Joni Mitchell. I didn't ask him anything personal."

"Joni Mitchell is a good sign." Her mother held up her hand to indicate she didn't want an argument over her musical tastes. "He doesn't like Dylan, does he?"

LouLou shook her head.

"LouLou, he sounds good. What scares you?"

LouLou gave her mother a look that showed she didn't like her mother playing dumb. "Mom, you know I can't have a normal life with a long-term boyfriend. Marriage and children are out of the question. I don't want to hurt him. I don't want to get hurt."

Her mother stood, sending Orchid to the floor, and hugged LouLou, who was still seated. "Sweetheart, being hurt is part of being alive. No one is talking about marriage and children. You've met a nice guy who shares your interest in music. You feel like it could be more than a casual relationship. You're thirty-one years old and never had a real relationship. Maybe it's time. Maybe he's the guy. Don't hold back because you're afraid. You have a mental illness, but you take care of yourself. I don't think you should deny yourself a chance with someone."

"Maybe I should talk to Dr. Youzny."

Her mother's features changed immediately. She looked directly into LouLou's eyes. "LouLou, you can't ask Dr. Youzny for permission to live an interesting life. I know you discuss how to handle certain situations with him, but this is a matter of the heart, not schizophrenia." She cupped LouLou's chin. "This is something for you to decide."

LouLou went to sleep thinking of what her mother had said. By morning, she'd decided to go for Gregg. She packed her small bag. Just before she left, her sweet father slipped her a fifty-dollar bill as he'd been doing since she'd turned eighteen. She'd never spent any of the money. She kept the bills in her white dancing ballerina jewelry box in her loft, lying face up in a smooth stack. "Just in case," her dad always said.

***

Back in Richmond, LouLou hoped she'd see Gregg at Vinyl. He pulled at her the way no one else had. She told herself he was a stranger she'd met for five minutes, but her mind and heart weren't in agreement. Monday afternoon, she put on a black cashmere sweater and black pants and headed to Vinyl.

Skylar greeted her with enthusiasm and a big hug when LouLou walked into Vinyl. "I sold The Beatles' *Christmas Album* the same day you brought it in. Made one guy very happy and two other guys sick. I did a straight auction to be fair. The winner knew exactly how much it was worth and then some. Me, I can retire off the sale." He walked behind the counter and absent- mindedly rubbed Robert's head.

"You're never going to retire, Skylar."

"Never know. Jagger is touring at seventy-one. That makes me dream. I'm a damn good guitar player." He played atrocious air guitar until LouLou begged him to stop.

"Skylar, Uriah Heep's still touring and you know they change band members every other week. Send them a demo." She looked around and saw a few browsers but not Gregg. She leaned on the counter. "What's Gregg's story?"

"He comes in every afternoon about the time you got here last week. Looks around like he hopes you're here. Then he makes selections, goes into the listening booth, and doesn't come out for hours. He's starting to feel like an employee. I confess I bought him some clothes. He looked like he was used to shopping at the Army-Navy surplus store. I like my customers to look cool. I bought him two pairs of jeans that fit and some tee shirts. I gave him a Vinyl tee shirt, too."

LouLou patted Skylar's hand. "That was good of you to do. He must be new in town." Taking advantage of LouLou's hand on the counter, Robert butted his head against it until LouLou massaged him thoroughly. "Did you tell Gregg the rules about tee shirts?"

Skylar snorted. "Of course. Never wear the tee shirt of a band you haven't seen live."

"Good. As long as he knows, I'll give him one of mine if he comes to a show."

"Anything coming up?" Skylar asked. He always attended LouLou's spins.

"No. I'm taking a break before the Asian tour, but I might do a run-through before I go. You'll be the first to know."

The bell over the entrance rang. Gregg walked in and smiled when he saw LouLou. "Hey, LouLou. Good to see you."

He was more handsome than she remembered. He looked hot in a Vinyl tee shirt and the dark wash jeans Skylar had bought, but she didn't want to seem like she was checking him out. "Have you made your way through the entire Joni Mitchell catalogue?"

"Just finished."

Skylar intervened. "Well, that calls for a celebration. Why don't you two get a fancy coffee at that new take-out bar off Strawberry Street? I've got accounting to do. No time for chatting." Skylar turned and walked toward his office. "Don't forget to let me know if you decide to do a preview before your tour, LouLou," Skylar called over his shoulder.

Skylar was an impish matchmaker. LouLou couldn't recall a time when Skylar had passed on the chance to talk about icons of the 1960s, a conversation which would inevitably lead to a homage to Bob Dylan. He couldn't have been more obvious as he hustled them out of Vinyl.

"Iced coffee sounds perfect. What do you say, Gregg?"

"Sounds good."

LouLou and Gregg walked the few blocks to Strawberry Street in silence. They turned the corner, where the bar was just a few doors down.

"My treat," LouLou said. "Anything fancy? Ristretto? Mochaccino? Chai Tea Latte?"

Gregg shook his head. "You pick."

When LouLou turned away from the counter with two iced coffees, she saw that Gregg had found a small bench next to a vacant storefront. She handed Gregg a tall cup with a straw and sat.

"I love this part of Richmond. There's a small town feel to it with a slightly cool vibe." She took a sip of her iced coffee. "This is pretty good. I'm mostly a black coffee woman, but in warm weather I like something cool."

"Thanks for buying. I'll get it next time."

LouLou toasted Gregg. "My town. My treat."

She noticed the neighborhood was quiet. They'd missed the lunch crowd, and it was too early for babysitters with prams out for their afternoon strolls. She and Gregg were the only people around. Sitting on the bench gave them privacy. LouLou felt more relaxed when the caffeine kicked in and started talking. She skipped over introductory details beyond the fact that she grew up in Paris, he in Norfolk, and went straight to music. Gregg talked fast and asked lots of questions. His excitement about music spilled out.

"Carole King's *Tapestry* is one of the best albums I've ever heard. I can't stop listening to it. Skylar told me to buy it before I wear it out."

LouLou laughed. "Don't listen to him. He's thrilled there's another aficionado in town. I consider *Tapestry* to be a landmark album. Hard to believe she and her first husband wrote jingles and songs for other people before she broke out." She sipped the chilled drink she found soothing. "That means you're moving into James Taylor and Carly Simon territory next, right?"

"On my list." He paused. "There's so much I haven't heard."

"Me, too," LouLou said. "People get into music at different times in their lives. I started at three on piano. I grew up listening to French pop with a sprinkling of what Americans call the British Invasion. My parents also had stuff imported from the United States—my mother's favorites like Debbie Harry, girl bands, and opera and my dad's obsession with Frank Sinatra, Ray Charles, and Tina Turner."

Gregg nodded his head enthusiastically. "Classical. I started there. Skylar has recordings I never dreamed I'd hear. Szell with the Cleveland Orchestra playing anything is spectacular." He continued to talk about the artists and works from the orchestral canon he liked.

LouLou noticed he was so enthusiastic about the treasures he'd found at Vinyl, he'd ignored his coffee. It sat untouched on the bench between them. She finished her coffee and eyed his.

"Please, finish it," he offered. "I don't want it to get warm."

She couldn't resist and took a long sip from his cup before speaking. "Music is who I am. I knew from an early age I could never do anything other than make music," she said. "What about you?"

"I started young in classical music. I play contrabass, oboe, and some piano, but I'm more interested in composing than performing. I hear entire walls of music in my head."

"You mean symphonies?"

He shook his head. "Tone poems. free dissonance, and atonality." He blushed. "Plus, romanticism."

"Are they only in your head?" LouLou asked.

"No, I've written big pieces, but ideas come every day."

"What about performances?"

He shook his head. LouLou was immediately contrite. "I'm sorry. That's like asking a writer if anything's been published or an actor if I might have seen any movie he's made. Forgive me?" She smiled from under her lashes.

"Of course." He hesitated and then pulled a folded, yellowed staff notebook out of the back pocket of his jeans. "I've never shown these to anyone. Maybe you could look at them and tell me what you think."

She hesitated. "Gregg, I'm a DJ. I make mix tapes of all kinds of music. I've no formal training past piano lessons. Surely, there are people far more qualified than I am to comment. Skylar knows several musicologists and composers."

"Skylar says you have an ear. That's what counts. That's the opinion I want."

The notebook lay between them on the bench like an offering. LouLou hesitated. If she refused to look at Gregg's compositions, she'd look like an arrogant ass. She'd hurt him. If she agreed, she'd give him her honest opinion. He spoke about music as though he knew what he was doing. Sometimes that translated to great music. Sometimes not. The worst that could happen was that she didn't like his work—a subjective opinion. LouLou took the notebook, tucked it in her red tote, and stood. "I'll look at it tonight. Same time tomorrow at Vinyl?"

Gregg looked enormously pleased that she was willing to review his work. He nodded.

"Tomorrow," she called as she headed home.

# CHAPTER SIX

LouLou couldn't wait to meet Gregg at Vinyl the next day. She issued a rare invitation to Gregg. Less than ten people knew where she lived, but LouLou emailed Skylar and asked him to send Gregg to her loft as soon as Gregg arrived at Vinyl. She didn't want to waste her precious energy going there only to walk back to her loft with him. She'd stayed up late playing and revising and replaying his compositions and still had questions.

She flung the massive industrial door open before Gregg exited the elevator. She was standing barefoot behind it wearing black pants and a comfortable old cornflower blue cardigan over a white tank top. She held out a mug of coffee.

Gregg put up his hand. "No thanks, I'm good."

"Okay, more for me." She shut the door, urged him inside the loft, and pointed to the concealed coat closet for his jacket. She headed straight to the piano. "Gregg, you didn't tell me your compositions were brilliant. Why did you need me to look at them? They're complex, perfectly voiced, and surprising. Orchestras should be playing these. Come here."

LouLou shooed Gregg onto the piano beach and sat beside him. She was eager to point out ideas that were particularly exceptional in her opinion. LouLou paged through the notebook to Number Three and played a section just after the introduction. "This is amazing. There are actually two key signatures and two tempi, yet it works. If that's not enough, it goes on to develop into a reverie that is heartbreakingly beautiful before the recapitulation. The coda is exquisite."

He bowed his head and spoke quietly. "You play exceptionally well. Twelve-part harmony is almost impossible to play with two hands."

"Gregg, you're missing the point. This is genius." Sitting next to him on the bench gave her goose bumps that she tried to ignore. "Now, walk me through the orchestration. The bass line, which stunningly is the main theme, obviously played by basses and cellos. Beyond that, I can hear brass, percussion, and winds. I don't hear other strings."

She faced him.

"There aren't any. I wanted human voices and bells for those parts. There's a thirteenth part for xylophone in the reverie."

She cocked her head as she imagined that combination. "Yes, yes, I hear that. It's perfect."

"So, you like it. You think it's good, that maybe I could publish it." He looked so hopeful and so clueless about the excellence of his work.

"I think you should hire an orchestra, make a demo, and send it to every conductor in the world.

They'll beg you to conduct premieres." LouLou's face was flushed with excitement.

Gregg shook his head. "That's out of the question moneywise. The constant artistic dilemma of not being able to get anyone's attention without making a demo that costs way more than I have."

LouLou got up and refilled her coffee. "Play that line for the xylophone." He did, and in a much higher register than she had. Yes. It made the contrast to the bass theme much more balanced.

"That's so lovely." She leaned against the bar that served as her kitchen table with her eyes closed.

"You really think it's good?" Gregg looked at her in a way that seemed almost desperate for her to say yes.

"Skylar surely told you I don't BS. I'm straightforward." She drank more coffee. "By the way, thanks for coming."

"No problem. I was surprised you invited me to your home."

LouLou shrugged. "Me too. I rarely have visitors, but I wanted to get you to a piano where you could fully explain things to me. I wanted to hear what you hear, but please don't tell anyone where I live." She pushed her cup aside. "What do you want to do with these? This work can't stay hidden in your notebook."

"I want you to play it," he said seriously.

"Me? I'm a DJ. I have exactly one contact in the classical world."

"It doesn't have to be treated as classical music. I didn't think of it as a particular genre. I just wrote. From what I understand, you lay down different tracks and modulate voicing and tempi and all kinds of technical things I don't know about. Couldn't you create a recording of one piece?"

She walked around the room. This would give her fresh material to blend into the album she was planning. She would perform slices of her last album in Asia, but she also wanted to absorb what was new there. Bells, chimes, and flutes were hallmarks of Eastern music. Something might click for Gregg's works.

"Okay," she said when she returned to stand next to the piano. "I've got three weeks before I leave for Japan. Let's put something together. I'll produce and perform. You compose and perform. Fifty/fifty split on anything we make, which could be zero." She laughed at the old joke amongst musicians who never knew if and when they'd be hired for a gig or signed by a label.

"I don't want any money. I just want it performed." Gregg's eyes shone with excitement.

"Never say no to money. First rule of being a working musician."

Gregg smiled for the first time. "Okay, I'll take my half of zero."

LouLou continued circling the loft. "We need to work out a plan—how many pieces we can do in three weeks, which ones, and what instruments we need. You can play five if we include various keyboards. We need two days of studio time. Then editing. We can probably get two done."

Gregg looked dazed. The naiveté and hope in those soft brown eyes tugged at her heart. LouLou wanted him to hold her close and kiss her in her soft places, but she put her hand on his shoulder to steady herself. Arm's length. "We'll make it happen. It's going to be awesome."

39

# CHAPTER SEVEN

## April

LouLou, Gregg, and Robert sat silently on the floor until Skylar finished listening to the demo. Gregg looked nervous. He sat on his hands. LouLou was as calm as she'd ever been. It was good. Great. Gregg needed to hear that from someone else. Robert sat next to LouLou and didn't do so much as flip his tail. LouLou relaxed and enjoyed the demo.

Tears flowed down the old man's cheeks when he emerged from the listening booth. He wrapped his arms around the two of them, pulling them in a group hug. When he pulled away, he said he needed to go up front to sit. All three followed Skylar in line like children behind their teacher.

"It's the stuff of dreams," he said as he continued to cry. "It's transcendent."

Gregg seemed to be dumbstruck. He didn't say anything.

"Good, right?" LouLou encouraged. She wanted Skylar to say it specifically and directly to Gregg.

Robert jumped on the counter as if to nudge Skylar into speaking.

"Gregg," Skylar said, "what you've written will be played for centuries to come. It's fine, fine work."

Gregg exhaled. "Thank you, Skylar. I trust your judgment. I'll let it be played in public." LouLou noticed he'd been holding his breath.

Skylar regained his composure and brushed the comment away with his hand. "Toff. The public doesn't know anything. They booed Stravinsky, Verdi, and Berlioz. What counts is the music. You've got a talent that far exceeds the public's consciousness."

"Hey," LouLou interjected. "The performer, not the composer, gets booed. Does that mean I— DJL—am going to be booed out of booths and stages throughout Asia?"

"Never. You are so delightful with such a good reputation that your choices are respected. You don't need me to tell you that."

LouLou gave Skylar a sly smile. "It's nice to hear."

Skylar nodded in acknowledgement. "Agreed. You're fabulous. I don't tell you often enough. Now, what's next?"

Gregg, who still seemed not to have regained the power of speech, leaned against the counter next to Robert. All three looked expectantly at LouLou.

LouLou ticked off her plans. "I'm burning copies today, and that's it for now." She didn't know what the three of them expected beyond that. "I've got to get my head around my set lists, review my itinerary, and pack. I leave for Tokyo on the thirtieth, which is six days from now. I'm travelling through Houston, so it breaks up the flight a little. I'll be back in early July."

Three months without Gregg. He was part of her everyday life now, and she'd miss him. They'd worked long hours every day. She made suggestions. He made them better. She felt like she was playing musical poker with a genius who constantly raised the stakes. Despite spending so much time together, Gregg hadn't made a romantic move. He focused on the compositions to the exclusion of everything else. He seemed to live on air, because he never suggested lunch breaks. LouLou insisted on breaks for her health. She couldn't maintain the pace Gregg set, but she worked diligently and efficiently. Nevertheless, LouLou knew Gregg felt a romantic pull to her. She was drawn to him. Something was growing between them, but it remained unspoken.

"Gregg, that means you'll be hanging around here, I hope."

"Skylar, I have to. LouLou's given me a list of pieces to tweak for her fall tour in Scandinavia. I've got so much music to hear. I haven't made it through ten percent of Vinyl. I have to absorb and write." Robert rubbed his head under Gregg's hand in approval. Gregg dutifully rubbed his ears. Skylar faked a pout. "Vinyl just isn't the same when you're not here, LouLou. All I have is an out-of-date headshot on my Wall of Fame."

"You're right about the headshot. I'll do something about that." LouLou playfully punched his arm. "You know I faithfully email you when I'm on tour. I'd never abandon you."

"Well, let's drink to your success before you go." Skylar pulled a bottle of Scotch from beneath the counter with three matching tumblers. He poured two and then poured warm ginger ale in a third. He handed it to LouLou.

The three raised their glasses. "To the art of music."

"To LouLou, my muse," Gregg toasted.

"Hear, hear," Skylar said.

"To the guys who make my work so much fun," LouLou toasted.

"And to the Fantastic Far East Tour," Skylar finished.

***

Gregg walked LouLou back to her loft although he admitted he felt like he could run all the way there. LouLou suddenly felt tired. Her sessions with Gregg had been productive, but now she felt brain-drained. The work they'd done was good and satisfying, but she needed rest and sleep. Stress, even if the stress came from intensity of working on something she enjoyed, and not enough sleep were a bad combination for her. Throughout her time at home in Richmond, she'd taken her meds, seen her psychiatrist weekly, and made sure she walked once a day. Roy and Sara made sure she ate properly. She didn't want to overextend herself right before her trip. She never wanted to see Sick again.

"What?" she asked. Gregg had said something

she hadn't heard.

"Do you mind if I come in to get my stuff?" he repeated.

"Of course not, but please be quick. I need to refocus." Once inside, Gregg picked up his music notebooks and the revised itemized list LouLou had made of things for him to do and stuffed them in the back pocket of his jeans. He'd asked LouLou to bring the oboe he'd rented for the month to Vinyl on her trip to Vinyl. He glanced around the loft. "That's everything."

"Good. Keep at it while I'm gone."

She knew he was going to kiss her, so she put her hand on his chest as he leaned in. "Gregg, I'm going to fall asleep standing up. I really need to rest. This has been amazing and I can't wait to play it on tour, but I need to be alone before I leave." She hated the hurt look on his face, but her health came first.

"Did I do something wrong? I know there's a connection between us beyond music."

"No. You've done nothing wrong. I feel something, too, but I have some…health problems. I can't get involved with anyone, especially someone as dear to me as you."

He seemed to like hearing that he was dear to her and dropped the topic. "I didn't mean to tire you. Get some rest." He turned toward the door. "I can't thank you enough. Kick ass in Asia." He kissed her softly on the cheek. "Good travels."

# CHAPTER EIGHT

## July

LouLou and Gregg became lovers the night she returned from Bangkok. Flushed with the success of her tour and Gregg's fantastic newest music that Skylar had forwarded, LouLou set herself free with Gregg. Their lovemaking was as exciting and passionate as their music with a tenderness LouLou had never experienced. She could only let it happen once. She couldn't let Gregg think they had a future together, but she didn't want to raise the issue immediately.

Gregg, Robert, and Skylar had met her at the airport with red roses. LouLou had emailed Skylar regular updates. In turn, he sent files of Gregg's latest compositions to download. She hadn't listened to it until her flight home. She didn't want to add new ideas while she was on such a successful tour. Skylar had discretely dropped Gregg and LouLou off at her loft and went on his way. Robert, who had sat on LouLou's lap in the passenger seat, seemed happy to have the seat to himself.

After making love with Gregg, LouLou slept thirty-six hours. When she woke, she realized Gregg had left a one-word note—

## Sleep.

Roy had stocked her refrigerator with mineral water, red grapes, two kinds of hard cheese, brie, and eggs.

LouLou ate a fresh banana from the bowl on the counter and pulled out her rig—her nickname for the syringe and meds she took twice a week in addition to four pills a day. She took every med she safely could at one time with food. Thirty-six hours was a long time. If she resumed the routine immediately, she'd probably be okay. Dr. Youzny assured her she'd be fine if she didn't miss a single dose going forward. Meds, plus rest, healthy food, and exercise would keep Sick at bay.

She stood beside the breakfast bar and inhaled the roses that sat in a crystal vase atop the bar. They were a lovely crimson and smelled luscious. She touched the fragile petals. She made a note to ask her mother how to make potpourri when she called her parents.

Roy pounded on the door. "Ah, you're awake," he said when she let him in. He gave her a one-armed hug because he was holding a glass of fresh squeezed orange juice in the other. "Sara and I checked on you yesterday, but you were snoring. You must have been exhausted."

LouLou accepted the glass. "This juice is just

what I needed. I had a long flight. The tour was a logistical nightmare but a success."

"Of course it was a success." Roy appraised the woman in front of him. "Where are you on meals?"

"I don't know. What time is it?" Long flights. Lovemaking with Gregg. Sleep. LouLou had no sense of time.

"About four on Thursday afternoon. Early supper?"

"Definitely." LouLou told him she'd slept through a cycle of meds and her psych had recommended exercise, rest, and healthy food.

"I know just what to get. Should I send Sara up with it to keep you company?"

"Oh, I'd love that, yes." She longed for her friend who'd talk about something other than the tour. LouLou enjoyed Sara's company in part because she was so serene. Sara loved and took care of her husband, her children, and her home. She treated LouLou like a younger sister.

Over a dinner of salad, bread, and spaghetti carbonara with peas substituted for bacon, LouLou debated whether she should tell Sara about Gregg. She decided not to because she and Gregg would never be a couple. They were a great musical team. That had to be enough.

***

Two weeks passed before LouLou felt like herself. She had a few rocky nights as the meds resumed their battle stations in her body against Sick. When she saw her psychiatrist, he cautioned her again about skipping doses.

"I know it's hard when you're touring, keeping odd hours, and changing time zones. I know you crash when you return, but you must set an alarm on your phone to wake you."

"I will," she agreed. "By the way, I had some trouble getting through airport security with syringes, even with your documentation and names of physicians in each city. Dr. Youzny, it scared me."

She didn't admit how much. Sitting in an airport interview room with two Chinese guards who debated with a third by phone as to whether she could keep her syringes was unnerving. She had an alternate medication in tablet form, but it wasn't powerful enough to be more than a temporary measure. After a three-hour delay, LouLou and her syringes were allowed to travel. She'd sprinted toward her gate before they could change their minds.

"If that happens, call the United States embassy. You're one of theirs, given your father's continued service. The embassy people will make sure you get what you need." LouLou's father had for many years been the United States Ambassador to France and remained a career diplomat. Any call from her would be taken seriously. She knew that. She didn't need Dr. Youzny to remind her.

"The alternative is to stop touring," Dr. Youzny suggested with his voice full of gravitas. She'd been Youzny's patient for so long she knew all of his pompous mannerisms and vocal tics. Her dad actually howled at her imitation of Youzny at his most profound. LouLou knew he'd say that.

"I intend to. My plan is to take at least a year off from international touring. I've got plenty of work in the States. All I have left is my commitment in Scandinavia. That shouldn't be a problem. At least I can communicate in English. Not knowing what the Chinese were saying was awful."

"I'm glad to hear you say you're taking some time off from traveling. Travel is stressful and is becoming increasingly so. You know stress is a trigger. I can't imagine too many things more stressful that being held in a strange airport interrogation room without a translator."

"Got it," she said as she left. LouLou despised Sick with growing anger. The meds themselves were now putting her in stressful situations. This disease had robbed her of her identity and control of her body and kept her from forming lasting relationships beyond friendship. She longed to love a man and be loved in return.

# CHAPTER NINE

After her appointment with Dr. Youzny, LouLou met Gregg at Vinyl and dropped off new treasure for Skylar. She didn't stay to browse. She was eager to get back to the loft and properly listen to Gregg's new music. He held her hand as they walked hurriedly to beat an impending storm. There was nothing lovely about mid-summer in Richmond. It was hot and humid punctuated by late afternoon thunderstorms. LouLou didn't notice much about her surroundings. She was focused on how right her hand felt in Gregg's.

The next thing she knew, LouLou was lying on the striped sectional sofa in her loft. Panic was her first instinct. This was how she felt when Sick took over, caused her to do something terrible, and departed leaving LouLou to deal with the consequences.

She didn't know how much time had passed, what had happened, or how she'd gotten home. Seeing Gregg sitting calmly beside her holding a cold compress to her forehead caused her to relax a bit. He seemed concerned but not alarmed. She sat up and accepted the glass of water with chunks of ice and two pain relief tablets he offered. She immediately swallowed the pills and held the chilled glass in her hands. Chilled water and ice always calmed her.

"Better?" Gregg asked.

"I don't know…" LouLou responded.

"I checked you over. Abrasion on your right elbow and a scrape on your right forehead. A long scratch on your tote. No vinyl LPs were harmed." He squeezed her hand. "Do you want to go to the ER? Get your head wound checked out? Check for a concussion?"

The sound of Gregg's voice triggered her memory. Something had freaked her out, something that made her wonder just how safe Gregg was and whether she could trust him.

"How did you do that?" LouLou demanded. She clutched the glass so her hands wouldn't shake. "That car hit you. I saw it aimed directly at you. The driver didn't stop to see what or who she hit. We've got to call 911. I got a partial plate." She was talking too fast. She knew it. Had. To. Slow. Down. Breathe.

"No, don't call anyone. I'm fine," said a completely unscathed Gregg.

"You can't be. You pushed me out of the way just in time. The driver came out of the garage too fast and turned left. She didn't look."

LouLou's heart was beating too fast. She reached in her now-scratched red leather tote and took a blue pill out of a slim silver container and placed it under her tongue. This med worked faster when it dissolved under her tongue rather than swallowed whole. Gregg reached for a throw to wrap around her. "I'm fine. You said you're okay. Try to calm down."

She couldn't let it go, but she had to remain calm. "Gregg, you're scaring me. Why aren't you hurt? I saw the car headed directly at you. There's no way you could've dodged that car."

He stared at her for what felt like an hour before he spoke. "There's no logical explanation."

His answer did nothing to quell her uneasiness. "No logical way? What does that mean? Is there some illogical way? If you don't tell me, you have to leave. I'll call the police and report the accident. Tell me, Gregg."

Although she never imagined she'd use it against Gregg, LouLou kept mace in her tote, partly because she was usually alone and partly because she might be faced with an over-zealous fan. There were three panic buttons in her loft. Her parents had insisted she have them in the event she felt Sick coming and didn't have time to call someone. One button was located just behind the end of the sofa, where she sat.

At the mention of having to leave, Gregg dropped the wet cloth he'd been holding against her forehead. He removed his hand from hers.

"LouLou, don't be afraid of me. I'm not going to hurt you. I'll leave if you want."

"I want you to tell me why you're not hurt when a five-thousand-pound car pointed directly at you slammed you. I didn't see you lying in the street.

You remained on the sidewalk with me. Tell me."

Gregg stood and backed away from the sofa. He held his hands by his sides. He looked harmless and vulnerable. "What I say is going to sound unbelievable. Please don't be afraid. If it's any help, Skylar knows about me. He's always known."

If he didn't spit it out, LouLou felt like she would strangle him in about two seconds. She threw the blanket off and sat with her feet on the floor. "Tell me." Her voice had a sharp edge that Sick often used.

"I don't live in human form," Gregg said quietly and firmly.

Human form. What's left? Animal, vegetable, mineral. "I don't understand."

"For lack of a better term, I'm a ghost." He stood still. He didn't make any motion toward her. He seemed afraid he might scare her.

She stood, felt dizzy, and sat. "A ghost."

For a nanosecond, she wondered if she'd taken the correct medication. Her blue pill was a sedative. The pills Gregg had given her looked like over-the-counter pain relievers. No, she wasn't tripping on drugs. This man she'd worked beside for months and made love to was telling her he was a ghost.

"What does that mean? You're going to have to be specific. Are you dead?"

His hands remained at his sides. He didn't try to approach her. "You'd say I was dead. I stopped living in human form when I was about thirty-two or thirty-three. What you see is the essence of me. I've poured my heart and my music out to you."

She remained seated and tried to focus. "Why

me? Why can I see you?"

"I was meant to meet you."

That sounded like something a man running a con would say. "And Skylar? Don't tell me he's a ghost too."

He shook his head. "Skylar is a Sensitive, a person who sees and is attuned to more than one realm."

She'd known Skylar since she was eighteen and had just moved to Richmond to attend Virginia Commonwealth University. She trusted him. She'd always suspected there was something more to Skylar than he let on—a sixth sense. Gregg, however, was a newcomer, and she hadn't felt anything more than a romantic pull toward him, nothing that made her think he was weird or paranormal. Questions whirred in her head in no order. She needed to ask the important ones.

"Do other people see you?"

"I don't think so."

She thought back to small things she'd noticed that seemed quirky. "Is that why you never eat? Don't carry anything? Don't drive? You don't need to eat, drink, and sleep, do you?"

He shook his head. "No," he whispered. "I don't."

She switched to the topic of visibility. "When we're walking together, what do other people see?"

"Unless they're ghosts or Sensitives, they see only you."

LouLou almost shrieked. "I look like I'm talking to myself while walking down the street?"

Still standing, Gregg kept his distance and spoke

with a quiet, even tone. "People notice a lot less than you think. If they do notice, they probably think you're talking on your phone or dictating a note." He reminded her that they didn't walk together often.

"What about in Vinyl? Don't people see you going through bins, or do they see the albums moving back and forth by themselves?"

"So far, no one's seen anything. I get there at the time you do for the same reason—it's slow. There aren't any customers. For you, Skylar has time to talk. For me, I have time to select what I need and hide in a listening booth."

This was too much to take in. Maybe she had a head injury. Maybe she should go to the ER for a CT scan. Pounding on the door made LouLou jump. She spilled water on herself and the sofa.

"It's Roy," the familiar voice called.

A feeling of relief washed over her. LouLou went to the door and let Roy in. He'd brought the first aid kit he kept in the deli/patisserie/bodega.

"Have you taken up being a paramedic?" LouLou asked in an attempt to hide her uneasiness. "Sit." Roy took her by the elbow and led her to the sofa. "Skylar called and said you'd been nearly hit by a car outside his shop. He said you were stubborn and wouldn't let him do anything except drive you home. He had to get back to the shop and couldn't stay with you, so he called me."

*Hmm.* The accident hadn't been outside Vinyl. It had happened closer to her loft. Gregg must have contacted Skylar to let him know what had happened while she was still groggy. Skylar, keeping Gregg's secret, sent Roy to check on her. Gregg still stood next to the sofa, but Roy didn't notice him. Gregg was invisible.

Roy fussed over her, took her pulse, reviewed her scrapes, and asked for the partial plate. He said he'd call the police and report it.

LouLou grasped Roy's arm with her left hand. "Please, don't. It was an accident. A bystander pushed me out of the way of the car. The push is what caused me to fall. I don't want to talk to the police. I certainly don't want them to come here."

She didn't hear Roy's response because she watched Gregg leave by walking through the windowed wall facing the street two stories below. He vanished.

# CHAPTER TEN

Sitting in one of the New York Academy of Medicine's marble-walled reading rooms at four in the morning, Bella wished she had someone with whom to brainstorm. She'd never needed a sounding board in her life as a ghost. She was a self-taught ghost who learned to get what she wanted through trial and error. Deep concentration controlled visibility. Visualization allowed space travel. Lying and stealing provided most human needs. She'd randomly seen other ghosts, but so far, none had been worthy of a discussion.

She'd never had a problem she couldn't solve. Even so, beauty, brilliance, and an impressive education and impeccable professional credentials hadn't led her to a solution that could legally get Daniel out of that hellhole in Petersburg, Virginia known as Commonwealth Psychiatric Hospital. He'd been there for almost two years, and she was no closer to her goal than when he'd been admitted.

The most frustrating thing was that Daniel knew how to get himself discharged. All he had to do was lie to a psychiatrist who would in turn call Daniel's criminal attorney, Nina Lombardi. Known as the Barracuda of Virginia, Lombardi would have him transferred, heard before a judge, and released as an innocent man in less than a day. A deal was already in place. All Daniel had to do was act.

He couldn't.

Daniel had lapsed into catatonia immediately upon admission to Commonwealth Psych and hadn't awakened. All that knowledge of how to help himself was on lockdown in his head.

In the early months, Bella had checked on him almost daily until she realized he was beyond her help. He needed a psychiatric genius. She'd searched for one without success. She'd met top psychiatrists in New York. They'd referred her to catatonia specialists in London, Vienna, and Johannesburg. Bella was so prepared for those meetings, she considered herself an expert on this condition first mentioned in Greek mythology and given a name in 1874. The specialists referred her to the best of the rarest specialists in Stockholm and Berlin, who narrowed her search for specialists down to one retired professor in Rochester, Minnesota. They'd all reviewed Daniel's medical records that she'd stolen, copied, and returned to the hospital and recommended no significant changes in treatment. Having seen the conditions at Commonwealth Psych and the almost complete lack of clinical staff, Bella had no confidence that the records were accurate regarding treatment.

Treatment. Daniel wasn't being treated. From what Bella could tell, Daniel was being managed.

His medical—which she now knew was medicalese for physical—needs were being met, but he wasn't receiving psychiatric attention beyond anti-anxiety medications. Any family doctor who prescribed Valium could treat him if that was the threshold.

Bella could do it. Her primary attribute as a ghost was invisibility. She was adept at stealing medication. She could go to the hospital, sneak Daniel out, and find a house for them. She could hire nurses. She could give him Valium, but she didn't want that. She wanted Daniel. Her healthy funny sweet Daniel. Her soul mate since they'd met when they were seventeen.

The only reason Bella was still living as a ghost was because she was waiting for Daniel. She couldn't be at peace until she'd gotten what she wanted—a reunion with Daniel Ramsay for eternity.

The fire at Commonwealth Psych had given her a new sense of urgency. Daniel was completely at the mercy of the very sick patients and indifferent staff. She'd taken time off in Bermuda to clear her mind and hope that a new idea might make itself known. Bella realized she didn't have time to rest. Daniel was in danger. She had to get him help.

# CHAPTER ELEVEN

LouLou awoke feeling fuzzy. Dinner with Roy and Sara and their three pre-adolescent kids just home from summer camp had distracted her from Gregg's revelation that he was a ghost. She wondered if what he'd said was true. Maybe she'd dreamed their conversation while recovering from her fall to the concrete sidewalk. Maybe Gregg, who otherwise seemed so serious and sincere, had a bizarre sense of humor. She could almost talk herself out of believing Gregg's admission except she'd witnessed him walk through her wall. She needed to talk to Skylar.

"I expected you earlier," Skylar said mildly when LouLou walked into Vinyl before lunch. Robert gave LouLou a short greeting and continued washing his face. "I assume you have questions for me." He seemed to be taking the temperature of her feelings.

"May we talk in your office?" LouLou wanted straight answers and hoped they wouldn't be outlandish enough to trigger a visit from Sick. She was nervous and annoyed, but she needed privacy. She couldn't be interrupted by customers. In order for her mind to accept Gregg's admission, LouLou needed confirmation from Skylar.

"Why didn't you warn me?" She pounced on Skylar before he'd completely closed the office door. "You, I suspected had something like a sixth sense, but I didn't get anything from Gregg. You know how easily Sick can be triggered. How could you let me walk into a relationship with him?"

Skylar eased into his chair and motioned for LouLou to sit. He poured himself a shot of bourbon and offered LouLou a bottle of water from his mini-fridge. "Haven't had all of my breakfast yet," he said about his drink. LouLou didn't care. She knew he drank, smoked weed, and had residual damage from who knows what he ingested in the 1960s.

"We're friends, LouLou. Let's not turn this into an argument." He drank his shot in one gulp and pushed the glass aside. "What exactly did you want me to say? The new guy in town is a ghost? Steer clear of him?"

LouLou, dressed in a yellow sundress, looked down at her lap. "Skylar, I don't know, but you certainly didn't discourage him."

Skylar looked around his office at pictures of his favorite bands as if they might offer suggestions. Apparently, he didn't get any answers, so he continued. "I recognized Gregg as a ghost. Period. In the few short conversations I had with him, I realized he was new at it. That's one of the reasons I bought him clothes. He looked like he was wearing whatever he had on when he passed. I brought him into the twenty-first century. That's it. I don't know anything about his past."

He stared at LouLou. "I saw what you did. He's a great musician who has a helluva lot of music in his head that he needs to get out. You were the logical person to introduce him to what music is like now. I couldn't have envisioned the genius of the music the two of you would create. The two of you appeared at Vinyl at the same time for a reason. I'm an observer not a participant or manipulator. Sick is part of you, but you're pretty and bright and sweet. You're also thirty-one. You don't need your hand held. I admit I noticed the spark between you two the day you met, but I also know you didn't dive in without checking the water level. You disappeared for a couple of weeks after you met him. I know that was to recover from the tour, visit your parents, and so forth, but you came back looking for him. He was irresistible to you. That means something.

"Beyond that, I don't think he knows what he's doing as a ghost. He appears here at the same time every day. Same goes for departure. I don't know where he goes when he's not here. I haven't asked. I've seen him make small mistakes, such as opening or closing the door to a listening booth when customers were here, and cautioned him about holding or moving things while invisible. I asked you to return the oboe he rented before you went on tour. I didn't want it to seemingly fly from your loft if Gregg brought it himself. I've made suggestions. Beyond that, I haven't interfered. I don't know much more than you.

"I've accepted being a Sensitive just like you've accepted Sick. I discovered it when I was a child. At first, I read about it and talked to other Sensitives and a few ghosts. I've had about seven decades or so to accept there's more to life than what we see. You just found out. If you need time to think about it, take it, but frankly, it doesn't change anything. You're not going to learn anything. There's a paranormal community of sorts and we help each other out, but we don't admit anything to humans unless we have a good reason."

Skylar focused his bleary eyes on LouLou. "Gregg is an extraordinary musician and from what I can tell, a decent guy. I don't pick up any bad vibes. I know he loves you and wouldn't hurt you."

LouLou sat back in her chair. "Loves me? He barely knows me."

Skylar shrugged. "Ghosts exist for a reason. At the time of their death, something was unresolved. They know what it is. I don't know whether it's voices in their heads or their hearts or whether they just know. My guess is that Gregg couldn't find peace until he met you, specifically. He also had to get that music that's been in his head for who knows how long out. The two of you make a great team."

Skylar reached into his bottom desk drawer and pulled out the bourbon bottle, poured two more fingers of the rich molasses-colored liquid, and again downed it in one gulp. "LouLou, walk away or not. I'm not going to ask him to stop coming to Vinyl. He's lost and needs help from other musicians. You're the best, but not only, musician in town. I'm not in the romance business." He waved her out.

"I have questions."

Without looking up from his desk, Skylar responded. "Ask Gregg. I'm not his spokesman." He lifted his head and seemed to realize he'd been too harsh. "I don't have Gregg's answers. If you want to know the truth about Gregg, the only way to get answers is to ask him."

# CHAPTER TWELVE

LouLou headed straight for Richmond's Lewis Ginter Botanical Garden. Aside from Vinyl, it was her favorite place in Richmond. With more than five hundred acres divided into gardens, there was always something in bloom. There was even a reading library where gardeners, botanists, and visitors could sit quietly and read about the wonders of the flower kingdom, as LouLou liked to think of it. It felt magical to her.

Even in July's heat, LouLou knew she'd find lilies, hydrangeas, and cooling water features. She headed to the conservatory pools, where she drew beauty and a sense of calm from the water lilies. They were lovely by themselves, but they evoked memories of growing up in Paris and going with one or the other or both of her parents to see Monet's works at his home in Givenchy. She'd no desire to garden, but she understood the restorative powers of nature. Flowers had a cycle. One bad spring might lead to a so-so summer and fall but a great winter. She favored musicians like Debussy who created music that she imagined flowers could sing.

After a stroll, LouLou found a shaded area and sat on a bench near one of the restaurants. She'd seen several photographers silently working in the conservatory. She'd never thought about bringing a sketch pad with her. Next time

She checked her phone that she'd turned off for her meeting with Skylar. When she turned it on, she saw that her dad had sent a text requesting she call him as soon as she could. Her heart stalled for a moment. He never called. She always called them. She'd just spoken to them, so she immediately was on alert. They were older than most couples when she was born. She knew their ages made them more vulnerable than the parents of her childhood friends, but there couldn't be anything wrong. There couldn't. She couldn't survive that.

Her mom answered. "LouLou, are you eating enough?" Things couldn't be that bad if food was her mother's main concern.

"Yes, Mom. I'm just getting ready to have lunch." She'd barely eaten breakfast because she was jittery about what Skylar might reveal. She'd have lunch here at the restaurant.

"Good. I'll let you speak to your father. He's standing next to me in quite a stir."

"LouLou," said her dad without giving her mom a chance to say goodbye, "You've become enormously popular, like Britney Spears popular."

"Oh, Dad, please don't compare me to her."

"Sorry. At least you wear panties. Brooks has been fielding offers for your new works like mad.

The stuff you debuted in Asia apparently has sent the music world into a feeding frenzy. They want to sign you, promote you, book you. Companies want you to be the face of their clothes, perfume, and cars. He's overwhelmed. He said he's never seen anything like it."

Probably not. Brooks was her lawyer and a friend of her father's. He fielded the occasional promotional and endorsement offers she received and reviewed all her performance and recording contracts. She had a booking agent to handle dates and fees. Brooks made sure her work was copyrighted and registered with the right associations to collect royalties. Otherwise, he was an intellectual property litigator who handled copyright and trademark infringements.

"Wow."

"That's what I said until he named the companies. They're major players. What do you want to do, LouLou? He's going to have a heart attack."

LouLou stifled a smile. "Dad, it's not uncommon when the industry sniffs the next big thing. Why don't I come up next week and meet with Brooks? The offers that are still on the table by then are legitimate. The rest are just noise."

"How can you be so calm?" Brooks had clearly passed on his excitement to her dad.

"I'm your daughter. I'm unflappable." She smiled even though she knew he couldn't see her.

"Aside from being my daughter, how can you be so calm?" She could hear him breathe a sigh of relief.

"It's the way the music industry works. Offers happen all the time. By the time whatever deals come to fruition, I may be old news. Legitimate offers are made for the long term. Tell Brooks to stall everyone. Tell them I just got off tour, I'm getting ready to go back in the studio, and I'll be available to review offers soon."

"That's it? That's what he should do?"

"Dad, do you think he should do something else?" She valued his input.

"I hadn't thought about it. Brooks is concerned you might lose opportunities."

"That's entirely possible, but you know my health comes first. I struggled after this last tour. Mostly, I'm focused on staying healthy and getting new stuff ready for the Scandinavian tour. That's all I can manage right now."

"I love you. I want you to be healthy. I don't care if you're famous or rich or the face of Chanel."

"Chanel?" she squeaked. "Dad, you didn't say Chanel called. Didn't you run these by Mom? She'd know that was important."

"Oh, yes, she did say to mention that first."

"Tell Brooks to stall everyone except Chanel. Get whatever they're offering in writing. I'll be there next week. Text me if Mom thinks anyone else is important."

"I will. I forget how alike you and your mother are sometimes. Stay healthy."

LouLou did a happy dance. She texted Sara and her best friend in Paris to tell them about Chanel. The men in her life wouldn't care a whit. Men. She'd included Gregg in that group even though she now knew he was a ghost.

BLIND TRUST

# CHAPTER THIRTEEN

With her decision to accept Gregg for who he was, LouLou invited him to visit that evening after she had an early dinner with Roy, Sara, and the kids. She was nervous but not stressed. She wore jeans and a white tee-shirt. She wanted to be comfortable.

The first few minutes after Gregg's arrival were awkward. They interrupted each other, talked about inane things like weather and the mayor's plans for new tolls throughout the city before they settled on the green striped sofa. Recognizing that she'd invited Gregg and he was letting her take the lead, LouLou got on with what could be a scary conversation.

"Gregg, I've got a lot of questions. I'm calm, but please be truthful. I hate liars. If you lie to me, I don't care what you are—human, ghost, werewolf— you're out of my life. If you don't want to answer something, just say so, okay?" She forced a smile.

He leaned back with his hands on his knees. "Deal, if you promise this isn't going to be an inquisition."

That made LouLou genuinely laugh. Gregg was a serious guy. She probably had made it sound like she was going to question him as though they were in a courtroom. She relaxed. She held a glass with iced water in her hands on her lap that calmed her.

"I don't know anything about you."

He shifted his position. "You know what matters."

She closed her eyes. She wasn't going to force him to talk, but she couldn't accept vague answers. She tried again.

"I need basics. Who are you? How long have you been a ghost? How did you become one? When did you become one?"

Gregg sat so still, LouLou wondered if he planned to answer. "My name is Gregg Waites. I was born and grew up in Norfolk. I drowned near here when I was about thirty-two."

"How old are you?"

"Thirty-two. I'll never be older than thirty-two." He seemed puzzled by the question and then amended his answer. "I guess I died about 1980."

LouLou thought about that in musical terms. "You were alive when all the music you listened to when we first met—Joni Mitchell, Carole King, James Taylor—was heard on every radio station in the country. You were what? Twenty-one? Twenty-two? How could you have missed them and all the great stuff around the late 1960s through mid-1970s?"

He looked down at his hands. "I'd like to save that for later. Ask me ghost stuff."

He wasn't lying. Okay. They'd go in the order that worked for him. It was his story. "Where do you go when you're not with me?"

He smiled. "I don't know. I'm with you, and then I'm not. I'm at Vinyl, and then I'm not. I haven't been anywhere without either you or Skylar."

"So, your mind is just blank then?"

"Exactly. Just blank. It's not like there's a club where ghosts sit around during breaks from human communication. I'd describe it as sleep, except I don't have a physical bed."

"Do you see other ghosts?"

"I think so. I'm not completely sure. It's not like heaven, where you see everyone who ever lived and died. Once, I felt like there was another ghost in the park near Vinyl. He was watching a bunch of kids having a birthday party and crying. I don't know whether he noticed me. We didn't acknowledge each other." He paused. "Do you mind if I stand? I do feel a little like I'm in a witness box."

"Sorry. I just have so many questions that aren't going to be answered in normal conversation. Ours isn't a natural situation. There's a reason I need to know everything all in one sitting. This can't be easy for you and I'm afraid of what your answers might be. I don't want to hurt you, but I'm cautious."

He nodded as if he understood. "Got it. What else?"

"What did you do before you died? Did you live in Richmond? Were you married? Did you have kids?"

"Softballs." He exhaled. "Fair enough. No, I was never married and never had kids. You're the only woman I've loved. Ever."

No man had ever told her he loved her. She was thrilled and frightened.

"How can you love me? I probably wasn't even born when you died."

He shrugged. "Everything after I died and before I found myself standing in Vinyl is blank. Deep inside me, I knew there was a woman I was meant to be with, to love, and to share music. When you walked in, I knew that woman was you. It sounds cheesy, but it was love at first sight."

LouLou shivered. She'd felt an immediate pull that was beyond lust. She hadn't felt she was destined to be with Gregg, but she wasn't a ghost who'd been waiting around for forty years.

"LouLou, I'm not good at being a ghost. All I know is I'm transparent and I show up at Vinyl at a regular time. I don't know whether I subconsciously control that or not. I don't know if I can. Tonight I found myself at Vinyl and then walked here. I didn't fly or space travel here.

"There was a TV show I remember called *Bewitched* about a witch married to a mortal. If she wanted to go from her suburban home to visit her uncle on Mars, she just twitched her nose and boom! she was on Mars, partying with her uncle."

LouLou excitedly moved forward on the sofa. "Yes. I've seen *Bewitched* in re-runs. The witch had an Aunt Clara who kept ending up in places when she'd intended to go somewhere else."

Gregg laughed. "Exactly. Clara wasn't good at space travel. I can't do it at all. Maybe, if I concentrate or find another ghost to ask, I might learn. I'd probably be like Aunt Clara at first, but eventually get the hang of it. I assume I'd think about where to go and transport myself there. Right now, I can't."

Gregg sat on the sofa. "I don't know anything else about ghosts. I'm Gregg Waites. Ghost. Between the time I was alive and when I showed up at Vinyl, time moved without me. I don't know about what happened in the world after I died. I only know what I knew when I was alive. That's true of actions, too. If I couldn't do it when I was alive, I can't do it as a ghost. I don't have special powers like laser fingers or mind-reading. I'm the same person I was, and that makes me about forty years out of date. Skylar has helped some. I've learned a lot about how music progressed from listening and from hearing what you do. I can't believe some of the gadgetry that exists. I feel like I'm a time traveler even though I'm not. Things like being able to listen to music on a portable telephone the size of a deck of cards is sci-fi to me. I grew up with rotary phones. You probably don't know what they are. I'm often confused. I'm awed. I'm sometimes overwhelmed."

What a hard time he'd had. LouLou leaned into him and took his hand. "That must be awful."

He squeezed her hand gently. "It's odd. Mostly, everything is wonderful, but I have to act normally. I can't act surprised when I see someone watching a movie on their phone. To me, movies are in theatres with popcorn."

"We're perfect for each other, then. I love movies in theatres. I love the smell of popcorn."

Gregg and LouLou sat in contented silence. Finally, LouLou asked the most important question.

"If you don't have human needs like eating and drinking, how can you have sex?"

"*Argh*. I knew that was coming and I don't have an answer except I really, really, really wanted to make love with you."

That was a pretty sexy revelation.

"Ghosts exist for a reason. We can't be at peace until we get what we need. I need you, and I need to put my music out there. You're the reason I'm neither alive or dead. I'm here to love you."

# CHAPTER FOURTEEN

LouLou wanted to fling herself in Gregg's arms and make love right then, but she held back. From what she could tell, Gregg had been candid with her. He'd told her he loved her. No man had ever loved her or told her he had because of Sick. If Gregg was brave enough to tell her he was a ghost, she had to explain why she'd not reciprocated his feelings. She stood and stretched. She headed to the bar to refill her glass with ice and water.

When she returned to the couch, she put on her comfortable cornflower blue cardigan that some said matched her eyes. She curled her feet under her and wrapped the sweater around her. When LouLou spoke, her voice had no inflection. She sounded as though she were trying to disassociate her voice and what she was saying from herself.

"Remember when I told you I couldn't get close to you? Before I left on the Asian tour?"

He nodded.

"I have a serious illness. It's about as scary as being a ghost. I was diagnosed with schizophrenia when I was sixteen. I've been hospitalized several times—sometimes for as long as two or three months. I haven't had an episode in almost three years because I take medication to keep the psychosis away. Every day. Several times a day. I inject myself just like heroin users do. It's powerful stuff. I live by the clock. I can't miss doses. If I do, I could have an episode. A violent episode.

"I call it Sick to separate the disease from LouLou. Sick haunts me because I do things I wouldn't otherwise do when Sick overtakes me. Anxiety that I might have an episode is always with me. Always. Nothing can get between me and my medication schedule.

"That's why I hole up before and after tours. Before, I check my itinerary against the amount of meds I have, make sure there are doctors I can see in places I'm playing, and rest. I always rest before a tour. The tour itself is fine. I give myself time between gigs, and the gigs are fun. They make me feel alive. After the tour, I inventory where I am on my medication schedule and rest. When I got back from Bangkok, I slept thirty-six hours straight and missed doses. I called my psychiatrist immediately and got back on track. I really live by my medication schedule. Healthy food—no junk, exercise, and a solid eight hours of sleep help. I stop what I'm doing and rest if I feel the least bit tired or exceptionally anxious."

LouLou had hunched herself in the corner of the sofa, so Gregg put his hand on her knee. "That's why the car accident frightened you. I thought you were over-reacting. Now, I understand why. My not telling you why I wasn't hurt must have scared you shitless. Sorry."

She nodded. "I took an anti-anxiety medication, but the longer you stalled, the more anxious I became. If Roy hadn't come when he did, I would've kicked you out."

"I'm sorry." There was nothing else he could say. He'd triggered her without knowing why.

"Roy and Sara are more than my friends. They take care of me. Not officially, but they keep an eye on me. Roy always, always has fresh, healthy food for me. He knows by now what's best nutritionally and for comfort. The two of them are saints. Their kids are angels. I probably wouldn't be able to live as independently as I do without them."

"Good." He nodded. "Good." He paused as though a light bulb had come on. "That's why you don't drink."

LouLou nodded vigorously. "Alcohol and those meds create an ogre."

"That's why you pushed me away romantically."

She nodded again without speaking.

"I don't understand. Don't people with schizophrenia have relationships? You have friends. Why not a man?"

LouLou calmed herself before speaking. Deep breaths. Sips of cold water with ice.

"Psychotic episodes are horrifying. When they happen, I truly believe whatever the voices in my head are telling me. They always say I'm in danger and must protect myself. The worst I feel is anxiety until the episode ends. When I'm well again, I don't remember anything that happened.

"I'm violent. I've committed crimes. Theft. Larceny. Arson. I hurt myself in committing those crimes. Scarred face. Broken ribs. Dislocated shoulder. So far, I haven't hurt other people, but my episodes have become increasingly violent. Everyone around me is in danger.

"My parents must have been traumatized over the years. They got me help as quickly as possible once they realized my illness wasn't behavioral. They made getting well easier. They were wonderful to me, but they must have been in pain seeing their daughter in terribly agitated states. They fear me. I recognize no one during the episodes. I wouldn't be able to stop myself from hurting them if the voices told me to. If I believed my dad was a ninja warrior who was going to kill me if I didn't kill him first, then I would kill him. It's horrifying."

She looked at her hands, the hands capable of doing irreparable harm.

"If I'm lucky during an episode, I can be loaded up with meds, put in a single hospital room, and have restraints. Even with soft restraints, I find what's left of wrist burn when I recover. That tells me I was thrashing violently. It takes about two months for a full recovery. Sometimes more. Even when I'm well, I feel just beneath the surface of life. I don't have clarity."

Gregg looked at her strong hands which could elicit such beautiful music out of the piano.

"So Gregg, I've never put someone I cared about in that path. It's too dangerous for a man and for me."

Gregg didn't speak for a few minutes. "Has an episode ever started around your parents or Roy and Sara?"

"Maybe around my parents when I was young and they got me to the hospital immediately. Never around Roy and Sara. Like I said, I don't recall anything after they're over. I've been told the most recent ones start in odd places after I've been off my meds. Until I was on my own, my parents always made sure I took medication."

"Couldn't I make sure you took it?" Gregg asked.

"It's too much. Too much responsibility to ask of someone. I've always wanted a lover, a man with whom I can be a partner. I don't want him to be my nurse. He'd resent it eventually, and I'd be humiliated. Sick runs my life, Gregg. I don't live normally. I tire easily. I can't be stressed. I have a rigid schedule of meals, rest, and exercise. "

He pulled her to him. "I'm sorry. I'm sorry you have such a monstrous illness."

"Monstrous, it is. A monster lives inside me, and I have to keep her at bay."

Gregg shifted to be closer to her on the sofa. She remained curled in the corner. "I'm different. You can't hurt me physically. You can think I'm a ninja, a space alien, or a serial killer, but you can't hurt me. You saw that car aim at me. It passed through me. You've seen me walk through the wall of your loft. I'm invincible.

"As for the rest, you don't need a nurse. You don't have one on tour. You're diligent. You have alarms and reminders and doctors to keep you on schedule. I don't care if you have to be on a timetable or need naps. Time means nothing to me. I couldn't resent you for what I don't know or feel.”

He pulled her to him and kissed her softly—her forehead, bruised temple, eyelids, cheeks, nose, and mouth. He held her until she was completely calm.

“I'd like for us to give a relationship a try.”

LouLou looked at him. Her tears were almost dry. “You're right. The obstacles to my having a relationship don't exist with you.”

“Does that mean you won't push me away?”

“Yes, I think we're a perfect pair,” she said as their lips found each other.

# CHAPTER FIFTEEN

Their secrets drew them closer. LouLou let Gregg lead her to bed. Her secret was exposed, and he was still here. His secret was out and she didn't care. Their lovemaking had a fresh intimacy that LouLou had never experienced. Afterwards, they lay entwined in bed. Gregg ran his fingers along her body. "Tell me about your ink."

"I love to draw. When I was thirteen, I started using my body as a canvas. This feather," she pointed to a single precisely detailed purple, grey, blue feather on her left arm, "was my first. It made me feel calm to look at it. Sometimes, I imagined it tickled. This was next." She took his hand in hers to trace an intricate vine of green and white honeysuckle winding from her right hand up to her elbow. "And this was third. Right before my first episode."

He traced perfectly peeled layers of a red onion with lines of white and purple on the inside of her left forearm. "Why an onion?"

"Because I was sixteen and thought I was deep

and complicated. Knowing me required peeling layers of defenses. Just like every other teenager who listens to brooding music, wears black, and reads Beat Poets."

"Who?" he asked.

"Ginsberg, Burroughs, Kerouac."

"I just thought they were post-World War II. I didn't know they had a name. Sorry, didn't mean to interrupt. Please show me the others."

"These," two matching razor blades drawn vertically along her wrists, "were done after I found out that schizophrenia meant medication for life, the never-ending possibility of an episode hanging over me, and never being normal. No happy family with kids. No full-time job. Devoting myself to staying sane."

"I'm sorry. It's awful."

"It is, but I've learned to cope. My parents couldn't have been better. They helped me through hospitalizations and medication adjustments, arranged for tutors so I could graduate with my class, and basically got me through high school. They encouraged me to maintain friendships, date, and do normal stuff. They didn't hover, although they must have been more terrified than I was.

"They suggested college outside DC in a sleepy city and a school that offered arts and music. I went to Virginia Commonwealth University for two semesters and had another episode. I never went back."

She looked down at her wrists. "People are wrong about cutting wrists horizontally to commit suicide. The razor has to be parallel to the vein to make a serious slice and bleed out. I put them there in case an episode was so bad that if I wanted to kill myself, I would know how."

"Oh, LouLou." Gregg kissed both her wrists. "You talk about this like you're detached from it."

"I am. Sick isn't me. It's an illness that has to be monitored, like diabetes. The psychotic episodes aren't me. The illness hijacks my body until I'm treated. I never remember anything about them."

"Tell me about the rest of your ink," Gregg whispered. She was grateful he didn't belabor the topic of Sick.

"After the diagnosis, I wrote phrases instead of drawing." She pointed out words in French, each phrase with a different script, crawling up her left and right sides. "I tried different styles of calligraphy with each."

"What do they mean?"

"This is *miles to go before I sleep*, this is *to die; to sleep* and that," she turned slightly, "means *life is rounded with sleep*. Those are on the left side. The heart side. They were done at different times, but I was fixated on sleep. I don't know whether I equated sleep with peace or with death.

"The darker ones are on my right. She rolled back and point to each—*weight of pain*. I purposely put *LOVE FADES* in all caps. *Demons in my head* is scrawled in bold.

"Now, the *pièce de résistance*." She flipped onto her stomach so he could see the beauty of her back. A phoenix rose from just above her waist until its red wings spread across her narrow shoulders. Its head raised itself up to her neck. The shadings of orange, pink, and red were delicately blended with traces of purple, blue, and yellow.

Gregg didn't say anything. He traced the bird with his finger from her waist to its head. "It's beautiful. I've never seen anything more beautiful. It's art." He kissed the head of the bird.

"Thank you," she said quietly.

"You did this?"

"I designed it and had a friend do the ink. It took several months. Both of us wanted to get it right." She loved having the phoenix on her back. She could always rise. No matter how bad things got, she hoped to rise above Sick.

"It's happy."

"Yes, I'm a survivor. I've had episodes that left me in a bad place, but I seem to overcome them."

She rolled over and kissed him. "I'd like to see your new compositions I missed when that car literally sideswiped us off track. Let's see how many pieces we can do. Come tomorrow before lunch and Gregg, please come through the wall. I don't want Roy or Sara to see the door to the building open without a person's hand on the buzzer."

# CHAPTER SIXTEEN

Lou and Gregg worked until mid-afternoon. The new pieces didn't require nearly as much revision as his first pieces. LouLou sketched out a schedule that would allow them to record four pieces for her to add to her tour program.

"I need a break. Roy left a fresh salad with tuna and avocado. Iced tea, too. Do you want to stick around while I eat?"

"Sure. I'll take another look at the coda."

She put her hand on his arm. "Rest your mind. Leave it."

Gregg looked around the apartment. "You don't have a TV."

"No. Never have. I get news from newspapers online. Roy knows all the local news. I listen to the radio. When I want to chill, I read."

"Do you mind if I turn on the radio to check baseball scores?"

"Help yourself."

LouLou savored her salad. She wondered if Roy and Sara had a secret vegetable garden or a really good produce provider. She speared a chunk of avocado and thought about what a good sketch a whole avocado would make—rich, dark green skin, lighter layers fading to a core. She'd ask Roy to give her a whole one.

"A final determination has been made about the fire at Commonwealth Psychiatric Hospital in Petersburg…"

LouLou shot off the barstool and shut off the radio. "I don't want to hear that."

Gregg stared at her.

"I spent time there. I know it first-hand. I don't want to hear or read about it either."

"You spent time at Petersburg?" Gregg looked shaken, or as much as a ghost could look shaken without changing pallor.

"Yes." LouLou fetched her iced tea and sat next to him on the sofa. "I told you Sick gets into trouble and LouLou deals with the fallout. I was a patient at Commonwealth Psych three times when I was nineteen and again when I was twenty-three. I went off my meds. I didn't hurt anyone—burglary, vandalism, larceny. Both times I took meds so I would become competent to stand trial. The first time I was found Not Guilty by Reason of Insanity, or NGRI as patients like to call it, and was sentenced to community service. The second NGRI landed me there for about nine months."

"Were you treated?"

LouLou shrugged. "I went to private hospitals first, so the worst of my Sick episodes were over. I got meds while I waited for competency hearings, but I think Dr. Youzny prescribed them. When I did my sentence for NGRI, I was on my standard psych meds to prevent episodes. I guess the answer to your question is no, I wasn't treated.

"I admit all of that was arranged by my parents. Private hospitalizations until the worst was over, supervision by a private psychiatrist which is unheard of, and then maintenance meds to bide time until a judge could consider the sentence long enough to fit the crime. I'm privileged. It made a difference. I'm not ashamed of having my father using his influence. I saw a lot of people who really needed treatment but weren't getting any."

"Why not?"

"No staff. No treatment plans. Most people got enough sedatives to keep them under control until someone declared them competent. I don't know about the NGRIs. They were pretty hard core and in seclusion most of the time."

Gregg stood and paced.

"Why are you so interested in this? I told you I'd committed crimes. I assumed you knew that meant jail or hospitalization for someone like me."

Gregg put his face in his hands. When he looked up, he was crying. "I spent thirteen or fourteen years in Commonwealth Psychiatric Hospital after I turned eighteen. I died the night I was released."

***

Gregg had a mental illness, too? Why hadn't he told her? LouLou didn't know where to begin.

"More secrets? Gregg, you're a genius musician and I thought you were a good man, but you know I need stability. Springing information like that on me is too much for me to handle."

She busied herself putting her salad back in the refrigerator, pouring water, and checking the clock for the amount of time before her next round of meds were due. She reached into her cupboard and took a mood stabilizer that would get her through the ninety minutes before her meds were scheduled. She knew she was being overly cautious. One missed or off-schedule med wouldn't necessarily bring on Sick, but she didn't take chances. Plus, she was angry and hurt that Gregg hadn't been completely truthful with her.

She returned to the striped sofa and curled into the corner, wrapping her soft blue sweater around her like a robe "This sofa is beginning to feel like Freud slept here. I'll listen to what you have to say, but I may not be able to hear all of it. I may have to kick you out. You may just be too much for me. Ghost or not. Your *raison d'être* or not, I'm human and a frail one at that. I'm always anxious about Sick. I can't handle you being a ghost with a mental illness, too. I protect myself. Some people are off-limits."

Other than the panic buttons, she wasn't sure how she'd protect herself should Gregg try to physically harm her. She forced that thought away and waited for Gregg to speak.

Gregg leaned against the counter and faced LouLou. "I'm sorry. No excuses. I didn't connect your Sick with Commonwealth Psych."

She stared at him. "NGRI patients go to Petersburg. You know that. Tell me your story. I think there are two parts. First, how you died. Second, what you were doing there, okay?"

"This is hard, LouLou. I'm reliving my death. Cut me some slack."

She nodded. She also thought "cutting some slack" wasn't a phrase he'd used when he was alive. Skylar probably taught him that.

"Sorry, Gregg. I can't. Spit it out or leave." She reached into her ever-present red tote and took out a blue pill and put it under her tongue. She felt it fizz some calm into her body.

Gregg remained standing, much as he had when he'd told her he was a ghost. He kept his hands at his sides and remained still.

"I'd been at Petersburg for more than a dozen years when I was released one night. I was pretty much the same guy I'd been when I got there. Maybe they needed the bed. Someone signed release papers, the gates were opened, and I walked out at midnight with two five-dollar bills the night nurse gave me.

"There was no moon. It felt chilly, but it wasn't raining. I was disoriented. I hadn't been outside the gates or seen anyone other than residents and staff for all that time. I knew the hospital was in Petersburg, which I thought was a twin city to Richmond like Minneapolis and St. Paul. I was from Norfolk and didn't know my way around any other part of the state. I didn't have a driver's license, so I didn't know the roads. I thought if I just kept walking, I'd eventually get to a road or town and take things from there.

"Ten dollars was a lot of money back then.

Enough for me to eat and buy a local bus ticket. I kept walking and walking, and then I stumbled and fell face first into a creek. I drowned. That's it."

LouLou tried to take it all in. More than twelve years in Commonwealth Psychiatric. Sudden release. Midnight. Dead.

"Didn't you have a discharge plan?"

"A what?"

"A plan the doctors make for what to do when you leave. Didn't you get one?"

Gregg laughed. "I don't think any doctors knew I was there. Like I said, a guy I'm not even sure was a guard woke me up, said it was time to go, and out I went."

"And you drowned."

He nodded.

LouLou processed that. She'd always been driven in and out of the hospital grounds and always had some sort of official paper. Maybe that wasn't done in the 1980s. He'd been treated terribly. He'd wandered around and drowned. Ghastly. She wanted to hug him until his tears stopped, but he'd been a patient. What kind of patient?

"That's unspeakable. I'm sorry."

"Yeah, it was. Looking back, I see how inhumanely I was treated, but it's too late. As for the rest of the story, I'll tell it. No interruptions."

She could do that, but she wanted to know his diagnosis first. "Why were you in the hospital? What was your diagnosis?"

"Nothing. There was nothing wrong with me. Back then, there wasn't a mental illness requirement to be a patient or an inmate. Being undesirable was one of the requirements. I was considered part of the undesirable population."

Despite the mood stabilizer and the sedative, fear crawled through LouLou's stomach up to her throat. He wasn't saying anything that made sense. She'd ask a few more questions and then he'd have to go.

"I've never heard of an undesirable patient. I know what the word undesirable means, but I never heard anyone at Petersburg say that was their reason for being there. What does that mean? "

He perched on the edge of the sofa as far away from LouLou as he could while still being on the couch. He looked down at his feet as he spoke. "I was admitted in 1968, the summer before I was supposed to start at Juilliard. I was with about seven or eight other guys standing outside the Trailways bus station in downtown Norfolk to go to Washington to protest the war. I was exempt from the draft because I'd had migraine headaches most of my life. Otherwise, I would have been a conscientious objector. Vietnam made no sense.

"We were waiting for the bus with tickets to DC, but the police said we were loitering and hauled us off to jail. We weren't there more than an hour before four of us were transferred to Petersburg by the sheriff's office. We were admitted and given cell-size rooms with bunk beds and told to follow the routine. We weren't locked up, but we weren't treated like patients either. I was there until I wasn't."

LouLou interrupted. "That makes no sense. The police can't just round up people and put them in institutions. You must have had a phone call or talked to a lawyer or something. Didn't your parents wonder what happened to you? And Juilliard. You were accepted to the best conservatory in the United States. That's major."

Gregg wouldn't look at her. "Forget Juilliard. Things were different in the 1960s. Really different. I mean, there was segregation for schools, bathrooms, restaurants. Everything. There was a black world and a white world. Surely, you know about the Civil Rights movement."

"Vaguely. I was raised in Europe. I went to high school in DC for two years and don't recall any history classes except for Western Civilization. I know a lot about French colonial states, but almost nothing about American history. I know who Martin Luther King, Jr. was and that there was segregation in parts of the United States. I've never thought about what it was like to live through it. You're not black. Why were you arrested?"

"They thought I was gay, although that's not the term they used. Long-haired skinny white boy. In jeans and a white shirt, they knocked themselves out laughing that they couldn't tell from behind whether I was male or female. The other guys who went to Petersburg with me were black."

LouLou's hands shook. Unbelievable. Could this be true? People were grabbed off the street because they were black or gay and put in the state mental institution?

Suddenly, Gregg laughed out loud. LouLou looked at him as if he really was crazy.

"LouLou," he gasped between laughs, "think about it. You're upset about Juilliard and the indignities of the pre-Civil Rights era but completely accepting of me being a ghost." She smiled. She did see the irony, but she'd also confirmed his ghost story with Skylar.

"It's a horrible truth."

Gregg sobered. "Yes, it is. It's how Big ended up there."

That got her attention. A detail she knew to be true. "You know Big? Of course you do. He's been there forever."

Gregg shook his head. "Not forever. Since the late 1920s."

"How do you know?" She turned to face him.

"I feel like I'm teaching history."

"I wasn't a great student, but I'm pretty sure what you're about to tell me wasn't in a French or American history book."

"You've got a point."

He rolled his neck from side to side, stretched his hands upward as far as he could, and exhaled.

"Involuntary sterilization was legal in Virginia until right before I was released. Petersburg was the place it was done. Half the psych patients at Commonwealth Psych were sterilized when I was there. Important people like Supreme Court Justice Oliver Wendell Holmes decided three generations of imbeciles was enough, so psych patients were prevented from reproducing.

"Hell, people didn't have to be patients to be sterilized there. There were whispers about Mountain Sweeps. A local sheriff and his deputies would go into mountain towns, round up black people, undesirable whites, and people they just didn't like and take them to Petersburg to be sterilized. Sometimes, they'd release them after surgery. Sometimes not. Big was picked up in a Mountain Sweep and stayed."

Her hands flew to her mouth. "Big? Sweet Big?"

Gregg nodded.

"Big looks about thirty-five. How could he have been hospitalized in the 1920s? Could Big be a ghost, too?"

He shook his head. "I don't know. I was alive and human when I was there. I wouldn't have recognized a ghost."

She was off-track. She had to get back to Gregg's story. Just Gregg. "Sheriffs just rounded up people they thought shouldn't reproduce and took them to Petersburg? There weren't any guidelines?" Of course not. What kind of guidelines could there be for having citizens taken out of their homes and sterilized? A wave of nausea hit. "What about you? Were you…sterilized?"

Another laugh. "No, they seemed certain I wasn't going to get any girls pregnant and bring more of my kind into the world, so they left me alone."

How this hot guy could be mistaken for gay for a long period of time was beyond her. It shouldn't have taken a doctor twelve or thirteen years to reach that conclusion. "Did you ever see a doctor?"

"No." He was back to speaking quietly and looking away.

"You never saw a doctor in a dozen years? Or a nurse?"

"No, LouLou. You've been there for treatment. You had a diagnosis and a court order. If you hadn't had a private physician, how often would you have seen a doctor?"

"Rarely." LouLou was treated because she was privileged and had a family with influence overseeing her. If other patients weren't treated, a person who wasn't a patient—part of a group of people some official didn't like—would never see medical staff. LouLou sat quietly in her corner and thought. What Gregg said sounded horrible, but it also sounded true. Without moving, she said quietly, "I'm sorry that happened to you. You spent half your life there. You lost your youth. You didn't go to Juilliard."

Gregg seemed eerily calm. Maybe that came with being a ghost. His past didn't affect him anymore.

"Doesn't matter. I composed. No one messed with my head. Music was always there and sometimes, I was able to write it down. And now you have it to play for the world. It turned out okay."

He looked at her, his eyes pleading her not to send him away because he hadn't spilled his entire story immediately.

"You're incredibly brave and not bitter at all."

"I can't be. I have a second chance. To love you. To share my music. It's all I've ever wanted."

She went to him and let him hold her. They were both on earth to make music and love each other. They were each flawed. Together, they were awesome.

# CHAPTER SEVENTEEN

### August

"Six weeks and done, done, done, done. Four beautiful, fabulous new pieces scored." LouLou and Gregg high fived each other.

"Finished early too," Gregg added. "I can't wait for Skylar to hear them. He's our best audience."

"No, he was our first audience. The music industry loves your work. The outpouring of offers I reviewed with Brooks last week were pretty amazing. I told you about them."

"The names of the companies don't mean much to me. They're all initials. I remember record companies with names like Mercury, Atlantic, and Decca. It's good to know professionals like our work, but my goal was to get it out of my head and give it to you. You ran with it."

"Gregg, we've got to talk about credit."

"No, we don't. It's all yours."

"But it's your music. I did some arrangements and produced. It's your legacy."

"I'm fine with just you and Skylar knowing that." He grabbed his jacket. "C'mon, we don't want to be late for the movie."

LouLou dropped the subject. She loved going to the movies with Gregg. They went to an art house that played indie and classic films during late afternoons, when the theatre wasn't crowded. She and Gregg didn't talk during the film because no one could see Gregg and she'd look like she was talking to herself or the screen. She felt normal at the movies. She and Gregg were on a real date. A normal, relaxing date. They held hands.

After the movie, they'd spend hours in her loft talking about film. LouLou loved film almost as much as music. Gregg was learning. He absorbed everything. He knew some of the classic films. Current films mesmerized him, particularly special effects, but he was awed by some of the stories told by foreign language films. He was stunned at how much movies had changed since he'd last seen one. The first time he'd seen nudity, he seemed to expect her to close her eyes. He couldn't believe the cursing and violence that was now acceptable. She thought it made him a bit uncomfortable.

This afternoon's movie was a desert movie—LouLou's weakness. She'd no idea why. She'd never been to a desert. There was something about a love story playing against the backdrop of seas of sand and the feelings of intimacy and isolation it stirred in her that always made her cry no matter how happy the ending.

After the movie, Gregg and LouLou returned to her loft. She was going into hibernation the next day.

"Do you have everything for the tour?"

"The CDs are being delivered to Roy's tomorrow. I'm trying a new company to burn and package them. The demo was good. I'm all set musically."

Gregg brushed a strand of blonde hair away from her eyes. "Tired?"

"Exhilarated about tonight." She filled a glass of water and plopped on the sofa. Gregg sat close.

"Tell me where you're playing again."

"It's a no-name after-hours blues club owned by my friend Clive and his wife, who is, believe it or not, named Olive. Mostly, the club attracts newcomers and old-timers. Sometimes, it turns into an all-night jam session depending on who's there. It's the only place to get a drink after two in the morning. I've heard some great stuff there."

"Sounds good."

"I'm going to eat now, take my meds, and nap until about midnight. I'll probably have a snack before we leave. Skylar's picking us, or shall I say me, up at about one. It's about a forty-minute drive from here."

"That's not much time before a show. Don't you have to do a sound check? Lights? Get dressed?"

LouLou laughed. "Clive's really is underground. I think it's a basement. There's two restrooms. Whichever one's not in use is my dressing room. The lighting guy is older than Skylar and he's been working longer. If he can't find me on stage, no one can."

"What about the turntables? The booth?"

"Prop turntable. No booth. It's as basic at it gets. There is a stage to separate the show from the crowd. No curtain to raise or lower."

Gregg looked thoughtful. "Kind of like a church basement."

"Exactly like a church basement if it had kegs, bottled bourbon, and tequila."

***

"They're going to boo me off the stage." LouLou adjusted her short-short backless yellow dress with red and orange flames shooting up from the hem and rested her hand on Clive's shoulder for balance as she put on one red stiletto and then, the other. Olive put finishing touches on her makeup and pulled a strand of blonde hair out of the way to better frame her face.

"Why would they do that? Your stuff's great."

"You're a blues club. I'm anything but blues. You gave me the prime two o'clock spot. How did I let you talk me into this?"

Clive kissed her. "Honey, you should know by now I can talk anybody into anything. Besides, most of them will be lit, and you're only on for twenty minutes." He walked onto the stage, mic in hand, and introduced "Richmond's own DJL."

The small crowd of music-lovers, some of whom had just finished their own shows in Fredericksburg and Virginia Beach, at the underground club went wild. LouLou gyrated her way onto the stage and started spinning one of Gregg's pieces. She quickly found her zone and soon had the crowd in her hands, making the audience dance wildly, sway dreamily, and bounce with freestyle abandon. With the lights flashing on her in various colors of reds LouLou was by turns fiery, seductive, and incandescent. She covered the length of the stage in Trey's choreography, which had required her to watch and imitate Michael Jackson's *Thriller* video too many times to count to do just one of his famous turn-on-a-dime pirouettes. In stilettos, no less.

She could feel the music inside her before it came through the house speakers. She modulated selections to fit her mood as she read what the crowd needed and wanted. She had hours of music to choose from, but she spun twenty-one minutes of pure gold. The house went dark, and LouLou snuck off before the house lights went up. The crowd wanted more and chanted her name—"DJL. DJL. DJL."

While the audience still remained hopeful, Clive walked back onstage, where he was booed. "Thanks, but if you want to hear more of DJL's newest EPs, you're going to have to go to Reykjavík, where she kicks off her Scandinavian Summer Solstice Tour. She was nice enough to give us a little *amuse-bouche*. For those of you who remain uncivilized, that means taste." He gestured off-stage. "Thanks, DJL, for a taste of what's coming out in November in the United States."

LouLou was surrounded by a few big names in music as well as appreciative audience members in the tiny hallway off-stage. They all talked at once, so she only heard snippets. "Cool. Wall of sound, man, wall of sound. Groundbreaking." The group spilled out into the humid night air. LouLou, hot from the stage lights, took deep breaths. She could've played for another two hours.

She noticed Robert spread languidly across the top of an upright piano just inside the stage door. LouLou rubbed his head. "Smart guy. You're not going out in that humidity. Enjoy yourself. We promise not to leave without you."

Skylar pushed through the crowd and hugged her. "She's the best. Didn't I tell you, Clive? I discovered her, you know," Skylar shouted over the crowd and the next act warming up.

Clive didn't let it go. "Did not. Known her since she was in knee socks. Always knew she'd be a star."

The two men slung their arms around each other's shoulders and headed to the after-hours bar. Neither had met her until she was eighteen. She hadn't been wearing knee socks.

Trey had a crowd of women gathered around him as he crowed about his choreography. "Choreography is everything. That, and good lighting." LouLou smiled to herself. Trey had been using that line since they were nineteen-year-old VCU drop-outs, and amazingly, it still worked.

Roy and Sara hugged her. "I'm checking your closets tomorrow. Hot dress. You were smokin'. I thought Roy was going to pass out when he saw you. Have your dresses gotten smaller and tighter over the years?"

LouLou whispered in Sara's ear. "Older. Gotta distract eyes away from the saggy bits."

Sara laughed. "Your legs go on forever. Why not show them off? Good for you."

From the corner of her eye, LouLou saw Gregg standing under a tree, smiling. She put on earbuds and went to him. He slipped his arm around her waist. "I've never seen anything like that. You were fantastic. The music combinations, your moves, your hotness. I heard some guy call you sex on a stick and wanted to punch him, but he's right."

"So you liked it?" she said as she moved in closer. To anyone watching, she'd look like she was talking to someone on her phone and stretching out her back against the enormous tree trunk.

"It was the best night of my life, LouLou."

Not daring to kiss him, she rubbed a little closer and whispered, "The best is yet to come."

It did. After staying to listen to a blues set by a new girl band, Gregg, Skylar, and Robert piled into LouLou's car for the ride home. Skylar snored in the back seat, occasionally mumbling blues lyrics. Robert sat on Gregg's lap.

After dropping off Skylar and Robert, LouLou carried her tote and one turntable into the loft with Gregg beside her. She saw that the lights were off at Roy and Sara's. They'd left after her set. Still, LouLou didn't want to take a chance that anyone might see Gregg invisibly carrying her gear.

Once inside, they fell on each other and made love that had a ferocity to it that LouLou didn't know Gregg possessed. Jealousy did that to guys. He'd also said seeing her onstage officially made her the hottest woman he'd seen in any lifetime.

The sun rose, and she knew it was time for Gregg to go and her to hibernate. She needed to stay healthy. She got up, took her meds, and then pulled Gregg down to her for their last lovemaking before her tour. She wouldn't see him for two months. She almost couldn't bear to go.

# CHAPTER EIGHTEEN

Bella Davis flung yet another dead-end medical journal on the colorfully inlaid mosaic floor. She wanted to kick something. Not that it would provide any stress relief. Being a ghost, Bella's kick would send her transparent foot through the wooden leg of the mahogany library table rather than making a satisfying smack or even a dent on contact. She could rip some journals. That would make the administration of the venerable New York Academy of Medicine take notice, but it wouldn't help her.

Bella had made a rare miscalculation two years ago. She'd arranged to send her Daniel to Petersburg for a three-month stint as revenge. He'd gotten cold feet and abruptly ended their affair after his father died. She'd killed his wife, framed him for the murder, and struck a deal to have the case against Daniel dropped at his first competency hearing after a short stint in Commonwealth Psychiatric Hospital. Bella underestimated Daniel's ability to endure the conditions at Petersburg. He hadn't been treated and released. He'd become catatonic and stuck there.

At a loss, Bella stood and walked around the windowless room, running her long, beautifully manicured fingers over priceless gold and bronze statues, along the leather spines of rare books, and on the soft velvet reading chairs. She stopped and pressed her forehead against one of the cool marble walls. She concentrated to feel the cold on her face, down the back of her neck, and into her spine. Sometimes, feeling just a little human would give her a creative spark. She closed her eyes and hoped the chill would jolt her brain into generating a new idea.

When she opened her eyes, she noticed she was standing next to one of the few laptop stations in the room. Quickly, she scrolled through medical journals published anywhere in the world within the last seventy-two hours. Within seconds, "Algorithms for Treating Catatonia in Clinical Settings" appeared on the screen. She quickly scanned the article. "Yes," she shouted to the empty room. Her triumph echoed around her. On the screen before her was a step-by-step treatment plan. The author was a psychiatrist who worked as a neurologist in Mississippi.

She'd done it. She'd found the doctor and the treatment. She'd have Dr. Mississippi personally treat Daniel. She'd see him today, even though she'd have to fly commercially. She had difficulty space traveling to places she'd never been to while alive. She'd formulate a plan during the flight using Daniel's attorney, his brother Rob, who was Dan's legal guardian, and as much money as Dr. Mississippi wanted. Bank-robbing and computer transfers of large sums of money were easy. Being on the opposite side of the law she'd enforced when she was a living securities attorney gave her a cheap thrill but nothing compared to the exhilaration of having Daniel back. He'd be healthy and hers in no time.

# CHAPTER NINETEEN

## October

The music in the airport lounge was chaotic. LouLou had learned so much from her Scandinavian tour, but this noise wasn't like anything she'd ever heard. Instead of cohesion or even dissonance, every line had a different wave length. Each thread separated from the whole and curled and snaked and snarled around itself with no indication it was going to resolve. Twelve or thirteen threads at once.

An attendant offered her something to drink. He handed her a glass of club soda, but it slipped from her hand and spilled on the carpet.

"I'm sorry," he said. "I'll bring you another. Why don't you move to the other end of the sofa so your feet won't be damp."

She felt very territorial about her seat. "No, I want to stay where I am." He gave her an odd look, and a second attendant brought her a club soda and placed it on the table next to her. There was a straw in the glass. "Is there anything else you'd like? Do you feel unwell?"

She stared at him. Unwell. Why did he think she was unwell? She had all her clothes on, was holding her tote, and had her ticket.

"I didn't get much sleep last night." She hadn't. She kept hearing all those guttural, incomprehensible sounds of Nordic languages racing through her head. Everyone spoke English to her, but she'd heard indecipherable conversations swirling about her for two months.

He sneered at her. "I hear that a lot, Ms. Fleming. I'll see that you're allowed to pre-board so you can make yourself comfortable before takeoff. The flight from Copenhagen to New York is just over eight hours, so maybe you can sleep on the plane. You'll have a personal canopy for privacy in International Class. You won't be disturbed."

She asked him to dim the lights in her area. He gave her a nasty look but turned them down. Everything here was made of glass. Everything. There was no escaping the light. Even when it was harsh and blinding.

The flight was a nightmare. As she walked the aisle to the restroom and back, everyone stared at her and whispered that she wasn't one of them. LouLou looked like them—blue-eyed, blonde—but she couldn't communicate with them. She must be Estonian. Latvian, maybe. English.

She knew the flight attendants had been warned by the lounge staff that she was an outcast. She huddled in her lounge seat and pulled the canopy closed. She didn't want anyone to see her. She refused all service—no beverages, meals, steamed towels. They were all poisonous.

The food and drink would kill her. If she put one of their towels on her face, she'd be burned with acid. She took a sleeping pill of her own but couldn't sleep. Nordic words spun around in her brain like LPs on a turntable. She put on her headphones without sound to shut out the words, but they kept circling faster and faster.

The two-hour layover at JFK felt like two days. She was disoriented. She stumbled down a long concourse and was blinded by neon signs advertising food, Vikings, and trolls. She turned and went halfway down another concourse and into the men's room. A nasty man in a suit called someone, and she was put in a cart on wheels and driven to her gate. She didn't know how the cart moved. There wasn't a horse to pull it.

She assured everyone who asked she was fine. Just eager to get home after a long trip. They all smiled condescendingly when she spoke.

A man in a uniform put her in the commuter plane seat and buckled her seatbelt. He tried to take her tote, but she hugged it to her. There was hardly anyone on the short flight to Richmond and no one bothered her. She heard them whispering, though. Foreigner. Alien. Immigrant. She put on her headphones to ignore them. They just talked louder.

When she got into a cab at the Richmond airport, she didn't know exactly where to tell the driver to take her. It was late. She was too tired to think. She was hungry, though. "Just drive along Broad Street," she said.

They drove for about thirty minutes before she recognized her destination. "Here. I want to get out here," she said excitedly when they passed a market with a familiar name.

"Lady, that store's closed."

"Not for me. They keep it open for me." She jumped out of the cab while it was still moving and ran to the door. She was banging on the door when the cabbie ran up behind her.

"You're not skipping out on the fare," he bellowed.

"I'm not going to the fair with you. Get away from me." LouLou kicked him in the groin. She screamed and screamed. The cabbie bent over, cursing. She had to get away. She picked up chunks of cement where the sidewalk was uneven and threw them at the store windows until one broke. She crawled in through the small opening and pulled her tote behind her into the darkened store.

Noise was everywhere. Elevator music. Sirens. Alarms. It was like a soundtrack of a movie about The German Blitz. She had to hide. She grabbed bags of charcoal and stacked them to cover the hole in the window. She was hungry, so she went in search of something to eat. She passed toilet paper and baby food and flour. She couldn't find food.

She ran down the flour aisle and stopped in front of cake frostings. She pulled a chocolate chip frosting can off the shelf, ripped it open, and started to eat it with her fingers. She needed something to dip in it. She ran up and down the aisles until she found radishes. She finished the frosting and radishes but was still hungry. She ate a jar of gherkins, a package of dry egg noodles, and was munching on dog food treats when she heard loud voices.

She had to hide while she planned her attack on the approaching voices. She grabbed a box of aluminum foil and a broom and ducked behind the seafood counter. She had to get to her ice fort, where they couldn't see her. The voices were coming from different directions, but not near her fort. She lay on the floor to make sure they weren't nearby, but it was fiery. The floor burned her stomach and made a hole through her skin. Her stomach was going to fall out. She had to get inside her ice fort.

She crawled toward the ice display case and climbed in. Good. She could hear the machine churning as it constantly produced fresh ice. Her fort wouldn't leak. She held her stomach inside her body with one hand and the foil in the other. She'd pull the weapon in behind her. Quickly, she papered the counter glass with foil so no one could see her. Pressing the tote against herself to hold her abdominal organs inside, she hauled the weapon inside and pulled the sliding panels shut. She lay on the ice that smelled vaguely of shrimp. She was safe.

# CHAPTER TWENTY

**November**

Damn. She was back in Petersburg. In bed. She rolled over. She seemed to have a lot of extra cushioning. No restraints except for an IV that was attached to a vein in her hand under a lot of gauze. LouLou saw a barred window. She was in a normal room—not seclusion—so they didn't think she would hurt herself or anyone else. She closed her eyes and went back to sleep.

"Good afternoon, LouLou," said Dr. Izari. He stood next to her bed. "I'm glad you're awake."

Her name must be LouLou.

"Give me the short version," she said with a thick tongue. She'd no idea how long she'd been here. It didn't matter. She'd be here a long time.

"According to your pharmacy records, you ran out of meds eight days before you left Copenhagen." He frowned at her chart. "You finished the tour but had a psychotic episode at the airport in Copenhagen. When you landed in

Richmond, you broke into a grocery store, injured yourself by crawling through a glass window, and ultimately assaulted two policemen with a broom. You also ripped off a cab driver and assaulted him."

Not terribly imaginative, but enough for her to have charges pending.

"You spent a few days at Richmond Memorial Hospital to attend your medical needs. You had glass shards embedded along your body where you crashed through glass. They had to be meticulously removed by hand. You still have bandages on your arms, sides, and legs above your boot tops. You're continuing on pain medication and an antibiotic to prevent infection from those lacerations. You were close to sepsis so you stayed longer than usual at RMH. Once that danger had passed, you were transferred here. You've been here four days. We've added a sedative, Clozopine, and Resperdal for Sick. We'll gradually up the meds."

"I know the drill. Two months, right?"

He nodded. "Maybe a little more. You can't let your wounds get infected. A private wound care nurse comes daily. Your parents arranged that."

"Can I leave my room?" She didn't really want to. She wanted to stay here and sleep with the meds running through her blood to her brain to kill Sick. That's why she was here. Sick had done something bad.

"No. You're taking baby steps. Walking to/from your bathroom, sitting in the chair, and walking around the room. You're not strong enough to leave this room. When you're more alert, you can take walks outside with an aide. After that, you can maybe go to the day room.

She was currently imprisoned in her room, but she would eventually get fifteen minutes outside in fresh air every day. She was at least a month away from the day room, where there were other patients. She was alone.

LouLou turned away from him. Tears ran down her cheeks.

***

On the first day she was allowed to go to the day room, LouLou sat cross-legged on a sofa, chipping at her nails. She knew she'd polished them a pretty apple green. She'd keep chipping until she found it. Big, the tallest and heaviest guy on the ward and someone she recognized from previous stays, gave her the rundown on her fellow patients.

"Most are like you. Here to get meds until you can go to court. A few NGRIs who almost never come in here. One does, but she's an older lady. Some head bangers. Two smack detoxes. And the zombie." He nodded in the direction of a man seated in a wheelchair by the smallest window in the day room.

"He's okay if nobody bothers him. Aides put him there every morning and return him to his room during the late afternoon. His eyes blink, but I don't think he sees anything. Doesn't respond to anything—touches, sounds, or smells. There was a fire here a while ago, and he never acted like he heard the alarm, which was off the charts, saw a dozen firemen, or smelled smoke that sent a bunch of people to the hospital. A couple of guys tried to escape with the firemen, and there was a brawl. He ignored it. Seems to like that window, though. He becomes agitated if he's taken back to his room early. Agitated is too strong a word. I sense it upsets him."

"What's his story?" she asked.

"Walked in as normal as any of us. Spent the first night in the Quiet Room. Been a zombie ever since. Been here about two years. "

"Faking?" she guessed.

"Nah, no one could fake it that long. He's the real deal."

"What if I go flash him? That'd wake him up." The hyper-sexuality that was part of an episode hadn't completely faded. Flashing a stranger appealed to her, although she'd never considered flashing the old man who took her for fifteen-minute walks outside every day.

"Those little strawberries? Doubt it."

"Just watch." Lou sauntered over toward the man. She wore low slung shredded jeans, a tank top over a Henley that wasn't buttoned, and flip flops. She stopped in front of him, blocking his view of the window. He didn't make a move or a sound.

She was about to start pulling off her clothes when she looked closely at him. He looked familiar, like one of her parents' friends. No. She'd seen him somewhere. Certainly not in a DJ club. Maybe in a doctor's office. When she recognized him, her facial features softened immediately. She crouched to be eye level with him.

"High Life? It's me, Lou," she said softly. "From

Richmond Memorial Hospital a while back. Your brother brought you tee shirts."

Dan, who she'd nicknamed High Life, stared blankly at her.

LouLou started to cry. "What happened to you, High Life?" She touched his arm. "How did you get here? How did you get so old?" She brushed his long, white hair out of his face. Her cries developed into sobs. She hiccupped. She sat on the floor and wept. An aide grabbed her still-sore arm and escorted her back to her room.

# CHAPTER TWENTY-ONE

"Lou, you're back." Big was holding court in his usual corner of the couch with his back to the wall and eyes on the door. LouLou sat next to him.

"Spent three days on stronger meds. I hate this Sick. I'm wild when I don't take meds and smudgy when I do. Sucks. Parents with the gene shouldn't have kids. I'm certainly not. Tubes tied when I was eighteen. Tried to get it done at sixteen, but no one would do it without my parents' consent."

Lou watched Dan staring, or seeming to stare, out the window. "Breaks my heart," she said. "He was a good guy. Depressed after his wife died. Nothing like this."

"Don't go too soft. He's here because he killed his wife. Waiting for him to become competent." This caused one of the patients awaiting trial to laugh hysterically. "To stand trial," Big finished.

"No way," Lou said. She looked sideways at Big.

"Way."

Lou wandered slowly over to Dan. She didn't want to spook him. Or maybe he didn't spook. She squatted next to the arm of his chair and looked at him.

"Bus," he croaked.

She patted his hand. He seemed like he was waiting for a response. She sat without moving for a long time before a smile crossed her face.

"Right, High Life. I'm the girl waiting for the bus. You cracked me up."

***

"Mr. Ramsay," said the nurse. "Mr. Ramsay, did you have something you wanted to say?"

Dan didn't respond.

The nurse looked at LouLou with his hands on his hips. "You said he spoke to you."

"Just one word. Bus. It came out kind of like a cough."

"Lou, he hasn't spoken a word in two years. Why would he say bus?"

LouLou couldn't contain her excitement. Her words spewed out. "We were at Richmond Memorial Hospital at the same time. He was there for depression, and I was waiting to be transferred here. He was really into exercise and walked around the halls four or five times every night. We talked one night, and I said I wouldn't see him the next day because my bus was coming. He didn't understand. He's this straight guy from the 'burbs. He didn't know I meant an ambulance or a police car. So,

119

three days ago, when I saw him, I said hi and today when I went over, he said bus. That means he connects me as the girl who was waiting for her bus."

"I think you're practicing wishful thinking. I've got fifty active patients to oversee. He's quiet, not bothering anybody. He's fine as he is," said the nurse as he walked away.

LouLou looked back at High Life. "I'm not being wishful. I know you spoke to me. We'll just keep it a secret." She winked at him.

# CHAPTER TWENTY-TWO

Damn Dr. Mississippi. He was more elusive than she'd expected. Upon arriving at the Mississippi hospital, where Dr. Harvey Chernoff practiced, Bella learned the doctor had taken a year-long sabbatical after the publication of his journal article. Answers as to his whereabouts were vague. Leads sent her on useless trips to Dr. Chernoff's elderly parents in Sacramento and a vacation villa in Baja. Finally, she learned he was spending the bulk of his sabbatical working with Borderless Medicine. Bella considered it a worthy organization, but she needed Dr. Chernoff more than it did.

He'd been moved twice to help with disaster relief in the Nepal earthquake to the conflict in South Sudan. Now, he was in Ethiopia working to halt the meningitis epidemic. Where in Ethiopia? Bella had impersonated a government official and shown fake credentials identifying her as a high-level staffer with the Department of Homeland

Security to finally meet the elusive Dr. Chernoff. She approached him as a representative of the United States government who required Dr. Chernoff's services for an unidentified patient important to the United States and its allies.

"I don't understand. I'm to be here for eight more months." The two stood outside the facility where people were lined up for vaccinations. Bella's heels sank in sand, but she was still almost eye level with Dr. Chernoff.

"Your commitment to the organization is admirable, Dr. Chernoff, but this is an official request from the United States government. It overrides any contract you have with Borderless Medicine." She was glad to be a ghost. A human would be sweating profusely in this heat. She appeared completely unfazed by the weather and her coolness added to her unflappable authority.

"May I see your identification again?"

Bella produced her credentials with the condescending attitude of an official accustomed to not having her orders questioned. She could tell the doctor didn't understand a word of the legalese she'd prepared.

"Where's the information about the patient? I must have that in order to treat this person. I might not be able to help them."

She had him. Keeping him was critical. She played the privacy card. All doctors feared sanctions for violating the privacy rights of a patient he or she wasn't officially treating. Federal penalties trumped even malpractice claims.

"Dr. Chernoff, all of that is classified

information until you are officially part of the treatment team. You'll be flown to Washington, where you'll be briefed and then taken to the patient, who is in a government facility."

"These people here need me. There's an epidemic. The world has forgotten Ethiopia," he argued.

Bella turned as if to walk towards the vehicle that would take them to the plane. "Dr. Chernoff, you're double-boarded as a psychiatrist and neurologist. You're vaccinating children. That task doesn't require someone of your experience and expertise. Your government has requested that your services be applied elsewhere. I'll escort you on your flight to Washington."

"But I must say good-bye."

"Dr. Chernoff," Bella commanded. "You're to leave with me now. Arrangements have been made to terminate your deployment here. A fee of $250,000 has been paid to the organization to release you from services. Think of the number of vaccines that will purchase. How many people will benefit." She firmly grasped Dr. Chernoff's hand. "Our car is this way."

Bella didn't relax until they were on the flight from London's Heathrow airport to Dulles International airport outside Washington, DC. Retaining Dr. Chernoff had taken a lot of effort. She'd hacked into the computers of Borderless Doctors to create a record of the termination of Dr. Chernoff's services and deposited $250,000 into its account with his name referenced. The money had come from the illegal off-shore account of a hedge fund manager who had eluded justice while she was alive.

Writing as a physician who'd been contacted in his search for a specialist in catatonia, Bella contacted Daniel's brother and legal guardian Rob to advise him that Dr. Chernoff was eager to consult on Daniel's case. She sent the journal article as an attachment. From there, all the pieces quickly moved into place like an excellent chess match— Rob through Nina Lombardi through the greased judicial wheels of Virginia that authorized Dr. Harvey Chernoff to treat Daniel Ramsay as a private patient at Commonwealth Psychiatric Hospital.

# CHAPTER TWENTY-THREE

On her good days, LouLou visited Dan in the day room. She'd told him she was a schizo the first time they'd met, but she reminded him. During the first weeks she visited him, she'd sit next to Dan and not say much. She'd angle herself so she could share his view. To keep herself occupied, she brought a sketch pad and crayons with her and drew whatever was outside. She hoped she saw what he did. Subtle changes every day.

She captured the subtle changes in the sketches she showed him. She drew melting ice puddles in the bitterness of December and the next day, starlings drinking the water. Dan seemed to like one of a black bird against the stark trees and dizzying whiteness. He reached for it when she showed it to him. She hadn't seen him move before. She gave him the drawing, and he held it on his lap even when he was taken back to his room.

Their communication went at a stuttering pace.

He would say one or two words in response to a string of sentences LouLou had said the previous day or visit. One day he said ink. He wanted to know about her tattoos.

She took his hand in hers to trace them. "Do you want a tattoo? Crayon tat?"

He blinked his eyes twice. She took that as yes.

"What do you want?"

"Run," he said decisively, but she didn't understand.

"Like escape?" She laughed. "We all want that.

"Foot. Race."

He was a runner. He probably wanted something to remind himself that he might get well enough to run again so she wanted to get it right for him. She sketched feet. Standing on tip toes. Flexed. Poised to run. Running. She left them with him and he looked at them all day. When she saw him before he left, he pointed to the sketch of a winged bare foot in motion that looked like it could fly.

"I like that one too," she said. "We'll start tomorrow."

She outlined, colored, and highlighted it on his left forearm with intense concentration during their next few visits. On the second day, he said, "Tickles." She laughed. "Yes, crayons tickle. They're sticky and smell waxy, but it's what I've got. I guess our keepers think crayons are less dangerous than pencils or paint brushes."

She made the final stroke on the wing. "Done. I hope you like it." Lou searched his face for any sign that he was pleased. Nothing.

When Dan left that afternoon, she sat next to Big

and sighed. "It's not wishful thinking. He talks. It's just delayed. Like it takes him hours to process what I said and for him to get a response to come out of his mouth. Sometimes it takes me a while to decipher what he means."

"You shouldn't do it if it makes you tired," Big said kindly.

"I like drawing. It passes the time. I'm sure it's more frustrating for him than me."

"What you draw is beautiful. You make magic from those delicate fingers."

She was surprised. Big never said anything personal. "Thank you. Do you want a tat?"

He grunted. "No, thanks. You can draw on the zombie all you want."

"His name's Dan. Don't call him the zombie."

Big put up his hands. "Point taken."

They sat quietly for a while before he spoke. "Lou, you're looking like a skeleton. Aren't you eating?"

"The meds make me nauseated. I'm getting IV fluids tonight. The nausea will go away in another week." She sighed. "I wish I could just go to sleep and wake up when the meds have kicked in. This is really hard."

"It's bad. I'm glad you can tattoo Dan to keep you busy. If you run out of space on him, I might think about letting you draw a small one on me."

LouLou started to cry. She thought of Petersburg as a place to fill with tears.

***

Dan didn't come to the day room the next day. LouLou was disappointed. Drawing things for him made time pass more quickly.

LouLou sat in his chair and sketched. She'd leave the sketches for Dan so he'd know what view he'd missed. She enjoyed the stillness. The evergreens were always different shades of green. She liked that Virginia had so many evergreens. They never lost leaves or turned brown or looked sad. Today, she drew just the tops. She had to use every green and blue in the crayon box, plus white and brown. She tried to mix colors, but the waxy crayons didn't blend. Even spitting on them didn't get the stuff to mix. She just drew and then tried to smudge where she could.

Voices floated up to her on the second floor. She looked down to the gravel parking lot and saw a slim woman in a black suit with an asymmetrical haircut. She carried a briefcase. She was with a man in a navy-blue suit who looked like Dan back when he was at Richmond Memorial Hospital, only slightly older. He didn't have white hair, though. She stood and got as close to the pane as she could to see what was going on.

The woman opened the driver's side door of the Mercedes sedan. The man looked around, as if he wanted to reassure himself it was okay to get in the car. He looked sad and tired. He glanced up and saw her at the window. He shook his head and looked again. LouLou put her hand up to wave. He froze. She could hear the woman urging him to get in the car. He didn't move. He kept staring at her. The look on his face was terror. Naked terror.

# CHAPTER TWENTY-FOUR

LouLou's stay was typical from what she recalled. She'd feel better, then plateau, and then relapse. There was no particular reason for the relapse—just the course of the disease. Time on medication—the correction medication, or combination of medications at the correct dose—was the only thing that would get LouLou back to a functioning person. Some medications took as long as a month to reach therapeutic levels. It wasn't like taking ibuprofen, which could make a headache disappear within the hour. In the meantime, she didn't remember what she'd done, nor did she think about anything. While recovering from the relapse, her life revolved around the four walls of her room and medication punctuated by doctor visits

Telling time was impossible, and she didn't really care about time. Mostly, she slept while Dr. Izari tinkered with her meds. She still got shots and a yellow tablet, but now she also got a white table four times a day. Meds. Shot. Sleep.

After she stopped sleeping around the clock, LouLou resumed her outdoor rambles. Early each evening, an attendant took her for a walk outside. LouLou walked listlessly beside the man. He was older and quiet. She liked that. She liked natural sounds whether it was silence or the crunch of her foot on a branch, the caw of a starling, or squirrels chasing each other and chattering. Outside was peaceful. Although she tuned it out, the hospital was never quiet. Arguments, fistfights, and voices over the intercom all day and all night filled the air. Someone was always yelling or crying or screaming. She was grateful that her aide wasn't one of those who constantly jabbered about nothing or worse, told her how soon she'd be well. She knew exactly how long it would take, barring any more setbacks, and it wasn't soon.

When she was well enough to return to the day room, she discovered Dan in his usual spot, but he sat in a chair, not a wheelchair. Had he walked? She sat next to Big. She wasn't up for an interaction with Dan. They were tiring, as Big had said. Trying to understand him and making herself understood was a bigger effort than she'd realized. She sank into the sofa next to Big and sat in companionable silence for a while before she asked what was up with Dan.

"Did he walk by himself in here?"

"Sure did," Big said. "New doc. New treatment. Got him up and walking in less than a week. Maybe talking will come next."

LouLou sighed. "That would be nice. I can't imagine being trapped in my body for years with no communication. I still don't think he killed his wife. He wouldn't have a clue how to do it."

"Could always hire somebody."

"Oh, Big. Where would he find a hit man? He'd probably look in the yellow pages for one, if yellow pages still exist. I suppose he could try Craigslist. Like they'd have a section of Hitmen For Hire. The man I met at Richmond Memorial was pure vanilla. He'd never hurt anyone and wouldn't be savvy enough to hire someone. "

"Innocent until proven guilty," Big said.

***

LouLou watched as Dan walked into the day room the next morning. She couldn't believe it. She wanted his doctor. He was a miracle worker.

Once seated, he looked at Lou and almost smiled. She walked over and sat on the floor next to him. He held the sketches she'd made of the evergreens the day he met his new doctor. "Pretty."

"I'm glad you like them."

He seemed like he wanted to ask her something. She waited patiently while he formed words in a sensible sequence. Hair. Cut. Sketch. Barber. The last syllable was pronounced as a question.

"You want to get a haircut?"

"Yes."

"You want me to sketch what you want to show the barber?"

"Please." It came out as two syllables.

"That's easy. Do you want to pose now?"

He nodded.

She got her sketchbook and quickly drew his face. It was oval, hollow-cheeked with small brown eyes and a high forehead. She showed it to him. He looked shocked.

"I forgot. We don't have mirrors. We all look different after time here. Mostly weight loss. We need to find you a style that looks good on you now. Okay?"

He nodded. Again, a movement he hadn't made two weeks ago.

LouLou moved to another chair by a larger window and drew the face with different hair styles. She only knew about styling techniques that were best for her long blonde hair. Thin white hair was another story. She wanted to make his hair look attractive. Or at least not awful.

She tried a style that was straight back off the forehead and ended at the ear, a Richard Gere layered look, a semi buzz cut, and a David Beckham/George Clooney look. She wished, as she did for herself, that he had some wavy texture. A shaggy Johnny Depp would look good and make him not look so old, but that was impossible here. He needed something low maintenance—wash and comb.

Late that afternoon, she showed him the sketches. He looked at the drawings and then looked up at her. He mimed pulling his hair back in a ponytail. "No way, High Life. Pony tails and man buns are out. You have to cut your hair to look current."

He looked surprised. Was it because she was bossy or knew trends? Either way, he decided on a short David Beckham cut and kept the sketch.

"Good choice. Your mind seems to be working just fine."

# CHAPTER TWENTY-FIVE

Bella couldn't believe this girl was allowed to go for walks. Skinny, stringy hair, bleary eyes. Too out of it to wear a coat? She probably wouldn't make three laps around the courtyard in this weather. Bella had gone to a lot of trouble to subdue the girl's regular aide, costume herself as a middle-aged Eastern European physiotherapist, and assign herself to LouLou. The fact that the girl was addled worked in Bella's favor.

"Where's my usual guy?" said the girl.

"Out sick. I talk better. Let's go." She started walking fast, chattering away about nothing, and forcing LouLou to hustle to keep up. LouLou put her hands in her pockets and shivered, whereas Bella had been smart enough to wear boots, a big down coat, a hat over a dark brown wig, gloves, and a plaid muffler. Dark sunglasses covered her unforgettable eyes.

"Come. Move. Walk. Don't you see puddles?

Why you walk through puddles? No boots in snow? Feet will be wet. You get cold. Go to infirmary. Many germs there. Many germs. You get sick."

She picked up the pace with LouLou trying to keep up.

"Come. Come. Finished one trip. Two more to go. Lazy girl. Walk. More. You walk with slow old man. Now you have me. Champion in my country. No drugs. No scandal. No doping. All lies. International committees say doping. No. Never. All me. In good shape. Best shape. Beat all other women."

She had LouLou breathing hard to keep up in her thin sweatshirt and wet tennis shoes.

"Walk with people like you slow me down. Gain weight. Big ass now. Men like big ass. Still not like I was with medals. Many men want me with medals. Many men.

"You. You have no men. Look at you. Do you have shampoo? Soap? Comb? You skinny mess. No man want mess like you. Okay. Finished two. Last round. Can you make it, slow girl? Slow, skinny girl with no man?"

LouLou was panting. They reached the halfway point, and LouLou stopped.

"Stop? Why you stop? Halfway to end."

"You're moving too fast. I can't keep up. I forgot my boots."

"Tomorrow you know to wear boots. After snow, always puddles. Mud. Slush. Don't you know anything?"

LouLou remained where she was, panting.

"Okay. I understand. Your father take care of

you. Tell you what to wear. Where is he today? Asleep? Let you go outside without coat? Boots?"

LouLou didn't move. "My father's not here."

"Liar. You and crazy father here together. Whole family crazy criminals. Mother crazy. Kills self. Father crazy. Killed wife. You crazy. Do many criminal things."

"What are you talking about?" The girl sounded exasperated. "My parents live in Washington, DC. They're perfectly healthy. They're not criminals."

LouLou looked worried, frightened even.

"Dan. Dan Ramsay. He your father. Crazy murderer."

"No, I talk to him in the day room. He's not my father." LouLou looked relieved, as though she'd explained everything.

"Liar. I see DNA records. Don't lie. DNA say Dan your father. You his daughter. Different last name. You must got married, so different last names. You born Ramsay. Why you lie?"

"You're the crazy one. My parents aren't here. I don't have a husband."

"Of course not. Husband run. See crazy criminal family. Get out. Smart man. No babies with crazy wife." LouLou looked frightened. One more push.

"Crazy mother. Criminal too. Suicide is crime, no? You inherit crazy from parents. Dan Ramsay and dead mother. You never get out. Never. Crazy criminal parents. Crazy criminal daughter."

"No," LouLou screamed. She ran, slipping and stumbling, to the door and pounded on it. The guard shook his head. She pointed at the aide in the black down coat. The guard shook his head again, but he opened the door.

"She's crazy," screamed LouLou. "She's saying crazy things to me. Lock her out. Lock her out."

Bella made herself invisible.

"There's no one there. Did you go out alone? I'm going to have to report this." The guard picked up his walkie-talkie. LouLou broke away from the guard and bolted to her room.

Bella smiled. Mission accomplished.

# CHAPTER TWENTY-SIX

LouLou locked the door behind her even though everyone on the staff had keys. The furniture, except for a single metal chair, was bolted to the floor. She jammed the chair under the door knob. The best she could do was hide beside her bed next to the wall.

She crouched behind it, thinking of the crazy things that woman had said. High Life was her father? No, that couldn't be true. It didn't make any sense. She was lucky to get away from her. Maybe she was a patient who'd gotten out and pretended to be an aide. Where was the old man? Had that woman hurt him? LouLou cried.

The supervising attendant knocked on her door. "Go away. Don't come in. I need to see Dr. Izari. No one else. It's started again."

"Lou, he's not here. I'll get another doctor."

"I'm begging you. Please get Dr. Izari. Please. If I don't see him, I think I might die." She made herself as small as she could behind the bed.

"What's wrong, Lou?"

"Call Dr. Izari. Please."

She could hear several voices outside. Deciding what to do. Finally, someone called to her.

"I'll call Dr. Izari. A nurse will stay outside your door. He won't let anyone in."

"Promise?" It was a trick. The nurse would break in. Why couldn't they do the one simple thing she needed?

"Lou, I promise. I'll call Dr. Izari."

She pulled the blanket off the bed and put it over her like a tent while she sobbed. She had no idea how much time had passed before she heard Dr. Izari's voice. She threw off the blanket and ran to the door, moved the chair, and pulled Dr. Izari into the room. He held her by her shoulders at arm's length.

"What's happened? Why are you wearing wet clothes and shoes? Why are you so frightened?"

"It's starting again. How can it start again when I'm on meds? How? Am I going to be here for the rest of my life?"

"LouLou, sit on the bed." She did. He pulled the chair next to the bed and sat.

"You can't have another episode while you're this heavily medicated." He gave her a blue pill and poured water into a cup from the plastic pitcher of ice and water next to her bed. "This will calm you enough to talk." He checked her vital signs and sat silently while they waited for the pill to give her some relief.

After about twenty minutes, he gently probed.

"You went for your evening walk."

She had to get this right. She wanted him to believe her. She had to stay calm. She held onto the paper cup. "Yes, but the guy who usually takes me wasn't there. He's a nice old man who doesn't talk too much. There was a new woman today. She talked nonstop. I tried not to listen to her, but she started talking about how my father should make me dress better since we're in the same hospital. She told me Dan—Dan from the dayroom—is my father. She said my mother committed suicide."

LouLou saw a flash of anger cross Dr. Izari's face, but he recovered quickly.

"She said it was in the records. That's when I knew I was hallucinating. I don't know if there was even a woman with me. I ran to the door and the guard let me in alone. I ran here and begged for you to be called. I don't want to be Sick forever."

"You're not hallucinating. You're doing well. A little dehydrated, but you're progressing."

"Then who was that woman?" A terrible thought crossed her mind. "What about the old man who walks with me? Have you seen him? She could have hurt him. She was big. Wide. With huge hands. Like paws, almost. Look for him, please."

Dr. Izari placed his arms on hers and held her elbows. He forced her to look at him directly.

"That woman is real, not a hallucination. If she's an employee, she'll be fired for upsetting you before I leave the building tonight. She may be from a temporary agency. We try to screen aides, but sometimes a bad one gets through. I'm sorry it happened to you. We'll search for your usual aide."

"I'm not getting worse?" LouLou asked softly.

"No, you're not." He stood. "Do you feel up to a shower?"

"No, I don't want to leave my room."

"Put on your pajamas and get into bed. We'll start a saline IV, and I'll give you something to cause you to sleep through the night. I'll see you first thing tomorrow morning."

LouLou was spent. She nodded in agreement.

"Dr. Izari, I'm afraid to sleep alone. Can someone stay with me overnight?"

"I'm sorry, but there's no staff to spare."

A nurse knocked and entered with an IV pole and two bags of solution. "Set that up. I'm going to add Haldol for tonight. Be sure no one enters this room. No one. Call me immediately if there are any problems."

To LouLou, Dr. Izari said, "Rest tonight. I'll see you in the morning. "

She nodded. She put on her pajamas and got in bed. She felt calmer when the nurse started the IV, smoothed the sheets and blanket on the bed, and gently washed her face with a wet cloth. She closed her eyes.

She heard Dr. Izari shouting as soon as he went into the hallway. "Where is that damned attendant? I want her in police custody, now. Start a search for the male aide."

***

LouLou slept until almost noon. She'd stirred once during the night and thought she saw Big sitting silently in the chair against the door. He must have been an apparition caused by the meds, but she slept without waking again.

She awoke the next morning feeling less anxious than she had during this stay. LouLou showered, shampooed and dried her hair, put a light moisturizer on her face, and dressed in clean scrubs and her dried white canvas shoes.

Given the amount of meds circulating in her system, she felt quiet. Almost still. Like she was in a stupor. She liked the feeling of being just under the surface of where humans lived. Feeling like a weight had lifted, she decided she felt well enough to wait for her appointment with Dr. Izari in the day room. She thought that was probably an hour from now.

"Lou, or shall I say Sleeping Beauty. Heard you were in a stir last night. You okay?" Big asked. He patted the space next to him on the sofa for her to sit.

"I think the staff is crazier than we are." She looked bewildered.

Big laughed with his deep, rich, bass voice. "Oh Lou, I agree. One hundred percent. I agree. Heard they found the elderly gentleman who accompanies you on your walks with his hands and feet tied with rope and a bandana in his mouth in the laundry room."

"Oh, that poor man. Was he hurt?" That nice man. How awful for him.

"Not that I heard. Shaken. Had a story about some big woman in a puffy coat mugging him."

"Then it's true. That woman who took me on a

walk yesterday said she was subbing for him. She was big with a black down coat, rubber boots, hat and scarf."

"What did she do to make you think she was as crazy as we are?"

"She scared me. Dr. Izari said he was going to have her fired and arrested."

"That's a new one. Docs don't usually get involved in hiring and firing aides. She must have been bad to the bone. Did she hurt you?" Big searched her face with his eyes for signs of trauma. LouLou had no poker face. Everything she felt could be read on her face.

"She had me panting, but she made me think I was having an episode even though I shouldn't because I'm on meds. I ran away from her."

"Sorry, Lou. A crazy staffer, man."

"When I think about it, she didn't look crazy. She said crazy stuff. She didn't even try to catch me after I ran away. It was almost like she was deliberately trying to scare me. Once she did, she left."

Big put his giant left arm around her small shoulders. "You're safe now."

Dan slowly made his way to them and sat in a chair next to Big. "Overheard. Not eavesdropper. Sorry." He sometimes spoke in longer phrases now but very slowly.

"Oh, High Life, don't be silly. Nothing's private here. Everything about her seemed wrong. I didn't want to go outside with her. Then when she started telling me crazy stories, I freaked."

"What kind of stories?" Big asked .

"She told me I inherited a crazy criminal gene. She said my father's a criminal with a mental illness, I'm a criminal with a mental illness, and my mother probably had a mental illness because she committed suicide. She said suicide is a crime. I don't think that's true. When I tried to argue, she just repeated herself."

"For real?" Big looked surprised. LouLou leaned her head on Big's shoulder, and he wrapped both arms around her. "That's a whopper of a story. Sounds like something from an old movie. She does sound crazy. Wonder why she picked on you?"

"I've no idea. All of it was a lie. There's no way she could've seen my records. I was born in Paris, and my birth certificate is in French. I doubt she reads French."

"Born in Paris?" Dan asked.

"Yes. Paris is my real home. It's the city where my mother and I really belong. DC is way too provincial for us, but it's where Dad works now."

"Sounds nice," Dan said. "Never been to Europe."

"Guys, that's another thing that makes her story so weird. She said Dan was my father."

Big guffawed, but Dan went completely still.

"High Life." She leaned forward from Big's embrace and put her outstretched hand on his knee.

"Month?" he whispered. "Birthday month?"

"April. Like *April in Paris*," she crooned.

Dan stared at her in disbelief. His eyes panned her face.

"Bella. Bella's eyes. Bella's mouth. Bella's daughter." Dan put his right hand to his chest, slumped in his wheelchair, and seemed to lose consciousness. He mumbled "Bella" over and over.

Big heaved himself off the sofa and crossed the room to press the panic button. Then he picked up Dan, who was as limp as a child, and carried him out of the room. "C'mon, Lou."

LouLou became alert and hurried after Big, who was moving quickly down the hallway to Dan's room. Big placed Dan in bed and told LouLou to pull the covers around him. She grabbed an extra blanket and tucked it around Dan. Big's large fingers were around Dan's wrist. "Does your chest hurt, Dan?"

"Yes," Dan whispered. "Am I having a heart attack?"

"Probably not, but we're going to the ER."

LouLou looked at Big in amazement. He knew what to do in a crisis. Big broke the glass door to the cabinet holding a portable oxygen tank and nasal canula. "Hook this up," he said to LouLou before he unlocked the wheels on the bed and wheeled Dan into the hall. When she had it ready, Lou ran after them, inserted the nasal canula, and attached the canister to the bed. A plastic packet filled with other emergency items had fallen on the floor when Big broke the cabinet open. She tossed them to Big.

"Push him. Fast." Big shouted. He dug into the pocket of his jeans and pulled out a handful of pills. All shapes, colors, and sizes. He picked a blue tablet and a white, round coated tablet.

"Swallow this pill, Dan." He put the white pill in Dan's mouth and watched him swallow. "Now, I'm going to put this blue pill under your tongue. Don't swallow it. Let it dissolve."

LouLou was blindly pushing the bed down the corridor as fast as she could. Big took a quick look at the plastic bag and threw it on Dan's bed, took over pushing, and said, "Make sure that canula stays in place. Nothing for us to use in that bag. Good catch, though."

Big broke into a run, and LouLou tried to keep up. Down one long corridor, around the corner to a glass corridor that led to a spoke with openings to each wing of the building.

Big yelled directions. "The ER is the far wing on the left."

They dashed through the concourse and through the swinging ER doors. No one stopped them. No one was there to notice them. Big pushed Dan up to a doctor and halted. By the time LouLou caught up, she was panting.

She heard Big talking to the ER doctor. "Collapsed seven minutes ago. Tachy. Chest pain. Semi-alert. Took aspirin, valium, and oxygen."

The ER doc and a team took over without so much as acknowledging Big and LouLou and pushed Dan behind a curtain. Big put his hand on LouLou's shoulder and guided her out of the ER toward the concourse they'd bypassed in their rush to get help for Dan. He found a bench and sat. People who weren't dressed as patients mingled around an area under a sign that read **'Information Booth.'** LouLou approached and asked if they had any bottled water. A bored teenager handed her two lukewarm bottles without looking up.

LouLou sat next to Big. "Here." She handed him a bottle. "What was that all about?"

Big didn't speak for a while. When he spoke, he looked like it pained him to speak.

"We had to get Dan to the ER. I've seen two people die in the day room because there was no response or a slow response to the panic button. One guy didn't get any attention at all for at least thirty minutes before a transporter came to take him to the ER. He was gone by then. The second was a woman who had a heart attack. A doctor was standing just outside the day room door and didn't rush to do CPR. It's called a Slow Code. The crash team runs a code, but so late that it does no good. She died too."

"That's…I don't know. Awful. Barbaric. Inhumane," LouLou stuttered. "How do they get away with it? I know the facility is understaffed, but to just let people die? That's monstrous."

"Ah, Lou," said Big as he put his arm around her shoulder. "This happens too often. More than we know."

He stood and held out his hand to LouLou. "That name—Bella—was what the guards found him mumbling the night he became catatonic. Must be important. What do you think?"

"Bella means pretty in Italian. Might be the name of something he likes that is beautiful or a safe place. Maybe it's his safe word."

Big patted her hand. "Time for us to go back. I wonder if we were missed."

# CHAPTER TWENTY-SEVEN

*Damn. I've been moved again.* There was a window overlooking a meadow. She opened her eyes completely and looked around. The room was spacious. The furniture wasn't metal and bolted to the floor. It was upholstered in a blue floral pattern. She couldn't be in seclusion. Where was she? Had she been kidnapped? Escaped?

"Good morning, Ms. Fleming. You're in Colonial Mental Health Center. I'll be your nurse for the first shift. Let me get your vitals." The nurse checked her temperature, pulse, and blood pressure. "Dr. Youzny will be right in."

Colonial was a private psych hospital. Dr. Youzny was her regular psychiatrist. What was going on? She was curious but not anxious. Dr. Youzny would tell her the truth.

He walked in on the heels of the nurse. "LouLou, you're now completely in my care. You've been transferred from Commonwealth Psychiatric.

There's no need for you to be there. Charges have been dropped, so there's no reason for a competency ruling. We're going to focus on recovery at your pace under my supervision. Understand?"

Something huge must have happened to get the charges dropped and a transfer to a private hospital. She nodded.

"How do you feel?"

LouLou took time to think. A little sleepy. Under water. Murky. She wasn't hallucinating and didn't feel anxious. "Better. I feel better."

"Good. Do you feel up to a talk?"

"Not really, but I don't think that's going to stop you."

She was tired of talking. She wanted to take her meds and do nothing until the meds were in full force and she could go home. She didn't remember where home was or what she would do when she got there, but the idea was to get well and get out.

He smiled. "You're perceptive, LouLou. Take a shower, get dressed, and I'll be back in an hour. Your mother sent clothes. They're in the dresser, and I believe there's a robe in the closet. "

Her mother? Her parents had never visited her during hospitalization for an episode. Even when she was younger, they'd been advised to wait until LouLou remembered them on her own. Maybe they'd sent things, though. She couldn't remember.

"Yes. I'll see you in about an hour."

At least she'd look stylish. Her mother had probably been on a shopping spree. LouLou hummed while she showered. The tune was uplifting and made her feel safe. She looked through the clothes. Black cotton slacks. Various acceptable tops. Her blue cashmere cardigan that always made her happy. One long-sleeved dress hanging in the closet. Canvas mocs and gym shoes.

After she showered, got dressed, and styled her hair, she reviewed the room. A nice view of a meadow with snow-covered mountains in the distance. Was the hospital near the Blue Ridge? Her sketchbook and colored pens and charcoals were in the drawer of her nightstand. She found an iPod with a single playlist—Beethoven's last three piano sonatas, orchestral works by Debussy and Ravel, and lots of Sinatra. Dad. He'd selected soothing and familiar pieces.

Exactly one hour later, Dr. Youzny returned. "You look good, LouLou. Have a seat and we'll talk for a bit and then you have visitors."

She sat on the sofa, and Dr. Youzny settled his straight-backed chair in front of her.

"You're here because an employee at Commonwealth Psychiatric recklessly disregarded your health. Several charges could be brought. If there's a trial, you may have to testify, but Dr. Izari and the Lieutenant Governor assure me that won't be the case. There's no reason for you to relive the trauma."

The Lieutenant Governor?

"Commonwealth Psychiatric is a state-run hospital, so the Lieutenant Governor was asked to oversee the investigation. Normally, it would be the Commonwealth's Attorney General, but I believe there's some conflict of interest. It's not important.

"What's important is that you move forward with

your treatment. I've asked your parents to come. Do you mind if they sit in on our meeting?"

"My parents? Won't it upset them?"

"They don't visit early in treatment because you may not recognize them and become distressed. They've visited you in later stages of hospitalizations at Richmond Memorial Hospital. You look normal, if underweight, and your room is attractive and comfortable. They've said they don't mind. They only want what's best for you. Do you want to see them?"

Tears formed. Yes, she wanted to see her parents. More than anything.

"Yes. Yes, I want to see them."

Dr. Youzny left for a few minutes, and her parents were with him when he returned. She flew into their arms. "I'm so happy to see you."

They hugged her individually and soon there were tears in both of her parents' eyes.

"Please, sit on the sofa. I'll sit between you. I can't believe you're here." She grabbed the hand of each once they were seated.

"LouLou, you look thin. Do the meds make you nauseated?" her mother asked.

"Yes, but I think the worst has passed. Will you be able to stay for dinner?"

"We'd love to," her dad said. "It's up to Dr. Youzny."

Dr. Youzny made some sort of doctorly non-committal noise.

After the small talk, Dr. Youzny prompted her mother to speak.

"LouLou," her mom said, "we withheld

information from you. We thought it didn't matter. It still doesn't matter to your dad and me, but you should know."

*Spit it out, Mom. You're scaring me. What do I need to know?*

"Before you were born, I had a miscarriage at seven months followed by a hysterectomy. We were devastated. We waited a year and then adopted you. You were two days old and the most beautiful baby in the world. I've never thought of you as anyone other than my daughter."

What that crazy aide had said was true? She was adopted? Her parents never told her? Dad would make this right.

"Dad? Am I adopted?" She kept her voice steady.

Tears streamed down his face. "Legally, yes you are. To me, you're my child. My only child, who I love dearly."

"You never planned to tell me?"

"No," her dad said.

"Did you buy me?" She hoped she wasn't some black-market baby from who knows where.

"Of course not. We merely paid a document tax imposed by the French government."

"Does anyone else know? Am I the only one not in on the secret? My grandparents, Uncle Collin? Aunt Deirdre? Any of your friends?"

"No," her mother said. "We'd never tell anyone and not tell you. Given that all our family was in the United States, keeping the secret from them was easy. Our Paris friends thought I was on bed rest during my hypothetical pregnancy to prevent another miscarriage. I didn't go out after the early months. When you arrived, it was a joyous time for everyone. Family and friends. But for no one more than your dad and me."

She was trying to catch up without getting side-tracked on details like how her mother had managed to fake her pregnancy. She had more important questions. She had to wait for them to be clear. Age. That was it. Why not?

"Why are you telling me now? I'm thirty-one years old, not five or six."

"That awful woman in Petersburg somehow found out. She called to blackmail us. We hung up on her and notified the authorities. Getting no money from us, she told you out of spite." Her mother was indignant.

"What she said was true?" She was incredulous. That horrible woman's story was true. She did come from a family of crazies. "Mental illness runs rampant in my biological family?"

Her dad spoke quietly. "The fact that you're adopted is true, and your biological father was hospitalized in Commonwealth Psychiatric. We didn't know anything about your mother except that she was beautiful, intelligent, and a gifted pianist studying at the Sorbonne.

"Daniel Ramsay, your biological father, didn't know anything about you until you repeated that woman's story in his presence. He'd no idea he'd fathered a child."

"What's wrong with High Life? Dan, I mean."

"Depression," Dr. Youzny explained. "He was suspected of killing his wife, but charges have been dropped. He had an alibi. The police over-reached. He got worse after he was admitted to Petersburg. He became catatonic after the first night. He's not crazy and not a criminal. He's a man who has had depressive episodes throughout his life."

"And my biological mother? Did you meet her?"

"Yes," her mother answered. "She was charming as well as beautiful and brilliant. The adoption agency checked everything about her family history. There was nothing suspicious. Certainly not mental illness."

"And her suicide?" LouLou looked to her dad, who had been crying. She watched him compose himself as she'd seen him do many times in diplomatic service.

"Dan's attorney gave us a file on your mother. She was quite accomplished, but she committed suicide during the week after 9/11. Her husband had died of cancer the previous year, and she knew hundreds of World Trade Tower victims because of her job. She was a securities attorney so she knew investment bankers and lawyers working in the WTC. She died of grief, not mental illness. She was thirty-one."

Good. Her biological mother wasn't crazy. Young. Grief-stricken. Poor woman, but not crazy. Dan was iffy.

She tried to process what she was being told, but her mind was blank. There were no rumblings in her stomach or headaches or anything that made her think an episode might be starting.

"LouLou," Dr. Youzny said, "do you have anything to say?"

"I can't think. I'm surprised. Stunned."

She sat silently and tried to think. Nothing. She didn't feel anything. Maybe she would later, but she was completely unmoved.

"I don't think it matters. Does it?" She needed some guidance. She looked at Dr. Youzny.

"That's a question only you can answer," he responded with his typically neutral psychiatrist tone of voice.

She looked at her parents on either side of her. They raised her, loved her to bits, and stood by her throughout her episodes. They encouraged her to be independent even though they must have been scared to death about what could happen to her.

Her schizophrenia could have been inherited, but her biological parents didn't sound like they had the illness. She wasn't going to have children. She wasn't passing any genetic atrocities to anyone. What did it matter?

"I don't think it matters at all." She reached over and hugged each parent. "You're my parents. I love you. Not Dan and his lover."

She looked at Dr. Youzny, who offered nothing. "You don't have to decide now if you want to discuss this further. It's often beneficial for adopted children to express emotions arising from being transferred from one family to another."

"Dr. Youzny, I'm thirty-one years old. I think there's a point where family is complete. My family is a threesome. It's always been that to me. The only way it could expand would be by marriage. So, whatever emotions other adopted children have, I don't feel them. Maybe, if I had learned this at three or four, but not now. My family is in this room." She looked at her parents. "Can they stay for dinner?"

# CHAPTER TWENTY-EIGHT

LouLou listened to Debussy on her iPod before going to bed. The meds were flowing freely at full strength throughout her body. She'd be discharged soon. She lay back, closed her eyes, and let the soft impressionist sounds flood her mind. A lovely flute solo merged into a violin, then it was joined by a viola, a sensuous cello, and a deep, steady contra bass. The bass drew everything together into a solid foundation.

LouLou replayed the piece just to hear that bass line again. The instrument was under-rated. It wasn't just a standing cello that players sawed to keep time. It required a dexterity equivalent to what was required for a violin. Even more so because the fingerboard was so long. A person had to move quickly and efficiently while simultaneously bringing out nuances of the musical line. Gorgeous. Dark. Like the depths of an ocean.

She opened her eyes. Gregg. Gregg played the

contra bass. Her sweet musical genius who loved her with his whole heart. He'd been pushed deep under Sick. She hadn't thought of him since…she didn't know. She thought back to her last memory before waking in Commonwealth Psychiatric.

Denmark. She'd had great success in Denmark playing all six of Gregg's pieces. People roared for more. She improvised a bit and then replayed them. The audience still wanted more, which was how she left them. She was onstage for three hours in Copenhagen. That was perhaps the best night of her musical life.

Did Gregg think she'd abandoned him? Would he be waiting when she returned home? She'd never leave without telling him. She'd never willingly leave Gregg. She wanted as much time with him as he was allowed.

Skylar would've explained that she might have been delayed by illness. Everything came back. Roy and Sara. Skylar. Her loft. Her Richmond life. Gregg. Her entire life disappeared during an episode and stayed away until late in her treatment. She was getting well. Every day thereafter, she had mini-mental status assessments. Did she know her name? Occupation? Where she was? Where she lived? Who was president?

The president question always made her laugh until she realized laughing about it made her sound odd, at best. She knew the president, vice president, members of the cabinet, and the senior senator from every state. She'd learned this almost as soon as she could talk.

Until she was fifteen and the family moved to

Washington, her father had been the United States Ambassador to France. He entertained constantly, and her mother taught her to be aware of who she might meet that evening during the cocktail hour before the adults adjourned to the dining room.

She'd enjoyed meeting senators because she could ask them what their states looked like. She wanted to hear firsthand tales of New York, Illinois, and Colorado, where the Aspen Music Festival took place every summer. She wanted to hear about University of Southern California and the Tanglewood Music Festival from the senators representing California and Massachusetts.

Once she taught herself not to get stuck on the president question during the mini-mental status test, she could ace the rest. As the meds worked their magic and she became more alert, she could answer questions about the season, date, time, and day of the week.

LouLou didn't know if these questions were supposed to help her remember, but they never had. One day something would change. A switch would turn on in her brain, and she would remember everything at once. Not bits and pieces. Everything. After tonight, she realized it was December. She may have missed Christmas, but the best present was knowing that she'd be going home soon. She desperately hoped Gregg would be there.

***

Dr. Youzny made their final session difficult. They'd talked about all the usual things—taking her meds, eating properly, exercising, and calling him at the first sign of trouble. Then he raised the topic of her adoption.

"Have you had new insights about being adopted?"

"No." She hadn't thought of it at all.

"My notes indicate you never mentioned it in group sessions," he stated.

"Dr. Youzny, I never thought about it after that initial conversation."

"Are you protecting yourself from disturbing thoughts?" he probed.

LouLou shifted in her chair and looked directly at the psychiatrist. "I've no idea. All I can say is my parents told me, it registered, and I'm getting better. Despite all the time to think here, that's not something I've thought about."

Dr. Youzny folded his hands flat on his desk. "That's a most unusual reaction, LouLou. For many decades, withholding that information was standard practice. Later, studies showed that the information almost never remained secret and when the adopted child learned the truth, there was a strong adverse reaction. Now, couples who plan on adopting go through considerable training before an adoption is finalized. Parents are encouraged to tell children as soon as they are able to understand so it becomes a normal part of their life experience. Your reaction is in direct opposition to the prevailing custom."

LouLou didn't know what he wanted her to say. "I didn't know there were rules about how I was supposed to react. I never would've found out except for that awful woman."

"The point is, just like almost every other adopted child, you learned of your parentage."

She didn't respond.

He pressed on. "Your parents were correct in thinking that you would never find out except in the most extraordinary circumstances. You did, however, experience those circumstances. Contrary to what we told you earlier, we now know the aide didn't find anything in your medical records.

"She discovered the familial connection from LIDS-CORIS. That's the Virginia version of a forensic DNA database. As you know, all patients at Commonwealth Psychiatric have a DNA swab taken. The match was noted after a routine computer run. Even so, the DNA samples are blind. Each sample is given an identification number that has three barriers to linking the number with the name of the patient.

"We're at a loss as to how she could have known about it unless she knows someone running the state database. It's being investigated. She may have blackmailed other people."

That got a small rise out of her.

"You mean this woman, who presumably has no skills beyond being able to walk a semi-stable psych patient to and from appointments and around the courtyard, is a criminal mastermind? When I consented to the swab, it was with the assurance that the information was private except for use by law enforcement. So, somewhere there was a major screw-up."

"Yes." Dr. Youzny nodded. "I'm sorry."

"That's why the Lieutenant Governor is

involved. He wants to cover it up. Dr. Youzny, I don't want an apology from you. I should have one from whoever is responsible for this mess, but I'm not expecting one. It was a complete fluke that my parentage, as you call it, came to light. My parents couldn't have foreseen DNA tests and databases thirty years ago and even if they had, no one was supposed to identify me.

"How could they have known that someone could criminally access my DNA? No one ever heard of DNA until the OJ Simpson trial, and forensic databases probably weren't around for another ten years after that. By that time, I was an adult. The odds of my ever finding out were nil."

"You don't feel betrayed by your parents?"

"I feel betrayed by the government and whoever allowed this to happen. I certainly don't feel betrayed by my parents."

"The bond of trust has been broken. Doesn't that lead you to question what other falsehoods you may have been told?"

"No, it doesn't. My parents wanted me to grow up normally. They stuck with me from the schizophrenia diagnosis through this minute. I trust them. I trust everything they've ever told me that was important. I trust them to have my back."

"I see," Dr. Youzny said.

"Do you really? You sound as though you want me to say this has devastated me, but it hasn't. Compared to the hell I go through living with schizophrenia, this is nothing. I'd be more upset if my name was misspelled on an album credit."

She was almost angry. Damn it, he'd outwitted

her. That's what psychs do. They push and poke and push until they get a reaction. This whole conversation was a test. A final exam before discharge.

LouLou deliberately sat still in her chair and allowed calm to overcome her. She spoke at a normal pitch and pace.

"Dr. Youzny, I understand exactly what this little session was all about. I'm responding normally to provocation. I can articulate my position. I'm not going to implode. I'm better.

"I want to make it clear that I don't want anything to do with Dan Ramsay or his family. And no, you'll never have my permission to write my case for a journal article or peer presentation. I won't hesitate to report you for violating my privacy rights as a patient if you do. I don't care that my response to being adopted didn't follow the adoption manual. I'm not in denial. I simply don't care. If there's anyone who has lost my trust, it's you. I don't want to continue treatment under your supervision. Please refer me to someone else."

She stood and left his office, returned to room, and closed the door. She leaned against it and exhaled.

# CHAPTER TWENTY-NINE

"Ms. Fleming, your car is here."

LouLou skipped out of the hospital, down the stone steps, and into a cloudless blue sky day. She wore a soft, blue knit mini dress her mother had left in her closet. Tights and boots kept her from being cold. She was happy to be free and headed home.

She stopped at the black sedan parked in the circular driveway. Odd. The uniformed driver usually stood in front of the car to greet her and carry her luggage. She'd been taking cars and limos since she was about ten and knew their protocol. There was no chauffeur in sight. She waited until she saw the driver's side door open and a pale-faced Skylar emerge.

She raced to hug him. He hugged her tightly. "Damn fool car. You're going to have to drive home."

He opened the door to the back seat, where Robert had spread his long, lean body and all four paws across the width of the car. Skylar squeezed in beside him. Gregg crawled out of the driver's side, hugged her, and then kissed her forehead, eyelids, nose, and lingered on her mouth. She had chills whenever he did that but especially today.

"What's going on?" She laughed.

"I couldn't use the passenger door in case someone saw it open and no one got out, so I had to come out through the driver's side. The car mostly blocks the view."

"Skylar," she stuck her head in the back door, "couldn't you put my bag in the trunk to pretend to be normal?" she teased.

"That was the plan, but I couldn't figure out how to open it from the inside and of course, there's no trunk lock. There's no ignition key, either. You just press a button and the car starts itself. It could drive itself for all I know. Wish it could. The two miles from the rental agency here were among the longest of my life, and that's saying something."

LouLou and Gregg were laughing so hard, they both grabbed their stomachs. "Those two miles felt like four to me," Gregg said, laughing.

"All right everyone," LouLou said as she tried to settle herself. "Gregg, crawl over the console and get back in the passenger seat. I'll figure out how to open the trunk. In the meantime, Skylar hold my bag."

She got in the car with its unfamiliar dashboard and it, indeed, took a while for her to find the trunk button. She pressed it. "Okay, Skylar. Put my bag in the trunk."

"Me? I'm an old..."

"Skylar, I'd like to leave before midnight."

The old man got out, put the bag in the trunk, and slammed it closed. He got back in the car, buckled his seat belt, and announced he needed a nap after his long drive. Robert immediately started howling and didn't stop until he'd situated himself on Skylar's lap so he could raise his head to look out the window should he choose.

LouLou was so happy to see Gregg, she leaned over and kissed him like she meant it. He responded. They were interrupted by a yowl from Robert and Skylar's announcement that he wasn't a voyeur and could they please get on the road. LouLou started the car and drove away from Colonial Mental Health Center. Forever, she hoped.

"I'm not going anywhere until you tell me the story of how you got here. Please tell me there's no body of a chauffeur in the trunk and no crimes have been committed."

"Nothing like that. We're not on the lam."

"Okay." LouLou headed for the highway.

By the time they were on the highway, Skylar was sound asleep. Gregg told the story. "Cancelling your car was easy. Skylar called the car service that was supposed to pick you up and said that he, your uncle, would do that and cancelled the reservation. He rented a sedan. All was well.

"We were a little nervous about the trip. Skylar had to drive because I'm a ghost and would be invisible behind the wheel. Also, I've never really driven and don't have a license. We rented a car here because there was no way Skylar's car would make the trip. We took the bus here despite a skirmish over Robert, who had to wear a yellow Emotional Support Animal vest.

"Things went south when we went to the rental facility and got the car we'd reserved. We got in. I was careful to climb through the driver's side. Robert hopped into the back seat. Skylar got behind the wheel and was overcome. He hadn't seen a dashboard since 1975, and he said it looked like airplane controls. I got the manual out of the glove compartment and read the basics aloud. First thing was to get heat going. It's much colder in the mountains than in Richmond.

"We couldn't figure out how to start the car, much less drive. Just when we'd decided that Robert should take over, I found the part about the keyless ignition and off we went. We drove about twenty miles an hour, but we made it. Skylar was white-knuckled all the way. In his defense, I've never seen anything so complicated. Skylar completely freaked when a woman started talking to him from the dashboard."

LouLou laughed. "GPS. He must have been scared witless."

"I wasn't too calm, either, and I'm a ghost. I don't scare easily."

"Oh, guys, thank you. All three of you. I've never had such a welcome."

# CHAPTER THIRTY

Cheers went up when LouLou, the guest of honor, and Gregg walked into Roy and Sara's house the next evening. The welcome home party was important because LouLou had been gone so long. Everyone wanted to hear about her tour. Gregg went to meet her friends even though no one could see him. He'd just watch and stay out of the way. The worst that could happen was that someone might sit on him and he'd move. They'd never feel a thing.

LouLou gave Roy a long-lasting hug and turned to his wife. "Sara, you have the best husband. I arrived after driving home and Roy handled my luggage, returned the car, and told me he stored all the luggage sent from the airport in the loft. He even filled the fridge. Unless you did that," she said.

Sara's eyes smiled. "I may have helped."

"When Roy told me that Skylar had driven you home, I almost fainted. When was the last time you drove?" Sara asked Skylar.

"I drive around town all the time, dear Sara, in

my own vehicle that has served me well. I'd never encountered cars that turn themselves on and women who speak from the dashboard giving me directions. It's like having a backseat driver in the windshield. Fortunately, LouLou was able to get us back without incident. Robert seemed quite pleased to have an outing. Now, if you'll excuse me, I'm the DJ tonight."

LouLou was pulled in different directions. Leonore, her best friend from Paris, was there en route to New York. "Please stay over with me," LouLou asked.

"I would, but I have to be on the set of a shoot at seven o'clock tomorrow morning. If I'm not there, the photographer and client will be at each others' throats. My job is to keep them as far away from each other as possible and convince each that their vision is being captured. We'll see each other soon enough. I hear you'll be in Paris soon. Chanel. That is a *coup, mon amie.*"

"I can't wait. It's only for four days. Mom is coming, and we might stay an extra night. We used to go at least once a year, but my tour schedule has gotten in the way for the past three years. This will be a vacation. A luxury vacation."

"Don't be too sure. Models work very hard for their money. And the artistic differences that surround them are *méchant*. Wicked crazy."

"I was surprised they hired me. I know they're changing their image, but that supermarket couture show was too much. This is Chanel. No gimmicks necessary."

"Don't get me started. Must dash. Take selfies of

everything you wear. Everything, especially shoes. Call me when you arrive. Love you, LouLou." They kissed on both cheeks. Leonore left in a flash of silk and exotic fragrance.

"Your friend is hot," Trey said.

"Of course, I surround myself with only beautiful people, including you. Please tell me you don't want to see me for at least two weeks. Your choreography is killer, and I'm out of shape."

"No, I don't want to see you until you're prepared. Take barre, jazz, and do yoga, if you insist. Then I'll see you."

LouLou stood on tiptoes to kiss his cheek. "Thank you for coming. I'm thrilled to see you."

LouLou headed toward the powder room, where Gregg lay in wait. As soon as she walked in, he closed the door and kissed her. She put her arms around his neck and swayed with him as though they were dancing.

"You have great friends. They love you. I mean, really love you. They're not fake social friendships." She put her head on his shoulder.

"That's what I need," she whispered so anyone outside wouldn't think she needed medical attention for talking to herself. "I wish they could meet you."

He kissed her neck. "I'm enjoying myself. I like seeing you happy. You're the most beautiful woman in the room."

They kissed quietly before LouLou pulled away. "I've got to get back. I'm the guest of honor."

"Allow me." He opened the door.

Clive grabbed her hand and pulled her into the dancing fray. "Tonight, you get to dance and someone else works. Skylar's a good DJ."

LouLou couldn't hear anything beyond that. She danced and danced and danced. She was sane. Safe. Happy.

After the party, Lou and Gregg returned to her loft. She snuggled as close as she could to Gregg in bed. "I think the best part of a party is this."

"Coming home to make love?"

"That is the absolute best. After that, it's talking about the party. Did you really enjoy yourself?"

Gregg got up, got a glass of water for LouLou, and returned to bed. "I did. I haven't been to a party since my junior prom, so merely going was a treat. I love that everyone dressed up, Skylar picked special music, and everyone was so happy for your successful tour. I even enjoyed the vicarious thrill of hearing how much everyone liked our music.

"I liked your yoga instructor and her husband a lot. Sweden, right? She seemed so pleased that you'd used her recommendations and taken an extra day to go to that sculpture garden outside Stockholm. Clive and Olive are great dancers. Trey is a terrible flirt. All wasted, because your friend from Paris had to leave early."

"Would have been wasted anyway. She's married with six-year-old twins. I'm godmother to one of them. Her husband is very dear and solid. A good man."

"The dancing was wild. No one had partners or cut in or even held hands. It looked like jumping jacks from Physical Education or improvisation."

LouLou laughed. "I love your interpretation of things I think are ordinary. That's what the crowd looks like at my shows. Aside from freestyle, the main dances are the slide, vogue, and lean back. Surely, there were dances when you were in high school."

Gregg rolled over to face LouLou. "I haven't thought about dance moves since high school. There was the twist. Then the mashed potato."

"The mashed potato? That's really the name of a dance? How do you do that?"

"It's like the twist, but you grind the ball of your foot like you're mashing potatoes."

She poked him. "You're making that up. Was there a song called The Mashed Potato?"

"Yeah, "Do the Mashed Potato" by Chubby Checker and "Mashed Potato Time" by a woman. I don't remember her name."

"I'm going to look those up. What else?"

"The Swim, where you pretended to swim with your arms and held your nose while you sank down to the floor. The Pony. Another Chubby Checker dance. Oh, The Frug and Watutsi. How could I forget The Jerk? That was just standing and jerking your arms around."

LouLou was crying, she'd laughed so hard. "Oh, you have to teach me those. All of them."

"I need music."

"I'm sure Skylar has all the basic dance tunes. Ask him tomorrow."

"I guess things haven't changed all that much. Those were all individual dances. Still, dancing without partners was considered scandalous. Only partner dancing was allowed at the prom."

She rearranged herself so her head lay on

Gregg's chest. "Who did you take to your junior prom? What did she wear? What did you wear? Who was the band?"

"Her name was Mary Lynn Bailey. She was a sophomore. It was a big deal for her to go with a junior. The prom was in the high school gym. One of the Tri-Hi-Ys was in charge of decorating."

"What's a Tri-Hi-Y?"

"It's a club. Sort of part social and part community service. Like a pre-sorority."

"What was the theme? There's always a theme."

"Camelot. The movie came out that year, and all the girls thought it was the most romantic story. I don't remember the decorations beyond a castle, a white horse, and silver stars hanging from the ceiling."

"Oh, that is nice. Camelot. What did Mary Lynn Bailey wear?"

"Something blue. I remember because I didn't know what color corsage to get. Back then, our choices were dyed carnations and pink roses. I opted for pink roses and she gave me a pink rosebud boutonnière. I wore rented black pants, a white dinner jacket, and whatever shirt came with it."

"Oh, that's sweet. You must have looked so handsome. I've never had a corsage. I've never seen a man with a boutonnière except at weddings."

"Bill Deal and the Rhondells played. They were a local band who had national success the next year. They were good. I'll bet Skylar has something by them."

"Yes. Yes, I want to hear them."

"It was a fun evening. We danced a lot, took

punch breaks, and were polite to the chaperones. I had Mary Lynn home by eleven o'clock."

"Eleven. On prom night?"

"It was small town Virginia, 1967. Not a lot going on."

"When did you have time to have sex?" LouLou asked thoughtfully.

Gregg laughed. "Sex? I'm sure Mary Lynn didn't have sex until her wedding night. We had a good night kiss. I tried for a French kiss, but she said she wasn't that type of girl."

LouLou rolled with laughter in bed. "No sex. No French kissing. That type of girl. What did guys do?"

"Naturally, we dated the other type of girl for three dates and then we were allowed to do more. A charm for her charm bracelet was usually expected."

"That's practically prostitution. Sex for a bracelet charm?"

"Probably, but that's the way it worked. Thankfully, anti-war marches attracted more free-spirited girls who weren't concerned with reputations or charms. They were liberated and bra-less."

"I'm not making fun of your teenage years, but things really have changed dramatically."

"They have, but there was an innocence about those times that I remember fondly. Doesn't make up for what went on in secret."

"That's right. In secret. You didn't do any of those horrible things. The worst you did was go to a segregated school, and you didn't have a choice about that. You're the best man I know. Remember more of the Mary Lynn Baileys, Camelot, and The Swim than anything else."

She'd known Gregg wasn't the most experienced lover immediately, but he was loving and passionate and a great kisser. The love they made now was their own. She pulled him to her.

# CHAPTER
# THIRTY-ONE

LouLou woke the next morning to find a package wrapped in white, non-acidic tissue paper tied with a red satin ribbon on Gregg's pillow. Her first reaction was that Gregg had gone, but she heard him open the refrigerator. He walked to the bed, kissed her, and handed her a glass of orange juice. "Good morning," he said.

"What's this?" she asked.

"A present. Open it."

"I love presents. Especially when they're beautifully wrapped. Scarlet satin ribbon. I don't want to know how you acquired that."

Gregg sat next to LouLou on the bed while she untied the ribbon and let it unfurl along the bed to the floor. She carefully peeled back the tissue paper only to find another layer. What was underneath caused her to scream with delight.

"Gregg! Piano works. You wrote them."

He looked shyly at her. "I had a lot of time while

you were away. I got the music out of my head and onto the page. They need some edits. We'll consider this the first draft."

LouLou pulled out the pages. A piano suite. Sonata. Four Ballades. Six Dances. Elegy. An amazing amount of music. As LouLou turned the pages, she saw not only musical genius but passion, longing, and fearlessness. Each work was dedicated to her.

"Don't cry," Gregg warned.

She threw her arms around his neck and kissed him while tears fell down both of their cheeks. She laid her head on his shoulder. "Gregg, you're a musical genius. Truly. I hope I'm up to playing them. You've got some wide chord spans and tricky rhythms. Thank you. Thank you for these." She carefully placed the manuscripts on the nightstand.

He pulled her to him and kissed her. "I'm so relieved. I thought you'd flip through them and say, 'Nice try, but start over.'"

"I don't believe you."

"I admit they came pouring out of me onto the page. I like them. I didn't know if you would."

LouLou got out of bed and threw on a robe. "I have to try them." She sat at the piano for the next hour sampling each of the works. When she finished, she turned to Gregg. "They're all wonderful, complex, beautiful, but the "Elegy." Ah, it breaks my heart."

"Mine too." He sat next to her on the bench.

She checked the calendar on her phone. "November. I don't see doing it earlier than that. Definitely not the summer or immediately after

Labor Day. Early November, before Thanksgiving."

"What?"

"A recital, of course. The public has to hear these. I think the Terrace Theatre at the Kennedy Center for the Performing Arts in DC would be best. We'll have to make selections. The recital can't be more than an hour or hour and fifteen minutes. Plus, one encore. Maybe I could do a series of recitals. At Georgetown, maybe. I'm thinking out loud. Pay no attention to me."

"I want you to pay attention to me. Special attention." He nuzzled her throat.

"Composers are notorious womanizers. Women can't resist them. All that passion, sexy…"

Gregg covered her mouth with his. She stopped talking.

# CHAPTER THIRTY-TWO

## March

He was waiting for her at their agreed-upon meeting point. Dan stood at the entrance to the West Island Garden at Lewis Ginter Botanical Park on Richmond's north side. It ranked number two on LouLou's list of favorite places in Richmond—a close second to Vinyl. She went to the conservatory on a regular basis to sketch flowers, vegetables, and visitors. She'd merely told Dan it was acceptable and she knew how to get there.

She pulled on her cashmere-lined leather gloves, not because she was chilled but because it would prevent any awkward handshakes or touches. She'd been reluctant to see Dan, but she thought he deserved a meeting. She knew the less available she was, the more intriguing she'd seem to him. Best to see him early.

He looked better outside the hospital. His hair

was styled in the Beckham look she'd suggested. His clothes didn't hang on him. He'd probably gained some weight, as all patients did upon discharge, and his clothes were probably new. He still had that sad look in his dark eyes, but he brightened when she greeted him.

"Good to see you," LouLou said.

"You're beautiful, Lou. You look well." He spoke slowly.

"I am," she said and started walking on the path that would lead through the garden. "And it's LouLou. Lou is my Sick name. I finished treatment at a private hospital and that certainly sped things up. Amazing what having one psych for four patients versus one for one hundred patients can do for recovery."

He nodded. He seemed nervous. He wasn't the determined-to-get-better guy she'd met at Richmond Memorial Hospital years ago. All that time in Petersburg had to have taken a toll on his body, mind, and life. He probably realized, as she had, that his life would be smaller than it once was. Fewer possibilities. Fewer friends. A small trustworthy circle of support. He was far from the physical fitness enthusiast she'd met as well. She slowed her pace to match his. She planned to let him take the lead in conversation. He wanted to meet. She'd merely agreed.

"I still have the sketch you drew. The winged foot tattoo. Maybe have it inked. If not. Matted and framed. Reminder. Things get better."

He'd kept the foot-in-flight sketch she'd made? That was nice. "Visuals help. I look at things I've drawn or written and am reminded of where I was and where I am now. Some tats are just peaceful, like my honeysuckle vine and my feather. They're soothing."

Dan smiled. "Never considered tattoos soothing. Never considered tattoos at all. Until I met you."

She had nothing to say. She walked silently. He'd talk when he was ready.

"Thank you for meeting me. Still don't quite believe it's true. One look at you erases any doubt. You look very much like your mother. Bella was the most beautiful girl I'd ever seen when I met her at seventeen and when I saw her." He hesitated. "When I saw a picture of her just before she died. She took my breath away."

LouLou couldn't say anything. Interesting, he was able to speak normally when talking of Bella. Apparently, she got her looks from Bella, but she'd never been described as breathtaking. She probably had just enough of Dan's genes to keep her from being beautiful. She'd been spared a life of constantly falling short of Bella's beauty.

"You scared my brother. Rob. The day he and my attorney visited to introduce me to a neurologist they'd hired, he glanced up at the day room window where I usually sat on his way to the car. He saw you standing at the window. You waved. He thought he was seeing Bella."

LouLou nodded. "He looked terrified." She remembered stark terror. That would be a normal reaction to seeing a dead woman.

"He thought he was looking at a ghost. I don't know why I never saw the resemblance."

"Dan, you were catatonic for a long time. I don't think you registered anything."

"I got the new doctor about the same time you befriended me. Mostly, I looked at the razor blade tattoos on your wrists and thought how delicate your hands were and what a talented artist you were. Making beauty from cheap paper and crayons. You captured the scenes outside that window and made them more vivid than they were. You saw things. You made me see things I didn't know were there.

"When you reminded me you had schizophrenia, I didn't really know what that was. I thought maybe you had multiple personalities. Or voices in your head. Or something that was even more awful that what I had. My mind couldn't process much. I thought of you as a kind, skinny girl who went out of her way to be nice to me. No one else had."

"I knew you from before," LouLou said. "It was natural for me to say hi. I was surprised when Big told me you'd been there for a long time and hadn't spoken or moved."

"Big was nice. He never said much, but he has this. Comforting. Presence."

"He also saved your life," she reminded him.

"He did?" A frown crossed his face and passed. "I don't remember."

LouLou felt a kinship. Patients don't remember what happens during a psych stay. Dan apparently didn't recall Big rushing him to the ER with chest pains. She hated losing chunks of her life. Three months, usually.

Dan slowed and stopped at a bench. "Do you

mind sitting? I used to run thirty miles a week. Now I can only walk about a mile."

She sat. "It takes time, but you know that."

LouLou could tell he was struggling to ask her something. He hadn't invited her to meet for no reason. He wanted something from her. It could be anything. She wasn't going to guess. She waited for him to speak.

"Do you mind if I tell you about Bella and me?" His voice was shaky.

"I really don't need the details, but you can tell your story. You might feel better once you say it out loud. If I want you to stop, I'll tell you."

He told her about meeting, loving, and expecting to spend the rest of his life with Bella. They had a connection that transcended everything. She was beautiful, brilliant, and talented. He wrote poetry, and she composed. Together, they'd written songs. She was a member of *Phi Beta Kappa* and *summa* at University of Virginia and had a fellowship to study at the Sorbonne after graduation.

"She wasn't certain what she wanted to do, mostly because she had so many opportunities. She definitely encouraged my dream. I wanted to own a talent agency for musicians and athletes. Getting them the best opportunities, guiding their careers, steering them away from mistakes. Bella encouraged me to apply for a summer internship with one of the biggest agencies in the business, and she polished and polished my application until no one else had a chance. I got the internship.

"That summer changed my life. I worked in the Los Angeles, Nashville, and Detroit offices and saw how the business was run from the inside. Just as I suspected, the best interests of the artists were secondary to the personal ambitions of individual agents and staying cozy with labels.

"It didn't have to be that way. My agency would be different. I couldn't wait to get started, but I needed an education in business principles. I'd applied for MBA programs my senior year. I had no experience. My grades were very good but not great. Bella asked me to take a gap year, go to Paris with her, and then re-apply to schools. She suggested getting a part-time job or a volunteer internship in Paris that would give me international experience. She believed that, plus summer experience at the agency and references from some of the biggest names in entertainment would make me a strong candidate for the best business schools. She had such confidence in me. She knew I could get into Harvard, Wharton, or the London School of Economics if I re-applied.

"I refused to wait. Instead of doing what she suggested, I stubbornly went to the only school where I'd been accepted. University of Miami. It's not a bad school, but it's not an Ivy. I was miserable. South Beach wasn't like it is today. It was filled with drug dealers, housing for the elderly poor, and sagging, empty buildings. I didn't speak Spanish and felt I was at a disadvantage. The classes didn't hold my interest. I hated it."

Okay, so things went south after college. He needed to move the story along or she'd ask him to stop.

"She wrote me. Her letters were filled with

longing. She asked me, almost begged me, to at least visit her in Paris. Now, I know why. She was pregnant and she wanted me with her. She didn't want to put it in a letter. She wanted to tell me in person, and she didn't want to risk flying herself. She probably knew very little about pregnancy and pre-natal care.

"I thought she was just trying to make me feel better. Her letters became more inviting, and I became more determined not to go. I thought I could carry a heavier load of course work and graduate early. I told her I'd come in the summer after school.

"She finally sent me a letter that essentially ended us. I now realize I could have gotten on a plane and talked to her. I would have been thrilled to know we were going to have a child. We'd be the happiest two people on the planet.

"I didn't go. I thought she'd met someone else. I lost my confidence and my trust in her. I tried to kill myself, but I woke up in the ER. That episode of depression lasted more than two years. I dropped out of school, lived in my childhood bedroom with my parents for three years, and wasn't able to work for about two years. I never saw her again."

LouLou's interest was fading. Cue Dan's tears.

"You moved on. You got married," she prompted.

"I didn't start dating until I was thirty and married at forty. My wife was younger. Bubbly, athletic, and a good antidote to my dark moods. She was murdered when we were going through a rough period. I think that's why the cops didn't consider any suspects other than me. I foolishly believed in the system. My brother Rob tried to get me to run, but I didn't want to leave my daughter forever. She was ten. I lost her anyway. Her mother's parents in Charleston have custody of her. I live with my mother."

Okay, she was done. She didn't need to hear about his daughter, in-laws, or custody.

"Sad, Dan. I'm sorry." She stood.

He followed. He seemed like he wanted her to take charge. Tell him what to do. About everything.

"Let's go to the Tea House," LouLou suggested. "I'd like some white tea. I tried it in Asia during the spring and loved it. You can get coffee if you don't like tea."

He followed her rapid pace to the Tea House and he arrived a little breathless. LouLou and Dan sat at a secluded table by the window overlooking the Asian Valley garden.

"I brought a picture of Bella and me. Would you like to see it?" He asked before the tea was served.

No, she didn't, but she knew her refusal would hurt him. He'd had plenty of hurt just like she had. "Okay."

He opened his wallet. It was an old snapshot of a young couple at an airport. They looked blissfully happy. The blonde, blue-eyed girl was a knock-out. She quickly handed it back.

"You looked happy." She couldn't think of anything else to say.

"My mother mentioned Bella looked radiant in that picture. Now, I know why. She was pregnant. That was taken at the airport on her way to the

Sorbonne."

The tea arrived. Dan put the photo away. As they drank, Dan asked about her life.

"I was born and raised in Paris. I had a dream childhood. Ballet and piano lessons, parties, lots of friends. I explored everything Paris had to offer plus vacations to nearby Spain, southern France, and Italy. We had semi-annual trips to London. When I was fifteen, we moved to Washington, DC, where I went to high school.

"I had my first schizophrenic episode when I was sixteen. That drove my life from then on. My parents did everything to keep Sick in check without hovering."

The rest she told in outline. She worked freelance and travelled at her discretion. This year to Asia and Scandinavia. She liked her life, her friends, and was close to her parents. No permanent boyfriends because of her illness.

He asked if she'd turn up on a Google search.

"Why would you Google me? I'm right here. What do you want to know?"

This kind of question made her nervous. She lived as privately as she could. Her mail went to a Post Office box or her attorney Brooks. Packages went to Roy. A handful of people knew her address. Fewer had her cell phone number. She changed it every three months anyway. Paranoia was part of schizophrenia, but she also had a job that attracted fans. Odd as it seemed to outsiders, she didn't care whether she had fans. Yes, she liked having a full house at shows, but that's where it stopped. She wasn't on social media. She didn't want fans to become too interested in her personal life.

Dan looked ashamed. "I don't have anything specific. I thought I might learn something about you I hadn't thought to ask."

"You won't find my address or telephone number if that's what you're looking for. About three people in the world know those."

She sensed he was getting agitated. "Why are you so private?"

"Why do you live with your mother?" she fired back.

"Touché. Because of my illness. It's easier."

"Exactly. My illness includes paranoia."

He looked into his coffee cup as he spoke. "I'd like to see you again," he said so softly she had to lean in to hear him.

"Dan, we need boundaries. I'm not Bella, even though I resemble her. I'm not brilliant. I didn't finish college. I have a life that I can live given my illness. I can't add anything to it."

He looked stricken but didn't say anything.

"I don't make friends with other patients and see them after hospitalization. It's the way I function. I have a Sick world and a healthy world. You're part of my Sick world."

He sipped his coffee loaded with cream and sugar.

"I named my illness too. Mørk. Short for the Norwegian word *Mørketid,* or Dark Night. It helps to name it, I think."

She smiled. "I think so too."

Dan searched her face as if he were looking for any sign of possibilities for the two of them. She didn't think he found any. He pulled two CDs out of his inside jacket pocket and put them on the table between them.

"Bella recorded these as soon as she got to Paris. She played them at a recital in New York before she left. They were her favorite pieces. Whether you want anything to do with me or not, I think you should have them. They're the last three Beethoven sonatas, Opus…"

"109, 110, and 111. They're my favorites too."

She stood, took them off the table, and dropped them into her tote. She offered her bare right hand to Dan to shake.

"Take care, Dan."

"You too."

She walked away as quickly as possible without breaking into a sprint. She couldn't bear to see the sadness in his eyes.

# CHAPTER THIRTY-THREE

Gregg knelt on the floor in the loft surrounded by handwritten notes. She saw he'd been listening to recordings of her tour performances. His eyes were red-rimmed and his nose slightly blotchy.

"I wasn't gone that long," she joked. "Crying because you missed me?"

He kissed her. "There are some moments where you and the music transcend time and space. Magic. I can't think of any word to describe those moments."

"That's why you're a composer. You don't need words. You have something better than words." She opened the refrigerator, pulled out a pitcher of orange juice, and poured a large glass. She flopped on the sofa. Gregg joined her.

"How did it go?" He put his arm around her. "Are you okay?"

"I'm fine. Seeing him was okay. I definitely had my barriers up. He'd like me to become involved with his life. He seemed lost and so lonely. It's heartbreaking to see him as he is now. He was recovering from a depressive episode when we met, but he's only about ten percent of what he was then, which was probably half of who he used to be. He's nice. Straight. Suburban. Good guy. I can't help him. I can't be part of his support system. I have to take care of me."

"Yes, you do. I'm sure you found a way to give him that impression without hurting him."

"Maybe. I explained I have two lives. My Sick life and my normal life. The two never meet."

"Do you think he got what he needed?"

"He wanted to tell me about his relationship with Bella. College lovers. Soul mates. Destined for great things. After college, she went to Paris. He went to Miami. She wanted him to come with her and after she arrived, she wrote him to join her. Even for a visit. She probably wanted to tell him about her pregnancy. He didn't go. She must have decided if he wasn't going to be part of her life, then she needed to give her baby to a couple who could love her.

"Apparently, Bella was the most beautiful woman in the world. I don't measure up. I resemble her, but I'm nowhere near perfection. Glad I didn't have to grow up hearing that."

"You're beautiful, LouLou. I don't care what some other woman looked like. No one can compare with you."

She stretched out her legs. "I got the impression those two would've been terrible parents. Their love, as he described it, went one way. To each other. When he talks about her, he almost goes into a trance. He speaks of her as a goddess and their love as something that was beyond earthly boundaries. He looks radiant.

"I don't think either one of them would have loved a child enough to make her feel secure, happy, and confident. I think any child of theirs would've been parked with nannies while they travelled the world fulfilling their dreams. I'm not saying what they wanted for themselves was bad. It's what I do, too. I just don't see how a child would've benefitted from being raised with them. She would always be third."

"Lucky you," he said.

"Very lucky me." She finished her orange juice and put the glass on the floor. "He asked if he could come to a show. That's when I told him I keep my lives separate. I can't prevent him from buying a ticket and attending. I wouldn't want to do that to him, but I don't want a groupie who wants to be backstage to hang with me."

"Can I do that?" he said with a straight face.

"Anytime. Just make sure no one sees you."

They dissolved into laugher that quickly turned into passion and lovemaking on the striped sofa.

# CHAPTER THIRTY-FOUR

Getting the gun was easy for Bella. The boy who guarded the rear door of the *tapis grossiste* in Paris fell asleep every evening before nine o'clock. The men inside bartering for rugs, weapons, and drugs wouldn't exit until midnight. Plenty of time to relieve the boy of his gun. He carried a Glock G26 9mm popular for its small size and light weight yet powerful eleven-round capacity. The recoil and accuracy were appropriate for the hand of a boy rather than a man.

The older boy, who patrolled the block as lookout, was equally lax. Wearing the traditional keffiyeh around his shoulders over Western clothes, he took a break to visit the hookah café around the corner between ten o'clock and eleven every night. Striking about fifteen minutes after he swaggered toward the café would be optimal.

The boy slept with a M70 assault rifle on his lap strapped over his turbaned head and around his shoulder. His child's hand rested near the trigger. The Glock was behind him on the small, dirty red carpet on which he sat in lotus position. His head nodded forward as he slept.

With one swift movement, she snatched the gun. The boy didn't stir. The Glock wouldn't be missed until it was on its way to Washington, DC.

# CHAPTER THIRTY-FIVE

LouLou turned the corner toward her loft after taking her daily walk in the park when Sara called to her. "Signature required mail," she called.

"Thanks," LouLou said as she followed Sara into Roy's. LouLou's packages and certified deliveries were addressed in care of Roy and Sara. She dropped the thick parchment envelope in her tote.

"Anything going on?" LouLou asked.

"It's that time of year when we have to decide what to do for vacation. The kids are getting older and don't think visiting grandparents is a treat. I want to sit in a lounge chair and read and have no one ask me a single question. Roy wants to taste exotic foods. We're at an impasse."

"Sounds like you're ready for a cruise. The kids can do their thing. You can chill. Roy can eat at restaurants in every port."

Sara smiled. "That's my thought. But where?"

"I've never been on a cruise, but I would say

anywhere. As long as Roy has new cuisine to try, the rest of you have what you need aboard ship. The Mediterranean, the Caribbean, and South America would work. Pick one and surprise him."

"Oh, no you don't. You know Roy doesn't like surprises."

"Well, at least narrow it down so he thinks it's his choice."

"Smart woman, LouLou."

***

Inside the loft, LouLou showered, tidied up, and got around to opening the large envelope. Return address was a law firm in New York. Probably a contract that should have gone to Brooks.

She'd just begun to read when Gregg returned. He gave her a lingering kiss. "Careful, or you're going to distract me from important contracts."

"Sorry, I'll sit quietly and read the latest copy of *Strings*. I can't believe such magazines exist. If they had when I was a kid, I'd never have done any school homework."

LouLou scanned the cover letter and stopped. "Gregg, this isn't a contract. This is a beneficiary letter. "

He looked puzzled. "Who died?"

"Bella Davis. The letter is from her attorney and trustee of a blind trust she established the year I was born. It was to be made available to me when I turned thirty. Apparently, it took a while to trace me from Paris to DC to Richmond."

LouLou sat. "It's a lot of money. A lot."

She showed Gregg the most recent bank statement. "Wow. Eight figures. Any catch?"

She read further. "No. It's an outright gift to me."

There was a smaller envelope tucked inside. It was addressed in beautiful handwriting to LouLou Fleming. "Gregg, I think it's a letter from Bella. Should I read it?"

"Yes. She's dead. She can't ask anything of you."

"I don't want my adoption to become a large part of my life. I know the truth. I listened to Dan. And now this."

"Why don't you just read what she has to say?" he said reasonably. "Better to know than waste time guessing."

She settled herself into the sofa and read aloud.

*To my daughter,*

*I am not able to raise you without your father and hope the Flemings will give you a wonderful life full of music, art, and happiness.*

*You are the child of two people who couldn't possibly love each other more. We are eternal soul mates. You were conceived in true love. Circumstances prevent us from being together.*

*I am saving money to give you when you are older. It is money that I alone have earned and want to share with you. I'm putting it in a blind trust so you'll be unaware of it until the appointed time. May it blossom for you.*

*I wish you love.*
*Bella*

"I think your hunch was right."

"You mean that the two of them wouldn't be great parents? Not exactly a warm, fuzzy note to the child you're giving away. More about Bella and Dan than me. She doesn't say she loves me. She wishes me love. Cold." She put the note down. "What do I do?"

"Transfer the funds to your account."

LouLou shivered. "This feels wrong. I don't want it mixed with my money. Maybe I could give it away."

"Put it in another bank."

"It would just sit there, haunting me. Every time I got a statement, I'd be reminded of Bella."

Gregg took her hands. "What bothers you so much about her?"

"They're strangers trying to insinuate themselves into my life. I don't want Dan and Bella in any part of my life. I have parents. I love them dearly, and they love me. Bella and Dan are intrusive. I thought I was safe from Bella because she's dead, but I'm not."

"I know nothing about money, but I know you pay bills online. Couldn't you set up a new trust with a different bank and ignore the electronic statements?"

"If I have to." She squeezed his hand. "I don't want to touch the money. It feels tainted somehow. I don't want to cause tax problems for myself, either. I can't pay taxes on that amount of money, especially if I don't want it. I need legal advice, but I can't ask Brooks."

She closed her eyes to think.

"I went to high school with a girl, Quincy, who is a partner with a big law firm in New York. She works in the Trusts and Estates department. She'll know what to do. I'll call her and email her the information if she'll take me as a client, which will cost money.

"Damn that woman. Once I get the trust sorted out, I hope it's the last I hear of Bella and Dan."

# CHAPTER
# THIRTY-SIX

"Quincy can see me this week. She just sent a text." LouLou put the phone down on the bedside table. She and Gregg were enjoying a lazy Sunday morning in bed.

"You have to go to New York?"

"Yes. I'm not a fabulously wealthy client who gets in-home attention." She rearranged herself to be away from the phone and closer to Gregg. "I have to spend at least one night there. I don't want to stress myself traveling."

"One night? That's all? People fly to New York and return the next day? Shouldn't you stay longer to rest?"

"Gregg, people fly to New York for lunch and return the same day. There are shuttles every hour between New York and DC and New York and Boston. No purchase in advance required. Air travel is not luxurious or a treat, believe me."

"Stay as long as you need. I don't want you to do

anything that could endanger your health." Gregg pulled her closer to him. "This is luxury. Sunday in bed with the beautiful woman I love while drinking coffee and reading the newspaper."

LouLou turned on her side to face him. "I'm the only one drinking coffee."

"I imagine it would be nice. I'm a low maintenance boyfriend. You never have to feed or water me."

LouLou put her hand on his arm. "Is that what you are? My boyfriend?" He stroked her face.

"Lover sounds like I'm a gigolo. Fiancé is inaccurate. Husband is never to be. What's left?"

LouLou couldn't think of anything. "I don't want to name it. Let's just leave it between us."

He kissed her. "Done."

"You're invisible. Aside from not eating, drinking, or sleeping, what else can't you do?"

"I do almost everything I did when I was alive," he responded. "Being invisible lets me do a few more things than I could do as a human, like walk through or go places when they're officially closed, but I also can't do as much if people can't see me. I don't have any other abilities. I can't foretell the future or rewind time."

LouLou sat up. "Can you travel?"

"I don't know. I know I can move around the general area. Tidewater, Richmond, and near the mountains. When we picked you up at the Colonial Center, Skylar, Robert, and I were on a bus and then in a car. I was aware of traveling slowly. I didn't expend any energy. I was able to appear to you."

"Could you meet me, say, in Paris?"

"I don't know. I've never been, so I have no frame of reference at all."

"Could you fly on a commercial plane? If we bought you a window seat and I sat on the aisle to prevent anyone else from sitting in your seat, do you think you would materialize once you arrived in Paris with me? Couldn't you stick with me and not disappear?"

"I've no idea. Before our trip to the mountains, I'd never been anywhere I hadn't been when I was alive or couldn't envision in detail. Skylar showed me Colonial's website and the town where the bus would stop and that we'd rent a car so they were implanted in my mind." He sighed. "I don't know any other ghosts to ask. We don't get a handbook. I've looked online for information about ghosts, but everything I've found is about sightings. I haven't found anything about ghost behavior."

"Would the risk of traveling with me be that you might disappear forever?" LouLou couldn't imagine losing Gregg. He was her only love. She'd never survive the loss.

"That, or I might disintegrate at thirty-five thousand feet, but I don't know for certain. I think ghosts stick close to where they lived or died."

LouLou sighed and flopped on her back. "I wish you could travel with me. I wish you could come to New York with me this week."

"I admit I'm envious. I'd love to go. The only time I've been is when I went for my Juilliard audition when I was seventeen. There's an energy and excitement that surrounded me there, but I don't want to risk flying if there's a chance I'd never see you again."

"No, No, No. I don't want to risk that. Ever." LouLou talked to the ceiling. "My only obligation for the rest of the year is the Chanel photo shoot in Paris. Did I tell you Mom's going with me? We're going to have an all-girls time with no stuffy diplomatic functions. Beyond that, I have to prepare for the recital in November and compose the music for Chanel's show at Fashion Week in January. Other than that, I'm free. You're free except for composing time. We have lots of time to just be." She sighed happily.

"LouLou," Gregg lightly touched her shoulder, "remember, we don't know how much time we have. I can't plan to be with you at a gig a year from now. I don't know if I'll be here tomorrow. I'm sorry."

"I don't want to hear that. I know it, but I don't want you to say it. Besides, you haven't finished your mission. We have work to do to get compositions published and albums released. I think you have more music that needs to be written."

"Yes, I do. It's leaping around in my head. I just need to play it for you and write it out."

"I think there are software programs now that facilitate dictation. You wouldn't have to write compositions out by hand and then have me play them to record. Check them out. It's worth a try. "

"I feel like I'm living on Mars. Such wizardry. Technology. Amazing things that can be done now."

LouLou moved as close as she could get to him. He held her tightly.

"Gregg, promise me you'll stay as long as you can. Please don't leave too soon."

"I promise, LouLou. I wish I could promise I'd be here forever. I love you."

She loved him in a way she couldn't describe. Love seemed too small a word. "I love you with my whole heart, Gregg." Time to bring up a topic she hoped Gregg would be excited about.

"I'm thinking of getting a new tattoo when I'm in New York. There's a great salon where most of my drawings have been inked. I'd like to get something that's meaningful to both of us. For us. Any ideas?"

"You'd be the artist to draw the design and someone transfers it?"

"Yes. I want something small and intimate. I'm planning to have it put on my left hand between my index finger and my thumb. It's a nice little fleshy place. I don't want anything obviously romantic. No hearts, infinity symbols, or swans."

Gregg leaned back and put his hands behind his head.

"Swans?" he asked.

"They mate for life. Over-used wedding cake toppers. Besides, I don't like swans. They look arrogant and condescending."

Gregg laughed. "Okay. No swans."

LouLou's mind was blank. She'd tried to come up with something and hit a wall.

"Owls. Owls mate for life," Gregg said.

"Perfect. They're feathery and beautiful and white."

"No, just some owls mate for life. Snowy owls are nomadic and mate wherever they happen to be.

Like a girl in every port."

"You're making that up."

"No. Barn owls are unusually beautiful. They have a white heart shaped face that looks like those masks you see in pictures of costume balls in Venice. Their stomachs are white, and their feathers are a range of yellow to gold to brown."

LouLou sat up. "I saw something like those in Japan. They're called Ural owls. The guide for the chamber music orchestra I was with pointed them out in a park at dusk. They mate for life and sing duets. The male has a deep voice and plays rhythm. The females have higher pitches and a husky timbre. Like Lauren Bacall as a soprano."

Gregg laughed and held her tight. LouLou was already plotting. "I'll have to look online for photos of each kind. Without knowing what a barn owl looks like, I'm leaning toward the one that sings."

Just before starting to touch LouLou's erogenous spots, Greg murmured, "Musicians who mate for life."

# CHAPTER THIRTY-SEVEN

"Shouldn't we be whispering?" LouLou asked when the conversation turned from catching up to the purpose of the meeting at Quincy's law firm in New York.

"My office is soundproof," Quincy said.

"You're joking," LouLou said before she saw the look on her friend's face. "I can't believe it. I mean, I knew the firm was esteemed old money, but this takes privacy to a whole new level."

"It's essential. Confidentiality is our highest priority aside from expert advice."

LouLou had no response other than to nod. Quincy continued.

"I believe everything has been done as you requested. I'll give you an overview and we can make any changes as needed."

LouLou nodded again and sat straighter in the beige chair. Everything in the law firm was beige. Carpet, walls, upholstery. Blonde maple for desks and doors. Completely bland. She was surprised Quincy wasn't wearing a beige suit.

"You're the beneficiary of a blind trust that will dissolve when the assets are distributed to a newly created blind trust. The trustee of the new trust will distribute the assets as you instructed. I've spoken to the development officers at both SchizoLife and Juilliard that you selected to receive disbursements. They prefer to use their donor documents, but this is a straightforward transfer of assets. They're each getting a nice sum. They'll accept bank transfers and whatever else we request.

"That's my recommendation for structure. You were notified beyond the expiration date to refuse the trust. You could challenge that and case law supports you, but doing so creates problems you don't want. If you refused the trust, the trustee would be forced to identify, notify, and distribute trust assets to your closest relatives—your parents—which you specifically said you didn't want."

"Correct." The last thing LouLou wanted was to involve her parents in anything to do with Bella Davis.

"My tax colleagues assure me that distributing the assets to a blind trust is preferable to distributing them to you personally. All transfers will be electronic. I have the documents to open an account for the trust at the bank we find most suitable for our clients. Once the bank account is funded, the amounts will be distributed to the bank accounts of SchizoLife and Juilliard, respectively. Upon confirmation of receipt of those funds, the bank account will be closed. The trust will be dissolved as well. Does that work?"

Everyone really had grown up except her. Here was Quincy, a partner at one of the most prestigious firms in the country, guiding her through a complex process and making it sound ordinary. Routine. It probably was for Quincy.

LouLou stopped herself from thinking about that. Quincy didn't live with schizophrenia. Their career goals had never matched. Quincy was one of the brightest members of her high school class and was destined to do what she wanted with excellence. Harvard. Harvard Law. Prestigious firm.

"Quincy, I don't know anything about finance."

"That's why I exist. You don't have to know when you have me." When Quincy smiled, she looked like the girl LouLou remembered from the sophomore volleyball team who could always be counted on at the right moment.

"What's a blind trust?"

"It means the beneficiary, in this case you, has nothing to do with trust administration. A trustee completely controls the trust with no input from the beneficiary. The trust established by Bella Davis was blind to you. You didn't know about it, didn't receive information about what assets it held, and didn't have any say in how those assets were invested. You were in the dark—or blind—to the trust.

"The successor trust I create to transfer the assets will also be blind. You'll appoint a trustee to manage the trust based on the instructions in the trust documents. You'll never have anything to do with it."

"Wow. What a great concept."

"Dates back to Roman emperors who wanted to keep ownership of their assets, usually real estate, secret. Who do you want to appoint as trustee?"

"You. Wouldn't that be best?"

"You can choose anyone who will act dutifully to carry out the terms of the trust. I can do it, but I'm obligated to inform you that the firm will take all fees to which its entitled as trustee. The administration fees won't be waived."

"Of course," LouLou agreed. If the fees were being paid from Bella's money, she didn't care how much they were. She also didn't expect Quincy and her firm to do her any favors. She was a very little fish in terms of their client list. She was lucky Quincy was handling this at all.

Quincy made a note on her tablet. "Then my name will appear on both the trust document and bank account. Acting as trustee, I'll handle all administration for the trust. You don't have to do anything."

"I won't get bank statements?"

"No, everything will come to me."

"What about your bill? You told me about your fees."

"The trust will pay it. Taxes, too, in the unlikely event there are any."

"So, I don't have to do anything ever? I'm done? Completely out of the loop?"

"Correct. That's the beauty of a blind trust."

"Quincy, could I have some more water, please. I need a moment to process this."

"Of course." Quincy walked to the bar in her office, poured water from a crystal pitcher over ice in a crystal glass, and placed it on a coaster. After she removed LouLou's original glass and returned it to the bar, she sat in the matching beige chair next to LouLou.

"Before you process, I admit I'd never heard of SchizoLife and did some research. It's a fine, well-managed charitable organization with the highest rating. LouLou, I know you have schizophrenia, but I've never thought about what it must be like to live with it on a daily basis, particularly the strict routine you follow and the number and quantity of medications. This organization funds medication, provides housing with a strict schedule for women, and offers all kinds of services to women who live independently. It's amazing."

LouLou patted her friend's hand. "Quincy, we're privileged. I see women in hospitals because they couldn't afford medication or maintain the routine because of other obligations. They are heroic, but they fail and most of them die or commit horrible crimes. SchizoLife offers exactly what they need. Exactly what I would need if I didn't have the parents I do. I like my life. I may have taken on too much with three big tours, including two international ones, but I won't do that again. I'm just as happy playing clubs around Richmond and Charlottesville. Of course, I did get that Chanel endorsement, which will be great fun and a chance to spend time with Mom in Paris."

"And the Juilliard instrument fund?"

"Same idea. Brilliance and privilege aren't

always matched. Musicians have had patrons ever since musicians existed. Orchestras always have endowments so their members play the best available instruments. Students are different. I think it must be hard to be talented enough to be at Juilliard and not have a great instrument when others do. The quality of the instrument really changes the sounds that can be drawn from it. I thought those two beneficiaries made sense for me given that I'm a musician and schizophrenic.

Quincy squeezed LouLou's hand before releasing it. "You're kind and thoughtful, LouLou. The donations are perfect. Now, I'll shut up and let you process."

LouLou clutched the iced glass and sat quietly, reviewing what Quincy had told her. LouLou trusted her friend. According to her, Quincy had extricated LouLou from any dealings with Bella's money. It was over. Bella Davis couldn't interfere in her life again.

# CHAPTER THIRTY-EIGHT

## April

LouLou twirled in front of the antique mirror in the suite she shared with her mother in the Hotel Grand Intercontinental just off the *Avenue de l'Opera* in Paris. She wore a midnight blue dress with a bateau neckline and a bare back that dipped just below her waist. The artistic director of her photo shoot profusely praised the design and colors of the phoenix tattoo on her back. He couldn't stop talking about it and finally took shots of LouLou wearing a white bikini bottom poised to dive into a pool that featured her gloriously vivid tattoo enhanced with make-up. He'd admired her new owl tattoo, but that was something she shared with Gregg. She didn't want it photographed. Still, she'd created a buzz within the House of Chanel.

Karl Lagerfeld himself had selected the dress she now wore as a gift—a rarity for anyone other than the most celebrated actresses and beauties in the world.

"*Maman*," LouLou lapsed into French, "I've never worn such an exquisite dress. I can't believe it. And *Monsieur* Lagerfeld selected it himself. I'm not famous. I'm a DJ who modeled something fun and will provide music for their next show."

"LouLou, you have style. That's what they love. That dress is like an award. You deserve it."

LouLou hugged her mother. "I'm so happy you came." She took another twirl in the mirror. "You weren't bored, were you? Tell me the truth."

"Bored? Don't be silly. I saw old friends. They took me to the opera while you were out clubbing until all hours. You and I had dinners in wonderful places. I still had time to have my hair cut by someone who knows what he's doing and shop. It's been a trip I'll never forget." She hugged her daughter close.

"Oh, but what are we going to do about packing?" LouLou eyed the suite. It was a mess of tissue paper, shopping bags, and boxes. Lingerie was strewn over chairs and the settee. Perfume samples in delicate miniature bottles lined the armoire shelf. Colorful macaroons were on a tray with champagne nestled in a crystal bucket of ice.

"We'll throw everything in at the last minute and sort it out at home. Let's have some champagne before dinner."

The house phone rang The *sous-concierge* announced Leonore's arrival. "She's two hours early," LouLou moaned. "Help me out of this dress."

"No, darling. Leonore will want to see it."

"Of course." LouLou answered the door before Leonore had a chance to knock.

"What's wrong?" LouLou asked. She pulled Leonore in quickly. "You look like you've just been robbed. Were you mugged? What is it?"

"Nothing like that. I'm fine."

Leonore perched on the edge of a gilt chair facing LouLou's mother and held LouLou's hand. LouLou and her mother exchanged glances as Leonore took time to collect herself.

"I have tragic news." She stopped before continuing. "I'm sorry. *L'ambassadeur est mort.*"

LouLou's mother cried out, "*Non, c'est n'est pas vrai.*"

"I'm sorry, it's most definitely true."

LouLou's mother sank deeper into her chair and started crying.

"I don't believe it. What happened?" LouLou said.

LouLou slipped out of her couture dress and pulled out a silk robe. The dress that had been the most important topic of the day was cast aside. It had lost its importance.

Leonore took LouLou's hand. "Your father is dead. The American Embassy will send someone over immediately, but I wanted to tell you. There aren't many details. He was killed in his dressing room before he went to bed for the night."

"No, this can't be true." LouLou's mother shook her head repeatedly. Leonore rose to sit next to her. "The police recreated his movements. He went to dinner and a performance at the Kennedy Center with a small group of friends. Were those his plans?"

LouLou's mother nodded.

"After the performance, he dropped Justice Bergen off at her house, then he went home and had a drink in his study while selecting a book to take upstairs. The book was on his nightstand with his glasses. He went into his dressing room of the master suite, where he was shot point blank with a pistol."

"A pistol? My husband was shot with a gun?" Her mother said it in such a way that she would have believed her husband had more likely been killed by an alien invasion than a common gun.

"No, that's impossible." She tried to turn away from Leonore. "We don't keep guns in the house." She looked to LouLou for confirmation. "What little we know about them we learned from the FBI when he joined the diplomatic corps. There had been a rash of kidnappings at the time, and there was a popular theory that we should know how to shoot. My hand shook so much just holding one I never learned how to use it."

"Perhaps it wasn't a gun from the house," Leonore said kindly. "That's all I know. The Embassy people will know more." She put her arm around LouLou's mother, who had yet to shed a tear. LouLou knew it was because she didn't believe it to be true.

LouLou herself stood frozen. She was terrified to move. This was the most shocking news she'd received in her life, and she thought she might break. She feared if she moved her shoulders, her legs, even a finger, they might break off like ice. Maybe she could speak without moving her jaw. She tried.

She called Leonore's name, looked at her directly, and spoke in French so as to eliminate any error. "Check my phone for a contact titled FrDoc and call her. Say I'm a patient of Dr. Vilak. It's urgent. I have meds in my bag, but I'm too upset to use them without making a mistake. Also, please call the concierge and ask them to send up the hotel physician until she arrives."

"Of course." Leonore made quick calls. "The hotel physician will be right up. *Madame Maillocheau* will be here within twenty minutes."

LouLou remained standing. She was aware of people from the American Embassy entering the room to speak to her mother. A representative of the president of France offered the president's condolences and the use of any governmental services, including a private plane, to LouLou and her mother. Security agents entered. They had little information to add.

"Where is my husband now?"

"Mrs. Fleming, the coroner is overseeing things at the moment. The ambassador has been removed from the house."

"*Mademoiselle Fleming?*" A red-haired woman dressed in a black suit and stilettos entered the room. "*Je suis Madame Mailllocheau, le psychiatre.*"

She quickly surmised that the frozen LouLou was her patient and guided her into the bedroom, where their conversation was conducted in French.

The doctor read LouLou's medical alert bracelet and immediately understood. "You're fearful you might have a psychotic episode brought on by shock."

LouLou nodded.

"You're alert and not delusional. That's good. Still, you've had a terrible shock. We'll not let that blossom into something larger.

"Sit, please." She took LouLou's vital signs. She asked what medications LouLou had taken that day and when. "I'll give you a booster as well as something to relax you. Please get into bed while I prepare the medications."

LouLou did as she was told. The doctor tucked an extra blanket up to her neck. A hotel aide or nurse or assistant opened a large medical bag and took out portable equipment to start an IV to keep LouLou hydrated. She was given oxygen through a mask.

"Breathe normally. Don't gulp."

LouLou was wild-eyed. "Hospital? Do I have to go to the hospital?"

"No. You have extra medication. You're warm. You have fluids and oxygen. Just rest."

LouLou felt fluids flowing through her body and the meds rushing to calm her brain. She forced herself to do a meditative exercise of mentally repeating one word like a mantra—Ice. Gradually, LouLou relaxed and fell asleep.

# CHAPTER THIRTY-NINE

LouLou's family home, which was on a quiet residential street in Northwest Washington, DC, was overrun with investigators and technicians. When she and her mother arrived, the person in charge corralled the crime scene staff to specific areas. LouLou's bedroom was one of seven and a distance from her father's dressing room in her parents' master suite. It was strictly off-limits.

Her mother was distressed that she couldn't enter her bedroom and lie among everything that was familiar to her life with her husband. She temporarily moved to a guest room next to LouLou. Family arrived. LouLou's Uncle Collin was waiting for his sister when she walked in the door and collapsed in his arms. *Tante* Deirdre, her father's sister, arrived from Montreal along with her husband late that evening.

LouLou and her mother had spent the night in Paris before returning to Washington the following day. LouLou's psychiatrist insisted she needed twenty-four hours before she could safely travel. Leonore had spent the night with LouLou in her bedroom. Her mother couldn't sleep and paced the sitting room all night.

Although Leonore offered to accompany them, only LouLou and her mother flew to Washington in a government aircraft with security officers. LouLou was vaguely aware of security. She had no idea or interest in which government's plane or what division's security officers were used. She continued to find comfort in thinking of herself as frozen. If she was frozen and didn't move, she couldn't get into trouble. Her mind calmed at the thought of cold water. Ice.

Once home, LouLou and her mother were required to sit in the rear living room overlooking the pool for a briefing. Tux, her dad's dog, sat on the floor next to LouLou. He seemed bereft without her dad.

LouLou held her mother's hand as the lead investigator stood before them. He'd introduced himself, but LouLou couldn't remember his name or even what agency he represented. There'd been a time before Sick when she remembered everyone she met and the purpose of every United States agency and some foreign ones. Before Sick. Before fifteen years of hard psych drugs had messed with her mind.

"Mrs. Fleming, Ms. Fleming, there was no sign of a break-in. Nothing was taken, so this wasn't a robbery. We can only surmise that Ambassador Fleming must have allowed his killer to enter."

"No," interrupted her mother. "Never. After an evening out, he wouldn't let anyone in except LouLou. He believed everything could wait until the next day unless the president himself called."

"I'll make a note of that," the officer said. "We investigated under the assumption that he admitted someone he knew, they followed him upstairs, and shot him at close range when he went into his dressing room to prepare for bed. A 9mm bullet to the heart. He died instantly."

LouLou gulped and held her mother's hand tighter. She felt like she was an actor on a TV crime show and believed she could anticipate the dialogue before it was spoken.

"We found a handgun and shell casing."

Her mother interrupted the investigator. "Isn't that unusual? For the killer to leave the murder weapon."

"We haven't determined that it was the murder weapon."

"Why not? Please be specific."

"Mrs. Fleming," the investigator said as he shifted uncomfortably, "until the coroner makes a determination that the ambassador was killed by a gun and not, for example, poison and then shot to cover it up, we can't say it's the murder weapon with certainty."

"Please sit down. Your fidgeting is annoying."

Her mom waited for him to sit before she continued questioning. "Humor me. Let's assume the gun was the murder weapon. Isn't it unusual for a murderer to leave the gun behind? Why would he do that?"

The investigator coughed. "Yes, it's unusual. The weapon could've been left because he knows with certainty it can't be traced to him, or he's framing someone else and wants the gun to be found or left as a message of some kind. In any case, ballistics will tell us more than I can speculate."

"Thank you. I understand."

Hesitantly, the investigator continued.

"Mrs. Fleming, the ambassador was vulnerable. He left his glasses on a book on his bedside table. Would he have been able to see much without his glasses?"

This was ridiculous. The investigators would look at the lenses and know immediately her father was far sighted and only needed glasses to read. Why put her mother through such a question?

"He only used them to read. He would have seen everything clearly."

"What was his bedtime ritual?"

"Very much as you described. We would come home from an evening out, he'd take off his jacket and tie, stay downstairs for a nightcap, and come upstairs about fifteen or twenty minutes after I did. He'd remove his cufflinks, watch, and money from his pockets and place them in the valet tray on the bureau. He'd put his suit and tie on the butler stand, his shirt and socks in the laundry, and leave his shoes by the door to polish first thing the next morning. Then he'd come to bed."

She was remarkable. Her mother was telling them everything in detail. LouLou was awed. She also realized that her mother seemed to think if she answered the questions correctly, the investigators would say it was a mistake and her father would come home.

"Did anyone else have keys to the house and know the alarm code?"

"No one except LouLou and our housekeeper Mrs. Morse."

"Could Mrs. Morse have made a duplicate?"

"No, it's a Medeco key. One that requires the owner's permission to reproduce."

"Other staff?

"We don't have staff. If we're hosting a party, the caterer provides servers. We've used the same lawn service for years, as do most of our neighbors. We have a pool and exterior maintenance contract.

"No one has a key and certainly no one knows the alarm code. It changes at irregular intervals. LouLou is notified by the security company. I tell Mrs. Morse directly."

LouLou kept telling herself to stay frozen. Frozen. If she stayed frozen, everything would be okay.

Her mother looked weary, but she was dogged. "Didn't the Supreme Court Police follow my husband home? They usually do after we drop off Justice Bergen."

"I don't have that information, Ma'am."

"What about security logs? Surely, the company can tell you when my husband entered the house and disabled the alarm and what time he reactivated it. We usually activate immediately after we've closed the door if we don't plan to go out again. We don't wait until we go upstairs to bed."

"Another team is following up on that. I have

just a few more questions. Can you think of anyone who had threatened the ambassador or might have wanted to harm him?"

"No, nothing personal. You'll have to ask the State Department if there was anything connected to his previous positions."

"This is a delicate question, but I must ask. Might the ambassador have brought a guest home for the evening?"

Her mother didn't respond immediately. When she realized what she was being asked, she was livid. "Another woman?" she shrieked. LouLou thought her mother might strangle the investigator. She'd never seen her mother so angry.

"Or man," he said neutrally.

Her mother stood, jerking LouLou, who was still clutching her hand, with her. "That's enough. I'm not going to answer any more questions. Please leave my house and take your technicians, experts, and photographers with you. I want all of you out. All."

"Ma'am, this is a crime scene…"

"Sir, you said the crime scene was my husband's dressing room. You don't need to look anywhere else. This house is off limits."

"Ma'am…"

"You've had forty-eight hours. That's enough. I want you out."

That was the last LouLou saw of him. He never returned. His replacement never questioned LouLou. She assumed she would be considered an unreliable witness. Schizo. Can't be trusted.

# CHAPTER FORTY

Uncle Collin was her mother's rock. By the second day, he'd hired cleaners to rid the house of all evidence of the murder and investigation, delegated one of Brooks' law partners to liaise with the State Department, and asked Mrs. Morse's daughter to handle visitors and deliveries that had been allowed beyond the check point. Security from some department or agency was posted outside. Too late in LouLou's opinion, but they kept gawkers away.

LouLou sat with the family around the dining room table for lunch. She kept movement to a minimum. Frozen. Frozen. Frozen. If she didn't move, she couldn't hurt herself or anyone else.

She sat to her mother's right and held her hand. Her mom seemed to be comforted by that. She looked deflated after the confrontation with investigators the previous day. Lunch was served, but LouLou couldn't eat. The thought of putting anything—salad, omelet, fruit—down her throat made it constrict. She'd not been able to eat anything. Aromas made her nauseated.

"Mom," she whispered, "please excuse me."

She left the table and the dining room and went outside to the pool area. She retched and then leaned against one of the columns of the rear patio and breathed deeply. She started to cry. She was useless. She couldn't even sit through lunch to support her mother.

"*Ma petite*, "said *Tante* Deirdre, "I brought you some water." She handed her a glass of water with ice in a crystal glass. No garnish. "I remember you don't like cucumber."

"Thank you." LouLou sipped slowly. "I'm sorry, *Tante* Deirdre. The smell of food made me sick. I couldn't stay." She drank more.

"Better?" Deirdre asked. "Why don't we take a walk around the back lawn." She slipped LouLou's arm through hers and walked slowly into the grass. They didn't speak for a while.

"You look so much like your dad. Those bright blue eyes and white blonde hair. Wasted on my brother. I got blue-ish eyes and mousey brown hair. You look lovely. Are you feeling better? Beyond this tragic happening?"

"Yes, I've been well and happy. The invitation to create runway music and model for Chanel was a fluke. Mom and I had such fun in Paris."

Deirdre nodded and smiled. "I like her new haircut. *Très chic*."

"She talked to dad twice each day. They loved each other dearly. I don't know how she'll manage without him. I don't know how I'll manage without him."

Deirdre put her hand on LouLou's. "We have to find a way. There's no option."

The two had reached a garden bench and sat.

"*Tante,* I'm so afraid. I'm afraid I'll have an episode and make things even worse for Mom. I keep telling myself to just stay frozen. Stiff. No movement. If I don't move, nothing can happen."

"Ah, *ma petite*, you suffer so much for one so young. For anyone. Have you seen a doctor since Paris?"

"Yes, I have a doctor here. He comes every day. He tries to be reassuring, but I don't believe him."

"Why not? Do you feel an episode coming?"

"No, but I have terrible anxiety that one will overcome me. The meds he gives me don't calm me."

"I don't think there is a medication that cures heartbreak. You loved your father, and he certainly loved you. Perhaps what you're feeling is not anxiety, but grief."

LouLou looked at her aunt. Traces of tears and sadness marked her face. LouLou thought it went deeper than the loss of her brother. She looked like she'd lost more.

"I think you're right. I've never known grief. Is this what it feels like?"

"Yes, I believe so. Your grandparents died at an old age of illnesses so the grief I felt wasn't as searing as with your father. Still young to me. Shot. Sudden." She seemed to drift in thought. "I remember our *Tante* Catherine. She was like you. She had schizophrenia. She was pretty and sweet, but she'd have these wild episodes where she couldn't be contained.

"Doctors wanted to permanently institutionalize her or perform surgery or put electricity through her brain. Her parents refused. The doctor gave her very strong injections that would calm her so much it would put her in a nearly comatose state, and then she would wake up and be herself again. It was frightening to your father and me." She gave a wry smile. "That's a childlike perspective. The poor girl must have gone through hell, and what I remember was how she frightened us.

"She died when she was about twenty-four. She never married. I don't know if she ever had a date. She had tutors and got an education certificate. She sang beautifully. A light soprano. Of course, she didn't have professional training, but her singing made her happy and that pleased her parents.

"She and her mother did charity work and went to teas. She was always kind to us as children. She must have lived in fear as you do. I'm terribly sorry, LouLou. I don't know why I brought that unhappiness up."

Her great aunt had schizophrenia?

"I've never heard this story. I thought I was alone in the family."

"Oh, *non, ma petite. Tante* Catherine was most certainly schizophrenic. Our father, your grandfather, had terrible dark moods when we were young. I believe that is a sign of depression or bipolar disease. I never asked, but I assume a doctor eventually gave him proper medication to ease his distress. He was about forty-five before his moods disappeared."

Her grandfather probably had a mental illness? Other relatives? Now she knew they weren't blood relatives, but it was odd that her father grew up around it and never mentioned it.

"Dad never told me any of this." It might have made things more bearable.

Deidre was thinking. Counting. Her head was nodding.

"*Alors*, your father was probably too young to remember anything more than fuzziness. He was not more than four or five when Catherine died. He might have been about eight when Papa's moods stopped. I was three years older so I remember more clearly. Your father probably didn't make a connection between Papa's headaches and depression. He cared mostly whether Papa was available to go riding with him."

"And you, Deidre? Do you have dark moods? I don't mean to be impertinent, but you look sad. Sadder than just about Dad."

"Not impertinent. We're family sharing medical stories. Yes, I suffer depression. It pushed my husband away. The pills made me gain weight and didn't always work. It is difficult for a husband."

"You're not fat."

"I don't have the girlish figure I maintained until I was forty. Even after two children. He loves me. He's just not faithful. It's not uncommon. You know that, surely."

"True, but I don't want it to happen to you."

"*Mais oui*, but it did. What your parents had was rare. You grew up in a very happy family. We must try to make things better for your mother. Neither of us can go too far, or we will damage our own health. That will help nobody." She stood. "Let's go inside. Perhaps you can try some broth."

# CHAPTER
# FORTY-ONE

Her mother was napping when LouLou returned to the house. Her conversation with Deirdre was startling. Her father's family had mental illnesses. Deirdre was probably right that her dad truly hadn't been aware of it and certainly never told her mother when they married years later.

LouLou sat in the kitchen alone and drank the broth Deirdre had made while nibbling at toast. She couldn't finish more than a quarter of a slice. She knew she had to eat. Perhaps the psychiatrist would have some suggestion for an appetite stimulant. Maybe she was suffering pure grief. Nothing psychological about it at all.

She slowly made her way upstairs to her room at the end of the hall. She passed her parents' room, where her mother had returned, and hoped that her mom would find some comfort there.

Gregg was sitting in her favorite blue upholstered chair by a window overlooking the pool when she returned to her room. She flew into his arms. He barely had time to stand.

"How? What? When?"

He wrapped her in his arms. "Sshh. I'm sorry, LouLou. I'm sorry about your dad." She put her head on his shoulder and leaned into him. He walked her to the bed and sat next to her.

"You traveled."

"Skylar got your text from Paris. We talked about getting me here and decided to give it a try. Skylar drove me. We took it mile by mile. We made it to Ashland, Fredericksburg, Quantico. I lost concentration near Arlington and became invisible. That gave Skylar a scare, but we got back on the road with the radio blaring. He said it was to keep me awake, but of course, I don't sleep. The noise forced me to concentrate.

"We each held our breath crossing into DC, but once we did, I knew we'd make it. Finding your house was tough. Skylar actually wished he had that woman in the windshield giving him directions. He'd never seen a city with such weird road patterns, and I was completely out of my element."

"Thank you, thank you, Gregg. Thank you for coming. I need you. I need us." She let herself dissolve into the tears she'd been holding for days.

There was a light knock at her door. "LouLou? It's Uncle Collin. Do you want dinner?"

He pushed the door open slightly. LouLou opened her eyes. "No, thanks. I'll come down later."

He nodded. "Let me know if you need anything."

She had exactly what she needed. She cried herself to sleep in Gregg's arms. She didn't want him to ever let go.

He kissed the top of her head and rocked her. "Sleep. I'm here."

***

When she woke, it was just after midnight. Gregg hadn't left. She hugged him tightly.

"I'm hungry. I'm finally hungry. Let's go downstairs and see what's in the kitchen," she whispered. "Remember not to help me. We don't want anyone to see the cream pitcher floating through the air and pouring its contents into my cup."

He took her hand. "I'm getting better at being a ghost. Don't worry."

She opened the door but didn't hear any noises in the house. The low lights burned in the hallway so she could easily make her way to the back stairs. It was faster than walking the length of the house to use the proper staircase.

She rooted through the refrigerator. Mrs. Morse's daughter had labeled everything. She selected a slice of spinach quiche to microwave and took a helping from the mixed green salad in a large wooden bowl. She tossed walnuts, cranberries, and orange slices on top and poured herself a glass of iced tea.

Gregg sat at the table with his hands folded in his lap. She smiled at his effort to show her he wasn't planning to scare anyone with floating objects. She joined him.

"Everything okay in here?" It was the security

officer stationed in back of the house.

"Fine, thanks. I missed dinner."

His eyes swept the room. "Let me know if you need anything." She nodded with her mouth full.

Gregg sat silently while she finished her meal. She rinsed the dishes, put them in the dishwasher, and filled a pitcher of ice and water to take upstairs. She signaled to him that she was ready to leave.

Back in the safety of her room, she asked Gregg why he came.

"I thought you needed me and wanted to be here if you did. Skylar and I read the papers and got the impression this was a big story, reporters were everywhere, and the cops didn't have any idea what had happened. I didn't know your dad was famous."

"Not famous. Just a recognizable name in DC. I never thought about reporters. I've been in the house since we got back from Paris except for an occasional walk around the lawn in back. I haven't seen any visitors. They're being screened. There's no one I want to see."

"Are you taking care of yourself?"

"A doctor comes every day. At first, I was terrified I was going to have an episode and tried to stay still. If I didn't move, I couldn't hurt anyone. That wasn't true, but it got me through a couple of days. After talking with *Tante* Deirdre—Dad's older sister—this afternoon or morning or maybe the day before, I know it's anxiety and grief. It has nothing to do with Sick. It's grief."

"Sounds reasonable. I know you're still on a regimen. Did you take your meds today?"

"Let me check." She looked at her pill box

marked with the days of the week and AM and PM. "No, I didn't take tonight's dose." She took out two tablets and swallowed them with water. "Tomorrow morning, I have to give myself an injection."

"It's so complicated. Plus, you have time zone changes. You're amazing." He took her hands. "LouLou, you can relax now. I'm here. I'll walk with you so you'll get some exercise and fresh air and remind you to eat. I can't do anything about stress, but I'm here. For whatever you need."

"I need you, Gregg."

"Then you'll be fine."

# CHAPTER FORTY-TWO

She slipped into her mother's room early the next morning. Her mother was sitting next to the window, close to her father's dressing room. There was a tea trolley next to her. Orchid was in her lap.

LouLou folded herself in her mother's arms. For once, Orchid didn't hiss at her as the interloper. They held each other silently. LouLou finally pulled back and looked at her mom. She'd changed. LouLou knew she was being fanciful, but her mother looked like she'd passed from her former life into a new, lonelier self. Part of her spirit was missing.

"Mom, have you eaten?"

Her mother waved at the tea trolley. "Tea, some toast. Have some. You need it to go with your meds."

LouLou poured herself coffee and put jam on a slice of toast. Some of her appetite had returned.

"I want to talk to you about plans for services. I

won't be pressured into making any decisions, and I want to discuss them with you."

"Anything, Mom."

"I simply cannot bear the thought of watching my husband being lowered into the ground. I don't care that women do it every day. I'm not one of them. I can't. Your father and I made funeral arrangements when your dad turned sixty. We left it to each other to decide what we could bear, but whatever we decided would be private. Your dad said he would appreciate a memorial service for his colleagues at Georgetown and in foreign service sometime. Not immediately and nothing showy.

"That's who he was. He was proud of his work, and he knew there was protocol to follow. He liked that. There were rules for almost everything. He said guidelines for memorial services for ambassadors are just that. Guidelines. Nothing hard and fast. He wanted formality but not pomp."

LouLou agreed. That's exactly who her father was—polite, serious, and unpretentious with outsiders and a happy, loving man with his family and close friends.

"LouLou," she said as she stroked Orchid, "I'd like for him to be cremated when the coroner has finished his examination and to ask Deirdre to take his ashes immediately to their family mausoleum in Montreal. I feel no need to accompany her. I don't know what you'd like to do. I just don't want to sit through a ceremony of any sort until the memorial service. I can't, LouLou. I simply can not."

Her mother was devastated. She, who had risen to duty as the wife of an ambassador in every circumstance, couldn't do this. She didn't want to watch the earthly door shut on her husband.

"I understand. I don't want to sit through a service, but I would if you wanted."

"I don't, LouLou."

LouLou reached for her mother's soft, beautifully manicured hands. "You don't have to. I think *Tante* Deirdre would be honored to do this for him."

"Then I'll tell Collin that's the plan. I don't want to receive condolence callers at a specific time. Close friends can visit, as they have been. I invite them or they call before they come. Do you want to see any friends?"

"No, Mom. My DC friends have scattered. My close friends are in Richmond now."

Her mother closed her eyes. She looked exhausted. "We'll talk about a memorial service later. There's no urgency."

LouLou nodded.

Her mother sighed as if she were steeling herself for resistance. "There is something else important. I want to leave this house immediately. I don't want to live in this enormous home that was already too big for two of us. Your dad and I were planning to move to a condo either here or in Paris or both. We didn't want to be too far from you. Now, I simply won't stay where an unsolved murder or possible terrorist assassination occurred.

"Terrorists? Mom, that's horrifying. Do the investigators think killing Dad sent some kind of message? Are we targets?"

"The investigators are leaning toward some sort of terrorist act. They think there are French connections, but they don't know who or why or how. The only place I can bear to be is your dad's dressing room. I've been sleeping on the divan there surrounded by his clothes, the smell of him, and things he touched daily. He has photos of the two of us and the three of us I find comforting.

"As for the investigators, I don't think they know anything." She reached to touch LouLou's hand. "I don't think we're in danger, and we have a lot of security surrounding us. The security team will brief you any time you ask. Don't let this upset you unnecessarily. I think they're grasping at straws, but I want to get out of this house as fast as our things can be packed.

"I plan to pack your dad's things and mine and be ready to leave when Deirdre heads for Montreal with the cremains. I'll sell the house furnished just as we bought it. Paintings, family things, and books can be packed and stored. I'll stay with Collin and Liz in Middleburg until I decide what to do. That's as far as I can get."

"Mom, that's plenty. Once you're out of here and living with Uncle Collin and Liz, I'll feel better about you. I don't want to think of you alone or in danger."

"Is all of this okay with you? Do you want anything from the house? The piano?"

"I'll check. I'll take things from my room and the music room, but all my memories are in my heart. They're not in objects. I don't know that I need two grand pianos."

"Need and want are different. It might be nice to have two for recording or teaching or playing duets.

It's up to you. You know what's best."

Decoded to mean only LouLou knew whether she could injure herself if she had a psychotic episode in her loft. It was minimally furnished with soft pieces and rounded edges specifically to protect her. Two pianos might be one too many.

Her mother cried softly. "I love you, LouLou. I think you're the best of each of us."

LouLou put her head on her mother's shoulder and still held her hand. "I think so too."

# CHAPTER
# FORTY-THREE

Discomfort gnawed at her. The timing was terrible, but LouLou didn't want any more family secrets.

"Mom," said LouLou as she sat back, "I want to update you on my adoption."

Her mother looked baffled.

"This isn't a great time, but I want you to know I saw Dan Ramsay. His doctor contacted mine. He doesn't know my phone number or where I live.

"He asked to meet, and I agreed to have coffee with him at Ginter Gardens, where I wouldn't feel trapped. He wanted to tell me his story. He never knew his girlfriend was pregnant. I listened and that was that. He gave me CDs that she recorded and he asked if he could come to zone of my shows. I told him I have a Sick world and a normal world and he's part of the Sick. I don't see patients I've met in hospitals after I'm released. He's no exception. He's lonely after his wife died, but I don't want to be sucked into his life. I work hard to maintain boundaries to stay healthy. Frankly, I'm in no position to help anyone, especially him, right now."

"Of course not. Your health is the most important thing. I hope he understood."

"I do too. I also had contact of sorts from Bella Davis before I left for Paris. I received a letter from an attorney in New York who was the trustee of a blind trust she set up for me when I was born. I wasn't to know about it until the money was distributed on my thirtieth birthday. The firm had trouble finding me. Otherwise, I would have learned about my adoption on my thirtieth birthday. I didn't want the money, so I asked Quincy to handle it."

Her mother's shoulders slumped forward. LouLou took her hand.

"Bella Davis was going to inform you of your adoption despite our agreement? She never told us about her plan to give you money or breach the agreement." She dabbed at her eyes. "Your father and I were naïve to believe you'd never find out. When you did, we took comfort in the fact that it was a fluke. A crime committed by a blackmailer who was probably doing the same to other families. Now," her mother placed her hands in her lap as though she were at a loss, "she was a lovely, lovely young woman. You say she set it up when you were born?"

LouLou nodded.

"Then she lied to us from the beginning."

"Mom, it doesn't matter. I know, and I don't care. I love you and Dad. Bella's dead, but I had to deal with the trust. Quincy set things up so the money never passed to me personally and went to SchizoLife and Juilliard to provide high quality instruments for students and alums. It was a lot— more than nine figures. It'd been growing for thirty years.

"A note from Bella was included in the papers. I read it and thought it was odd. I got the impression all she cared about was Dan. I think the two of them were so wild about each other, a child would have been ignored. You and Dad rescued me from that.

"I shredded the note after I read it. I felt contaminated by it. There was something off about it, about her, and about Dan. I don't want anything to do with them, but I was sucked in. I'm done with both of them now."

Her mom was tired. She was almost whispering. "That must have been unbelievably stressful. It must have felt like a lightning bolt."

"It did, but not as bad as if I didn't already know. It felt calculated, as if she's trying to control me from the grave." She shivered. "Bella and her money are gone. I hope Dan leaves me alone too.

Her mother looked at her through broken-hearted eyes. "One thing I know for certain is that we can't control other people. Concentrate on yourself and your music. Keep your friends close. You know I'm always behind you."

"I do, Mom. Thanks." LouLou stood and kissed her mother's soft cheek. "I'll check out the music room to see what I might like to keep and let Uncle Collin know you're ready to speak to him. Please try to get some rest too."

# CHAPTER FORTY-FOUR

"This was yours?" Gregg wandered around the music room with his hands in his pockets and his eyes taking in everything. LouLou pressed a button, and a symphonic playlist came alive to cover any conversational sounds.

"It's where I practiced. Dad played piano and alto recorder."

"You were literally surrounded by music." Gregg looked at the floor-to-ceiling walls of scores, books, and LPs. Recording equipment was neatly stacked behind closed doors. A grand piano sat next to a bay window wall and window seat overlooking a rose garden. Folding music stands and chairs were stacked neatly to one side. Comfortable sofas and chairs were arranged for listeners to sink into. The lighting was perfect.

Gregg eyed the instrument cases. "I guess a flute, viola, and recorders. Is that a contrabass recorder?"

LouLou nodded. "I'll take it with me for you."

She'd told Gregg about her mother's plans and her opportunity to take things from the music room.

LouLou ran her fingers along the spines of musical scores. "This could fill a music library. Perhaps it should." She selected volumes of piano scores that weren't duplicates of what she had.

"The wall of honor," Gregg called. Gregg pointed to a section of wall near the piano.

"Oh, that's my parents' doing." LouLou was embarassed of the framed certificates, awards, and competition medals.

Gregg whistled. "Three Presser Music Awards. Second Prize, Dallas. Audience Favorite Prize, The Arthur Rubinstein International Piano Master Competition. That's awesome."

"More like People's Choice Awards." She saw Gregg didn't understand. "Like Miss Congeniality in the Miss American pageant."

"Sixth prize, Chopin Competition. LouLou, I said you were extraordinary. You're too modest. These are the most prestigious competitions in the world."

"They were fun when I was younger and before Sick. I love to perform, as you know, and it was nice to get cash. Beat babysitting, for which I wasn't equipped at all. I really wanted to compete in the Chopin. It's the only one I did after my schizophrenia diagnosis."

"That ended your piano performance career?"

"That, and all the other kinds of music exploding around me. I love pretty much everything. Also, to be a pro I would have to travel constantly and play concerti with orchestras. It's brutal, lonely, and not very much fun. The touring I do now is for a specific release. An EP or CD. There's no season. There's always a club or concert venue that needs music. I control where I go for the most part. There's no politics and sucking up to conductors."

"You sound flippant, but it's the way you keep music in your life with Sick, isn't it?"

She nodded. He put his hands on her waist and kissed her. "Play for me?" He turned off the CD.

She sat at the piano. She didn't hesitate. A Bach prelude and fugue was drawn into the air by her agile fingers. When she finished, LouLou looked at Gregg with tears running down her face.

"I hate playing Bach. It was Dad's favorite. After Sick, it was impossible for me to play Bach. So much math. You know how Bach liked his word and numerical puzzles—spelling out B-A-C-H on the keyboard and assigning numbers to notes and writing codes. I'd only see the math. Bach was no longer music to me and more like a crossword puzzle. I can get through something now, but I was never a fan so I don't count it a loss. I know, I'm bourgeoisie."

"LouLou?" The door opened, and Uncle Collin walked in. "Well-played," he said. "Mrs. Morse asked me to let you know dinner is in about half an hour. Do you feel up to joining us?"

"Yes. I'll go change." She stood and started toward the door. Collin put his hand on her arm to ask her to pause. "You mother told me her plans. Are you okay with them?"

"Yes," she said, breathing quietly. "I can't bear watching him be put away from us. Mom needs to get out of this house. Do they really think this was terrorism?"

"That's the theory. There was nothing in his personal life, and it wasn't random. Somehow, this was a message. The CIA, Homeland Security, and State Department have to figure it out. I'll be frank. Witness Protection was discussed for you and your mother, but ultimately dropped. The target was your father, not his family. Even that doesn't sit right with me. He'd been retired for a while and was teaching at Georgetown. He wasn't involved in espionage."

"What about one of his students?"

"It's someone else's job to investigate. In the meantime, stay with Liz and me for a while. Help your mother and Orchid get settled. We'd love to have you."

"Thank you, but I want to go home and get back to my routine. Orchid isn't going to approve of anything I'd do. You'll take care of Mom, won't you?"

"The best a big brother can."

# CHAPTER FORTY-FIVE

"Terrorism?" Gregg almost shouted when they were back in LouLou's room. "This was an assassination?"

"You heard what I did. I don't want to know any more than that. I think they concluded it had to be a professional job because there was no sign of entry anywhere. Whoever did it must've come in with a deliveryman or behind a service tech and may have hidden for days before acting. Otherwise, it was Houdini or a ghost." She looked at him. "Sorry, no offense."

"It could be a ghost. I don't know how he'd get a gun, but it could be done. I'm an amateur ghost compared to some."

"A ghost who had something against Dad?"

"It's possible. Just saying."

***

After dinner, Collin asked LouLou to play. "I haven't heard you live in ages. How about some Chopin?"

"Sure," she said. Chopin was her dad's favorite after Bach, and she thought Uncle Collin was hinting that her mother might find it soothing. "I'll go set up. Everyone's welcome."

LouLou had worn a dress to dinner out of respect for a family in mourning. She slid onto the piano bench and played some Scarlatti etudes to warm up. Gregg sat on the window seat behind her.

Her mother, Collin, Liz, and Deirdre sat expectantly in the music room. She played a Chopin Scherzo and Ballade.

"That was lovely, LouLou. Your father and I both love Chopin. You do, too, don't you Deirdre?"

"Yes, but not to play. I prefer the impressionists."

"Let's play some duets, *Tante*," LouLou suggested.

"I haven't played in a while."

"We'll play Debussy and Bizet. I saw a score of four hands one piano this afternoon." She stood, selected the volume, and placed it on the music rack. "Warm up a bit," she encouraged Deirdre. "Scales. I love hearing other people playing scales."

Deirdre tentatively played a C major scale with her right hand. Then both hands. Then arpeggios.

When Deirdre indicated she was ready, LouLou directed her to the bass register, and she sat at the treble. "Let's try Debussy's *Le Petite Suite*. Start with *Bateau* and skip to *Ballet*."

She counted off, and they started. Deirdre made

some rumblings in the bass, and LouLou carried her forward and wouldn't stop. They moved on to the next, and Deirdre started to find her groove. They played highlights of Bizet's light-hearted and enjoyable children's games. Deirdre mostly kept up.

LouLou nudged Deirdre. "Ready for *Galop*?"

"I'm game. Just keep playing if you lose me."

*Galop* was exactly what its name suggested—the sound of galloping horses growing faster and faster. Deirdre and LouLou were laughing by the time they reached the end. LouLou directed *encore,* and they took off at an even faster pace. Both were laughing and crying simultaneously.

"*Brava*." Deirdre's husband had come into the room unnoticed and rose to applaud and cheer his wife. Deirdre blushed. LouLou hugged her and forced her to come from behind the piano and take bows with her. Twice. Everyone in the room talked and laughed and enjoyed moments of being a family together.

LouLou's mom cried unabashedly. "I'm so pleased to hear laughter and music in this house. Thank you."

LouLou saw Gregg smiling in his window seat. He mouthed, "*Brava*." She caught her mother's eye and telegraphed her thought.

Her mother agreed because the next thing she said was. "Deirdre, please take the piano. It would give all three of us great pleasure to know it's with the family and being used by someone who loves us and knows what she's doing."

Deirdre was too overcome to speak. Her husband came toward her, put his arm around her waist, and kissed her cheek. "I accept on behalf of Deirdre. She's an artist who should have a wonderful instrument, one played so beautifully by her brother and niece and loved by her sister-in-marriage."

This time when LouLou looked at Gregg, he mouthed, "Matchmaker."

# CHAPTER FORTY-SIX

### June

"They're here. They're here," shouted Sara when she got off the elevator and walked into LouLou's apartment carrying a large brown paper bag.

LouLou looked up from a score long enough to ask what was here.

"Magazines with the Chanel ad featuring 'The always *au courant* DJL.'" Sara fanned out *Vogue*, *French Vogue*, and *Marie Claire*.

LouLou picked them up and turned to the pages Sara had marked with pink sticky flags.

"They used a different shot in each magazine. Too funny. Don't you love these shoes?" LouLou said as she pointed to the ones she'd modeled in *French Vogue*.

"Love? I adore them. Did you get to keep the shoes?"

"No way. They were a full size too small. That's

why I look so casual with one dangling off my toe. I couldn't bear to even sit in them."

"Ah, LouLou, you've ruined the magic of fashion for me. I love the Chanel headphones and the mini dress. You've got great legs."

"Probably air-brushed to be five inches longer than they are. I wish the headphones were real and not a prop. I'd wear them all the time. Cool colors."

The two women dissected each of the three pictures. LouLou selected *French Vogue* as her favorite. Sara selected *Marie Claire*. "Will you autograph one? I want to frame it and hang it at Roy's. He gets a kick out of having customers asking about celebrities who visit his sandwich shop/patisserie/bodega."

LouLou laughed. "Of course. Anything to keep the man who feeds me happy. Do you think he's ever going to settle on just what it is he owns?" She took out a black marker and signed 'Love, LouLou' on the magazine page. Sara sat. "Who knows? I keep telling him to call it a specialty coffee shop and market like Dean & DeLucca, but he thinks that will discourage tea drinkers."

"Sara, secretly I like the way it is. Always a surprise in stock."

Sara leaned closer to LouLou. "You sound good. How are you doing?"

"I hate to jinx things, but there hasn't been a catastrophe in my life since Dad died. That's unforgettable. I think of him every day, but I haven't had an episode or had to tour or do anything other than what I love. It feels nice to be normal-ish for a while."

"Good. Don't forget. Dinner on Thursday. I'll have this framed by then. Later."

***

"You have to frame one of these for Skylar." Gregg looked at the magazine photos carefully. "I can't believe I'm dating this hot celebrity DJ. I wish I'd seen the one Sara liked."

"Gregg, you can go to the newsstand and peruse women's fashion magazines until you find *Marie Claire* and make a purchase."

"And scare the owner to death when a magazine floats onto the counter with exact change and walks itself away?"

LouLou laughed. "I keep forgetting you're a ghost. Sorry. I'll buy it myself so you can see. Then you can pick one for Skylar, and I'll have it framed." She went to the kitchen and poured a glass of water, added ice, and grabbed an apple from the wooden bowl she'd taken from the house in DC. She flopped back on the sofa.

"How was your day?"

"Good. I've finished inventorying the LPs from your family music library for Skylar. He starts to cry every time he looks at some of them. He'd no idea your parents had French pop music and British Invasion works with original UK cover art and liner notes. Once he put the word out, people started calling him right away. He's making brisk sales with classical music to everyone from obscure orchestras to superstar violinists. He has contacts at universities all over the world swooning over these finds. Still, he keeps at it. He says things like I might be receiving something you might like in the near future, or I've come across something that might tempt you and two or three other serious collectors. He's a salesman, but a well-intentioned one. He wants to make great matches."

"I'm glad the music is going to good homes. What about your listening education?"

"I can't stop listening to recorder chamber music. I enjoyed the evening when your father's recorder quintet played for the family. They were all interesting people who just happened to play the recorder for fun. I wish I'd been able to ask them questions. I know the recorder is an acquired taste, but after discovering the contrabass recorder, I can't stop listening. So much could be transposed for the double bass. And then my mind goes off into compositions, arrangements, and orchestrations."

"To state the obvious, Gregg, you're a composer. That's what you do."

"True." He got up to get his composition notebook from the countertop. "LouLou," he suddenly sounded serious, "I thought you shredded this. I know you did."

"What?" LouLou replied offhandedly.

He showed her an envelope. It was the one that had been included in the documents from Bella Davis's New York attorney.

LouLou's stomach lurched. "Is it empty? Maybe I only shredded the letter."

He opened it and took out the note. Intact.

"How can that be?" She wanted to shout. Freeze. Freeze. Freeze.

"Could there have been two letters?" He read it. "Word for word, it's the same as the one you shredded. Did she send two copies of the same letter? Where's the large envelope it came in?"

"I shredded that too. It was empty." Freeze. Freeze. Freeze.

"What is this, then? It's not a photocopy."

By now, LouLou was sitting perfectly still. Gregg sat beside her.

"Let's think aloud. There might have been a second communication that was overlooked. You had a lot of mail—mostly condolence cards and letters—Roy held for you."

"No, I recorded each on a spreadsheet and included the date I sent an acknowledgement. Did it come through the Post Office?"

"No. It's addressed to LouLou Fleming. No street or PO address. No city or state. No return address. No stamp. It had to have been inside something else."

"But what?"

"Did Dan send you a condolence card?"

"No. I was afraid he might. As far as I know, he still doesn't know where I live. He'd have to follow me. The obituary was carefully worded to include me as daughter LouLou of Washington, DC. I didn't want any fan sympathy mail, either."

"What about that awful aide at Petersburg? Were there any names you didn't recognize?"

LouLou shook her head.

"LouLou, don't over think this. There's an explanation." He squeezed her hand but knew not to do more. "There are only a few people who know about the circumstances of how you found out about the adoption. Dr. Youzny, the blackmailer, her accomplices, and Dan. Anyone else?"

"I forgot." She looked horrified. "I forgot to ask Dan to keep it a secret. He could have told his family. His friends. Anyone."

"Do you think he'd do that?"

"Yes, he was ecstatic that he and Bella had a child. He had to tell his brother who saw me at the window in the day room at Petersburg and thought he was seeing Bella's ghost, the resemblance was so strong."

"But you said Dan has a child. A child from his marriage. He might not want her to know. He wouldn't tell his family and expect them to keep it a secret from the child."

"Dr. Youzny said my parents were unusual in keeping it secret. The prevailing wisdom is to tell the adopted child and everyone on the planet so the child grows up knowing he or she was chosen. Siblings and half-siblings are supposed to be told immediately too. That's probably what Dan thinks is the right thing to do."

"That still doesn't explain the letter."

"I didn't find out about the trust until after I met Dan to hear his story. Maybe he got a letter from Bella too."

"And then did what? Mailed it in another envelope to you?"

"It's the only thing that makes sense. Maybe he thought it would be the only way I'd know I was conceived through soul mate bliss."

"What are you going to do?"

"Shred it. Ignore it. I don't want to think about it. What time is it? Can we still make a movie?"

# CHAPTER FORTY-SEVEN

LouLou didn't like the presence of another letter from Bella. She shredded it before they left for the movies, emptied the shredder into her kitchen waste can, and dumped that plastic bag into a garbage can on the street.

She liked the movie and that she could snuggle next to Gregg. The theatre was almost empty. On the way home, they stopped at a newsstand so LouLou could look through magazines for her Chanel ad. She purchased *Marie Claire* for Gregg and discovered another ad in *Harper's Bazaar* and bought that too.

Gregg thought Skylar would like the *French Vogue* ad best, and LouLou agreed to have it framed the next morning before she met Gregg at Vinyl. She hadn't seen Skylar or Robert for almost a week.

She felt sassy and wore a sky blue dress and gladiator sandals. Summer was on its way. Robert accepted her long-delayed massage. Skylar was in a listening booth. Gregg was packing orders for shipping.

"I can't believe Skylar has you doing manual labor," she said as she kissed him.

"I don't mind. Besides, I do this ten percent of my time and listen the other ninety percent. I learned how to print postage paid mailing labels on the computer. I'm a whiz now."

"You're constantly learning something now. It's a delight to see things through your eyes."

"LouLou," Skylar said as he bounced out of a listening booth. "I believe you now. I listened to that recorded but unreleased Björk album, and it's a treasure. I'm going to think about who I'll offer it to. It has to go to someone appropriate and appreciative."

"Lou?" said a voice from the front of the store.

LouLou and Skylar walked toward the front counter. Robert was complaining loudly that the newcomer wasn't paying attention to him.

LouLou stopped before reaching him. Dammit. He'd found her favorite place. She felt he was contaminating it. She tried to hide her anger. "Dan. Remember, my name is LouLou. Lou is my Sick name."

"Sorry. This is a nice surprise," Dan said.

Was it? Was he following her?

"Hi, forgive LouLou's manners. I'm Skylar, the proprietor of Vinyl." He held out his hand to Dan.

"Dan Ramsay," he said and shook Skylar's hand.

"My partner Robert feels dissed because you didn't introduce yourself." Dan clearly didn't understand Skylar was referring to the cat, but

Skylar plowed on. "How may I help you today?"

Dan seemed to have trouble focusing on Skylar with LouLou there, so she stepped into a listening booth but didn't completely close the door. Eavesdropping was fair if Dan was following her.

"I'm learning to play the guitar. I want some simple songs that I can play and sing. I thought about maybe Bob Dylan or Pete Seeger. Would you have recordings by them?"

LouLou groaned. If things weren't bad enough, her biological dad was a Dylan fan. She knew Skylar was in heaven as he led Dan to the correct section and advised him on the pros and cons of each possibility. This was basic stuff, though. Dan could have easily downloaded Dylan and Seeger. He didn't need Vinyl or Skylar's expertise. Flimsy.

Gregg, who had been in Skylar's office, came out. "All deliveries for today are ready."

Skylar and Dan looked up. "Thanks. You've saved me hours of procrastination and frustration."

"Hi, I'm Dan." He held his hand out to Gregg.

Without showing any surprise, Gregg shook his hand and said, "Gregg, nice to meet you."

"Do you work here too?"

"No," Skylar interrupted. "Gregg is a composer who is also a computer wizard. He likes to show off his skills from time to time to keep things running smoothly."

LouLou pulled the door closed on the listening booth. She couldn't listen anymore. Dan could see and touch Gregg. How could that be? What was that word Gregg used for Skylar? A Sensitive. She couldn't take any more surprises from Dan. She wasn't going to hide in the booth until he left, so she joined the trio.

"LouLou, I understand you and Dan know each other," Skylar said mischievously.

"We've come across each other in hospitals. I hope we don't do so again. I don't plan to be a patient any time soon. I hope you don't do anything foolish that would land you there either, Dan."

She kissed Skylar on the cheek, gave Robert a rub, and waved to Gregg. "See you next time." LouLou casually walked out of Vinyl and sprinted away as soon as she turned the corner.

# CHAPTER FORTY-EIGHT

LouLou slowed and walked to the Jefferson Hotel. It was a landmark best known as the prototype for Scarlett O'Hara's staircase in *Gone With The Wind*. It was pricey, classy, and quiet. She went into one of the rare private phone closets, took out her cell, and called her mom.

"Mom, have you seen the Chanel ad yet? I've seen it in four magazines. *French Vogue*, *Vogue*, *Marie Claire*, and *Harper's Bazaar*. They used three different shots. Air brushed like crazy."

"Fashion doesn't come to Middleburg. Maybe Collin can get them when he goes to DC."

"I'll scan them and email them. Sara asked me to autograph one for Roy's coffee shop. How are you?"

"Okay. I take long walks. Liz rides a lot, but horses scare me."

"Nothing scares you, Mom."

"Don't like is more apt. I like the horses. Riding

them is nerve-wracking. How are you?"

"Good. I was excited to see the ads. We had a great time in Paris. It was what happened after that was so awful. We have to remember the good."

Her mother didn't respond.

"We had a lot going on in DC, but do you remember the conversation we had about Bella and Dan interfering in my life?"

"Of course. How could I forget something like that? You're my daughter."

"I think it's escalating. Today, I found a duplicate of the letter Bella Davis sent me on my counter. I shredded the original. I know I did. Sara was there when I did it." It was Gregg, not Sara, but she could hardly tell her mother that. "I think Dan sent it to me. I met him for coffee before I learned about the trust. Maybe he got a letter from Bella, too. I think he mailed it to me in something else like a card or a business envelope or something that I didn't notice. It wasn't in any of my condolence correspondence."

"I didn't think he knew where you lived."

"He doesn't unless he followed me or bought one of those information packages online that sell people's information for $29.99 or hired a private detective."

Her mother was silent. When she spoke, her voice seemed small. "That doesn't make sense. You said Bella's plan was for the trust and presumably, the letter, to be given to you on your thirtieth birthday. Because you were no longer in Paris, the law firm couldn't find you until more than a year later. If you and Dan were supposed to open the letters at the same time, Dan would've gotten a copy on your thirtieth birthday, not now."

LouLou thought about that.

"True. Dan was a patient at Petersburg on my thirtieth birthday. I assume his brother or lawyer handled his mail. He and I were transferred from Petersburg at the same time. I was discharged from Colonial in January. I don't know how long he'd been out of a hospital when I met him in March, but he must have had time to read his mail. He told me he wouldn't have known about me except for the blackmailer. Of course, Bella has proven herself to be a liar. Why not him? My birthday was in April, and he didn't contact me. I didn't think about it, but he seems sentimental. If he'd known the date, he might have tried to contact me on my birthday. It makes no sense why he'd send me Bella's letter now—more than a year after he should've received it, even allowing for his hospitalization."

LouLou pressed her forehead against one of the panels of the phone closet. Thinking through this puzzle was exhausting. Finally, she said, "Mom, there's more. Just now, I went to Vinyl to see Skylar. He loves all the music we placed with him from the estate. He can't part with some of it, but I know what he is parting with is going to universities and knowledgeable collectors. Anyway, I went in and less than five minutes later, Dan came in. Skylar had never seen him before and welcomed him. I said hello and then went into a listening booth and looked industrious.

"When enough time passed, I left. On my way out, Skylar said something that made it clear that Dan had told Skylar we knew each other. I corrected him and told Skylar we'd been patients at the same hospital and hoped we both stayed out of them. I left. I think I walked out normally, but then I ran. I'm at the Jefferson now."

"Are you on your cell?" When LouLou said she was, her mother insisted on calling her back on the hotel's phone. She asked for the number. All LouLou could think about while she was waiting for her mother to call was how much she hated Bella and Dan. She didn't want anything to do with them. Now, she was getting duplicate mail from Bella, and Dan was following her. It made her sick.

The phone rang, and LouLou picked up immediately.

"I don't want you wasting minutes when there's a landline. I think it's more secure anyway. I don't like the sound of this. Maybe you should hire a private investigator to see if this man is stalking you."

"I think he's at least aware of my favorite places. More importantly, I forgot to ask him to keep the adoption a secret. His brother saw me at Petersburg and thought he was seeing Bella's ghost, I look so much like her. I'm sure Dan told him.

"Dr. Youzny said adoption experts encourage parents not to keep it a secret. Dan has a child from his marriage. He may have told that child and everyone he knows. The fact that he and Bella had a love child sent him into orbit."

"Darling, would it be so terrible if people knew that you were adopted?"

LouLou started to cry. "Yes. You and Dad are my parents. I don't want some college kid and his girlfriend claiming any hold on me. I love you. No one else."

"What matters is who you consider to be family, but if this investigation into your father's death drags on, we won't have a shred of privacy left. The authorities may be looking at the same DNA database that revealed your biological parents. It may not stay secret."

She hadn't thought of that. *Tante* Deirdre thought she got her blonde hair and blue eyes from her dad. She'd be heartbroken to know that wasn't true.

"Should we tell the family now to prevent them from hearing about it some other way?"

"No. The family has had enough. Canadian investigators interviewed Deirdre and her family. Collin and Liz and their kids have been interviewed and researched. Truly, it makes me want to run away to Iceland or Lapland or the Faroe Islands, away from this intrusiveness."

"I'd no idea they were looking so widely. It's ridiculous. My concern is you. Are you really okay in Middleburg?"

"Yes, I am. It's quiet and peaceful. Even though my friends are in Washington, I don't want to go back there. I went to DC for lunch with close friends one day and had a terrible time staying at the table. I wanted to jump and run out of the restaurant. They were being kind and wonderful and protective, but I couldn't wait to leave. Everything reminds me of your father."

"Your times were good there, though. Did you close on the house?"

"That was the easiest thing I've done. The bidding war tripled the price. The buyer paid cash, and it closed last month. I'm free of it. Like you, I have the memories of our time there in my heart. I'd love to see you. Come stay here. You might be smart to stay out of Dan's town for a bit. He sounds a bit desperate and possibly unstable."

"Mom, he was at Petersburg for two years. He is desperate and unstable. I don't even know his diagnosis beyond what Dr. Youzny told us. Whatever it is, Dan may not be as diligent as I am about continuing treatment and medication. I don't know, but I think I need to find out."

"Be careful."

"I will, Mom. It's getting dark. I need to head home. I'm going to splurge and take a taxi.

"That's my sensible girl."

# CHAPTER FORTY-NINE

"Here, let me help you." Roy helped LouLou out of the taxi. "Cabs are a rare treat for you. Everything okay?"

"I think so, Roy. It was getting dark, and I didn't want to walk home. I'm fine."

"Let me know if you need anything."

LouLou nodded and headed to her loft. She could feel Roy's eyes watching until she was in the elevator and lights came on in her unit.

Gregg was standing at the door. "Are you okay? You tore out of Vinyl."

LouLou put her tote down, unlaced her sandals, and poured herself a glass of iced water. She'd kept eight crystal high ball glasses from the DC house.

She went to Gregg and kissed him. He responded ardently. "I need you," she said. "Now."

Their clothes were off in seconds, and they were in bed. LouLou needed the feel of his skin, his probing kisses, and his deep thrusts. She needed his tenderness too. Afterward, she lay spent as he kissed her softly in all the right places. He knew instinctively where they were. He was the most generous lover she'd ever had.

"Want to talk?"

"Dan at Vinyl? That was High Life."

Gregg sat up immediately. "Do you think he followed you there?"

"That was my thought. Who needs Vinyl to find some easy Dylan and Seeger? He could find it on YouTube if he wanted to learn chords. And that wasn't even the most upsetting part. He saw you, Gregg. He shook hands with you. Does that mean he's a Sensitive like Skylar? "

"Definitely. Do you think he's stalking you?"

"It's starting to feel that way." She reached for her glass of water and sipped. "I called Mom immediately. I wanted to hear her voice. I told her about the magazines, and then I told her about Bella's duplicate letter and Dan showing up at Vinyl on a flimsy pretext."

"What was her take?"

"He's unstable and desperate. I mean, I met him at a psych hospital. He spent a long time at Petersburg. Who knows how catatonia messed with his mind? I don't know that his depression or whatever else he may have is cured. He may no longer be in therapy or taking meds. He's a wild card.

"I also told her that he may be spreading news about the adoption. That didn't bother her. The investigation into Dad's death includes looking at every aspect of his life. She thinks the investigators already know whatever they need from the DNA database."

Gregg turned on his side to face her. He cursed. "That isn't over yet?"

"The theory is there's a terrorist cell in France targeting US and EU diplomats. No reason given. She said she feels so hounded she wants to live off the grid in Iceland."

Gregg shook his head. "That's a thought. What about you? Do you feel safe?"

"I'm edgy. Mom invited me to Middleburg, but that's a temporary solution. I think I'm going to hire a private investigator to get a read on Dan. If he's stalking me, I'll press charges. I may be unreliable due to my mental health history, but a report from a PI would be sufficient to get a restraining order and charge him with stalking. Even if it's cyberstalking.

"What did Skylar make of him?" She was curious.

"Do you have to ask? A man comes in and wants to talk Dylan? He thinks Dan's the angel Gabriel or Michael or whichever one is the top guy."

"What about Robert?"

"Pissed he didn't get any attention from Dan. Hissed a couple of times."

"I trust Robert. I'll call a PI tomorrow."

"And tonight?" Gregg reached for her.

"Tonight is just for us. Just let me check messages." She turned from Gregg, picked up her phone, and read texts.

"This may be the answer," she said to Gregg.

"What is it?"

"A text from Dan Ramsay's mother asking to

meet me. The text was from Dr. Baldwin's office, so Mrs. Ramsay doesn't know my phone number."

"Do you think it's safe to meet her?" Gregg brushed a wayward strand of hair from her face.

"She's got to be eighty. She might tell me more than I can find out from a PI. I'll meet her."

***

LouLou savored her big cup of Roy's chicory coffee. She'd treated herself to a second one after finishing the breakfast of egg whites, fruit, and whole wheat toast he'd presented her. Sipping it slowly gave her time to watch the deli/patisserie/bodega's breakfast crowd empty. Caesar was handling the few latecomers and ringing up sales of dishwashing liquid, deodorant, and diapers—the best-selling mid-morning items in the bodega.

Roy walked to where LouLou sat at the far end of the counter. "Busy morning. Unusual for mid-week."

"The word is out, Roy. Best breakfast in town. You're going to have to name this place soon."

"I'll get around to it." He wiped his hands on his apron. "I've got a feeling you don't want to talk to me about names."

LouLou could tease him, but she was serious. She didn't want to waste time.

"There's a guy who might be following me. I don't think he knows where I live, but he may know I come here for breakfast if he's studying me."

"A fan?"

"No. He's a man in his fifties. A psych patient I met first at Richmond Memorial Hospital and then at Petersburg."

"Commonwealth Psychiatric? I don't like the sound of that. What was he in for?"

"Competency hearing like me, except he lapsed into catatonia after his first night there and ended up staying more than two years. He came out of it while I was there."

"Why's he interested in you?"

She'd never lied to Roy and Sara. She'd fudged about Gregg, but that was different.

"There were some rumors an aide started. She was fired, but she told people he was my father. He believes them."

Roy cocked his head. "Father."

LouLou nodded.

"So he doesn't want to hurt you. Nothing romantic."

"Roy, I don't know what he thinks. Coming from me, this sounds weird, but he's a psych patient. That can mean anything. He may be cured. He may be sick. He may have a doctor or not. Not everyone is as diligent as I am about fighting the disease. Not everyone has a support system like you and Sara and Skylar. I don't know anything about him."

Roy nodded his head. "No one takes better care of themselves than you do, LouLou. You're right. You're probably exceptional, but why now? Why are you telling me this now?"

LouLou inhaled the aroma of her coffee, took a last sip of coffee, and swallowed. She pushed the cup away. "He showed up at Vinyl yesterday at the same time I was there. The same time I'm always there."

"Could it have been a coincidence?"

"No, Roy. He had some flimsy pretext about wanting to learn to play the guitar and getting some Dylan records. Beginners don't buy LPs; they download. Suburban guys like him buy CDs."

"You're right. He could learn how to play basic chords from YouTube and buy or download songs from plenty of sites. He didn't need to go to a store for aficionados to get basic information. What did you do?"

"I hid in a listening booth until it looked like he was going to stay as long as I was there. He told Skylar he and I were friends. I headed out, but I corrected him and said we'd been patients at the same psych hospital and hoped we didn't do that again. I left and took a long route with a couple of stops getting home."

"Ah, that's why you were in a cab."

"Right."

"What about Skylar?"

"I emailed Skylar and told him the guy was stalking me and to call the cops if he shows again. Skylar got it. After the euphoria about Dylan cleared, Skylar realized how weak the guy's pretext for being there sounded."

LouLou reached in her tote and pulled out a sketch she'd made the night before of Dan as he'd been at Vinyl. Beckham haircut growing long, white hair, and gaunt. "I made a sketch. If you see this guy anywhere near here, lock your doors and call the cops."

Roy shifted on his feet. "Are you sure? Do you think he's dangerous? Are Sara and the kids in danger?"

"I don't know. From what I saw yesterday, he's not as well-groomed as he once was. He might be going off his meds. He may not even have meds, but he's sniffing around me and that's unacceptable. I don't know anything about violence or weapons. I had to warn you. I hope it's a false alarm, but you need to know."

"What about you? Have you been to the cops yet?"

"I'm meeting someone in a few minutes who knows him better than I do. I'll go to the cops after that. I may go stay with my uncle for a few days so I have all my meds with me. Nothing's in the apartment. I'll let you know if I'm not going to be home tonight. I don't want you to worry. In the meantime, I want you, Sara, and the kids to be safe."

She leaned over the counter, held his head in both hands, and kissed the top of his bald head.

# CHAPTER FIFTY

The elderly woman extended her hand when LouLou walked into the dim lounge of a suburban hotel. Her hair was short, silver, and stylish. She was seated in a club chair and had on a tailored pink dress and low-heeled pumps.

"I'm Selma Ramsay. It's nice to meet you, Ms. Fleming."

LouLou shook her soft hand. She smelled of sandalwood and Iris. *Shalimar*, she guessed. "Please call me LouLou."

"Then you must call me Selma." She pointed to the chair next to her. "Please sit. I've ordered tea for myself. What would you like?" she asked in a soft, southern voice.

"Club soda with lime, please." Selma discretely relayed the order and a glass was placed in front of LouLou. "LouLou, you're a beautiful young woman."

"Thank you." She sat silently. Selma would get around to asking her something eventually.

"I'm told you're an artist."

LouLou nodded. "I draw. I drew all my tattoos. I like to capture moments on paper. I'm not a painter or sculptor."

"I don't think that matters. You take pleasure in it."

Sensible. Reassuring.

"My son told me how kind you were to him during his hospitalizations. He said you drew sketches so he could get a haircut that wasn't hideous."

LouLou nodded. "Always best to take a picture to a hair stylist."

More silence. LouLou waited her out.

"Please forgive me, but was there anything in particular that caused you to be kind to him?"

"I'm a kind person. I've lived with schizophrenia since I was sixteen. People who've had perfectly normal lives have no idea what it's like to live with a chronic illness, much less a chronic mental illness. I assume we're all doing the best we can until proven otherwise."

"What a thoughtful way to live." Selma smiled in appreciation.

"When I first saw him at Richmond Memorial Hospital, he was walking laps around the floor as part of his routine to stay healthy. He seemed determined to get well. I liked that. His clothes attracted me."

Selma raised an eyebrow. The skin of her eyelids were wrinkled with powder.

"He seemed so out of place on a psych floor. He looked like a middle aged suburban guy, but he was wearing something like high school gym shorts and a tee shirt with a beer logo that read High Life. I'd only been on meds for a few days and that struck me as hysterical. He said his brother supplied his clothes and he wore them without looking at the slogans. When I arrived at Commonwealth Psychiatric he'd been there for about two years. I thought I could scare him out of his catatonia. I went over to him, intent on being naughty and then when I looked at him I realized I knew him. Like someone's father or a professor or neighbor. I finally realized he was the man I called High Life and reminded him I was Lou from Richmond Memorial Hospital. The next time he saw me, he indicated he understood what I'd said."

Selma visibly relaxed. "So I have you to thank for getting him on the road to recovery. After he showed signs of awareness, we were able to retain a neurologist who specialized in the rare condition he had. Now, he's able to live a mostly normal life, but what's normal? He's alive and not behind bars. Thank you."

LouLou sat straighter.

"Please don't thank me. As patients in psychiatric facilities in the region, we recognize familiar faces and bond for the duration of our stay. There's a man at Commonwealth Psych who always looks out for me. There's a woman I saw during two stays. We smoked cigarettes together, made jokes about the staff, and speculated about the first thing we'd do when released. We'd reconnect again if we were to be hospitalized at the same time. It's a way to get through the agony that is hospitalization, but it stops at the hospital door. I have a Sick life and a real life.

I don't mix the two."

Selma sipped her tea and refilled her cup from the small teapot on the table.

"Is that a polite way of saying you don't want anything to do with Dan or me?"

"I told Dan directly. I have two lives. I don't mix them. He's part of the Sick life no matter what biology we share."

"I see." Selma put her cup down. "Why did you agree to meet me?"

"To satisfy your curiosity." She was matter of fact.

Selma looked taken aback, but LouLou continued. "It's natural that you'd want to know what your biological granddaughter looks like and get a sense of her. I don't have a cold heart. If I could meet you without harming myself, there's no reason not to do it." LouLou took a sip of her club soda.

"You're forthright," Selma said. "Not a lot of Southern charm."

"No, but then I wasn't raised in the south. I lived in Europe."

"What do you mean you'd meet me if it didn't mean harming yourself?"

"I protect myself from unnecessary stress. Adding Dan's family to my life and pretending there's a family connection would be extremely stressful. I won't do it. I spend all day every day checking the time for meds and injections and making sure my phone is charged. I have alarms set for times to eat and exercise. I keep the same doctor's appointments once a week. I take naps. I avoid stress. I have a rigid schedule."

Selma seemed to be listening carefully.

"Selma, I've known since I was diagnosed at sixteen I would never have a normal life. I could never marry and inflict possible psychotic episodes on a man I loved. I certainly wouldn't have children. I'll die younger than most. Women with schizophrenia live abut twenty-five years less than women without it. Schizophrenia is one of the rare mental illnesses that can actually cause death and be considered a natural cause. It took me a long time to accept those facts. I've endured hospitalizations and experimental medications.

"Were I to include Dan's family in my life, I'd be a curiosity. I'd feel constantly compared to Bella and always falling short. I don't want to fill in gaps for Dan. I don't want to share my childhood memories with anyone other than my parents. I've no interest in Dan's life. All of it would be too stressful for me. I'm simply not going to jeopardize my health."

Selma stretched her hand and rested it on top of LouLou's.

"Nor should you." She kept her hand on LouLou's. "Your life sounds very complicated with a terrible illness."

Selma didn't speak for a bit. LouLou did.

"My parents are perfect. I love them with all my heart because they taught me how to love. I'll never think of anyone else as my parents. Ever."

"LouLou, I think you're a remarkable woman. You're very adept at describing your feelings. I see a watchfulness in Dan now. To a much lesser extent, of course, but he's vigilant against anything that might bring on a depressive episode."

She removed her hand from LouLou's and placed it in her lap. "I can't say I didn't have sentimental expectations that you'd embrace Dan as a family member. He was devastated when Bella left. He lived with his father and me for almost three years and I frankly didn't think he'd survive. By the time he did marry, he was much less than his former self. Had he known about you, I think his life would have been so much better." She had a wistful look, as though she truly wanted to turn back the clock.

"Maybe, Selma, but mine wouldn't have been."

Selma's composure dissipated.

"From what little I know from Dan and now you, I think I would have been a lost child. Dan and Bella were so obsessed with each other, there wasn't room for a child. Certainly not one with schizophrenia. If I hadn't already been banished to boarding school, I would've been sent to a psychiatric facility. Plush, no doubt, but a permanent institution nonetheless. I'm grateful Dan never knew and I was adopted by people who wanted and cherished me. I know I wouldn't be alive if it weren't for them. So, no, I'm not going to help your fantasy come true."

That was probably too harsh, but she wanted Selma to understand she wasn't going to change her mind.

"Obsessed. Interesting word choice. Dan's father and I used to say he was possessed by Bella." She sipped more tea, but her hand shook as she held the cup.

"Selma, I know Dan has a mental illness. I don't know what and don't want to know. I know he needs supportive friends and family. I'm simply not healthy enough myself to be of any assistance to Dan. He would drag me down with him. I understand you're Dan's mother. You want to help him, but I'm not an option. All of my love, loyalty, and very survival are due my parents. Do we understand each other?"

Selma lowered her eyes, and when she raised them to look at LouLou they were brimming with tears.

"LouLou, you must have remarkable parents. You're a brave young woman with a loving spirit."

"I owe them everything."

Selma placed her cup back on the tray along with her napkin.

"I don't want to be disloyal to my son, but you are my granddaughter. You raised a topic I worry about. I think Dan is becoming pre-occupied with you. Not to the extent he was with Bella. Far, far less than that."

That gnawing feeling started in LouLou's stomach. This is what she'd feared. She slipped her hand into her tote and grabbed a blue pill. She placed it under her tongue and took a long sip of club soda.

"Are you saying I'm in danger, Selma?" Freeze. Freeze. Freeze.

"Not danger, no. He doesn't want to hurt you. He wants to see you. You're his child with Bella, and he can't stand that he never knew about you. He's frustrated that you won't see him."

"Is he a threat to me?" This was exactly what she knew would happen. "Is he going to hound me until I say yes, have a psychotic episode, and possibly kill both of us as well as innocent bystanders?

Selma made a startled noise.

"That's what would happen, Selma. I'm not exaggerating. My psychotic episodes are violent. Before my last episode, I'd only committed property crimes. Vandalism. Theft. Arson. The last time I assaulted a cab driver and two policemen. My psychiatrists have warned me the violence will escalate should I have more episodes. My delusions and hallucinations will become darker and darker. The fact that he can't accept my boundaries frightens me. It should frighten you too, for Dan. Does he know where I live? Tell me the truth."

"No, he contacted you through your doctor, just as I did."

"Is he stalking me?" Freeze. Freeze. Freeze.

"No. He lives with me in a gated retirement community. He takes long walks around the grounds with his dog Ivan. He sticks to a routine. He doesn't have a driver's license so his brother drives him when he leaves the community."

"Do you know if he's told his psychiatrist about me?"

"He hasn't told me that."

"Does he spend a lot of time on the computer? He could be cyber stalking me."

"He uses a laptop, yes."

"He knows who my parents are, right?" No. No. No.

"Yes. Your father was a public figure." Selma

pushed her empty cup aside. "This is beginning to sound like an interrogation."

"You, Dan, and I could be in danger if this is some kind of set-up. Did Dan put you up to seeing me and then plan to make an appearance after you paved the way?"

"No. Certainly not." The elderly woman seemed surprised and then frightened.

"Does Dan know you were meeting me today? Did you drive here? Where does he think you are?"

"I told Dan I was going shopping. I drove the only car we have. He didn't seem the least bit suspicious. Short of taking a taxi, he doesn't have transportation. He couldn't have followed me."

LouLou had already put her napkin on the table. She was ready to flee. "I appreciate your telling me this. I'll let my psychiatrist know. Who is Dan's therapist?"

Selma reached into her handbag, pulled out a business card, and handed it to LouLou.

"My psychiatrist will speak to his and make him aware of this near-obsession with me. That may send Dan back to a psych hospital until he realizes he can't turn back time and that I'm not Bella."

"I hope that doesn't happen, but I don't want either of you to be in danger."

LouLou needed to make this elderly woman understand what a dangerous path her son was taking.

"Selma, hear me. My psychotic episodes are violent and escalating. If Dan pursues me, he's putting himself and the rest of his family at risk. My mind is turned over to the voices in my head and my body does whatever those voices say. If those voices were to say Dan was my enemy and he and his entire family had to be hacked to death with a hatchet, I'd get one and kill all of you, including his child."

Color drained from Selma's pleasant face. Her hands flew over her mouth to stifle a scream. She'd been graphic, but Selma had to know how serious her illness was and how dangerous it would be for Dan to push her into an episode.

"Be afraid for your family. Dan's heading to dangerous territory."

LouLou left and jumped into the first cab waiting in front of the hotel and went straight to the Jefferson Hotel, where she took another cab to Vinyl. Once she was with Skylar and Gregg, she'd be safe.

# CHAPTER FIFTY-ONE

LouLou relayed what Selma had said to Gregg and Skylar as soon as she arrived at Vinyl. Skylar led her to the room behind his office, where she sat on a zebra-striped velvet sofa. "From my LSD days," Skylar said. Robert settled himself on her lap.

She took another blue pill and drank it with ice cold water. Ice always soothed her. Gregg sat next to her on the sofa and held her hand. Skylar sat on a neon lime beanbag chair close to her. LouLou wondered if Skylar had bought the furniture while he was on an acid trip or if he'd taken acid because he lived with the furniture.

"What do we do now?" Skylar asked. He transformed into full attack mode, ready to fight demons.

"I'm headed to my psychiatrist's office. I'll call the cops from there."

"What will your doctor do?" Gregg asked.

"She'll assess me and make sure I'm okay. She'll contact Dan's therapist and fill him in. It's up to his therapist as to what to do next with fourth-hand information. All mental health professionals, whether they're psychiatrists or psychologists, have a duty to warn others if there's an immediate possibility of the patient doing something dangerous. Some therapists are cautious about the word immediate or imminent or whatever the exact legal term is."

Skylar stood. "That's not good enough. Call your uncle. Unless the cops say no, get out of town. Stay in Middleburg with your mother and your uncle's family."

"I intend to." She looked at Gregg. "I'm sorry, but I have to leave. If Dan's made it to Vinyl, my loft is probably next. I don't want anyone to get hurt. His mother didn't have a clue as to whether he was even on medication."

Gregg stood and hugged her tightly. "I love you. Don't let Bella and Dan take you away from me."

"Nothing will, Gregg. I love you."

Skylar tossed Gregg keys. "Put the closed sign on the door. You and Robert mind things here. I'm going to the doctor with LouLou in a cab."

***

LouLou's psychiatrist Dr. Baldwin didn't seem to notice Skylar sitting in the waiting room with LouLou. She was intent on hearing LouLou's story about Dan.

"Dr. Baldwin, this is my friend, Skylar. You can

tell him anything you need to help me. Do you want me to sign a release?"

"We can do that in my office."

In the exam room, Dr. Baldwin took LouLou's vital signs, did a mini-mental assessment, and asked if she felt suicidal. "Your blood pressure is high. So is your temperature. Your pulse is fast. How do you feel?"

"Scared, Dr. Baldwin. Terrified, really, that I might have an episode at any minute. I don't want anything to do with Dan Ramsay or his family. His mother said he was obsessed with Bella and almost died of grief when she left him. He attempted suicide. She said he has a pre-occupation, at least with me, but I don't think she's fully aware of how he spends his days. He's cyber stalking me at best." LouLou handed Dr. Baldwin the doctor's card Selma had given her along with one of the sketches she'd made of Dan. "Here's the card for his doctor. I've been giving the sketch to people at places I frequently go. This is what he looked like as of yesterday."

Dr. Baldwin accepted both without comment. "I'm going to give you a sedative and a booster injection of one of your anti-psychotic meds. Then we'll talk."

LouLou started to sweat. The sedative and shot came as a relief. She wanted to feel the flow of her ammunition against an episode. Knowing that it was channeling through her veins against one was comforting.

"Let the meds work and I'll make some phone calls." With Dr. Baldwin out of the room, LouLou was pleased not to be alone. Skylar's old hippie personality comforted her.

When Dr. Baldwin returned, she was pleased to have spoken directly to Dan's doctor.

"I advised Dr. Ramsay's physician of Mr. Ramsay's obsession with you. Most obsessives are good at hiding that inclination. I specifically warned him of your precarious psychiatric state and the danger of Mr. Ramsay pursuing you. The information flow was one way. Mr. Ramsay's doctor didn't give me any indication of his condition, treatments, or whether he was keeping appointments. He was following the privacy regulations to protect his patient. He can be much more forthcoming with the police than with me.

"I also contacted the Richmond Police and Lieutenant Douglas Winston of the Virginia Bureau of Criminal Investigation, in part because I've worked with him and found him to be an excellent investigator who takes threats seriously and because he'd be responsible for any investigation that might cross city and county boundaries. Do you know where Mr. Ramsay lives?"

"No. His mother merely said a gated retirement community," LouLou whispered.

"I sent along copies of the sketch. That was smart thinking, LouLou. Your mind is working. You're protecting yourself."

There was something Dr. Baldwin wasn't saying.

"Dr. Baldwin, please tell me what you know."

"It's merely my professional observation. It corroborates what you suspected. The man in that sketch has either not been treated for a while or has abruptly stopped. He's deteriorating. Nothing new. Nothing you didn't already know.

"Your uncle has asked a government agency to drive you to Middleburg with a psychiatric nurse practitioner. LouLou, you're safe. You're going to remain safe. You're going to be with your family. You haven't missed any medications. I've given you a booster and will give you something to add to your daily medication. The chance of you having an episode is low and contained.

"If you need to be admitted while you're in Middleburg, go to Shepherd Hospital in Loudon County. It's small, private, and bucolic. I have privileges there, but I also know every one of the doctors. They're all good. I don't think it will be necessary. You need time for stronger medication to become effective and a place to quiet yourself while the police do their job."

When the car arrived, Skylar hugged LouLou and reminded her how much he needed her to keep Vinyl going. She knew he meant he loved her.

"Please call Roy and let him know I decided to go out of town. He knows why. Take care of Robert. I'll be back as soon as I can." She was not going to let Bella Davis or Dan Ramsay take her down.

# CHAPTER FIFTY-TWO

LouLou's mother met the car in the dark, cool night. She hugged her daughter close. LouLou held on tight to her mother. Collin came out, chatted with the driver, and invited the nurse inside. Tux wagged his tail as though he was happy to see someone who might belong only to him.

Liz greeted her at the door with a smile and a hug. "You've got time to shower and change before dinner. We're on our own tonight and are going to eat a little late. Do you want a snack now?"

LouLou calculated when she'd last eaten. "Yes, Aunt Liz, I would. Something like cheese, crackers, olives. Nothing fancy.

"Coming right up." Liz left for the kitchen.

LouLou's mom followed her to the guest room next to hers, where she'd be staying. She hugged LouLou again. "Are you really all right? That man doesn't know where you are, does he? He's not going to hurt you?"

"No, Mom. Dr. Baldwin assured me getting out of town was the best thing to do, and she gave me additional medication. I'll be fine. I just need time to let the cops do their job."

LouLou's mother sat in one of the blue cushioned chairs. "I think it's more than the police. Your uncle was on the phone with all kinds of government agencies this afternoon. I think the FBI may be investigating. Or maybe Homeland Security. I don't know. I just know some federal agency is on the case."

"Good. Let's not talk about it anymore." She looked inside her tote. In addition to sketches of Dan, all she had were meds and changes of underwear. She had one knit dress she could just pull over her head. It would have to do.

***

"How's my girl?" Collin boomed when LouLou came downstairs. He kissed the top of her head.

Liz and her mom were having drinks in the family room. Orchid shared her mother's chair. Tux wagged his tail until LouLou sat and he settled himself beside her.

"Shaky."

"Let me change and we'll talk." He mixed himself a scotch and headed toward the bedroom.

"When's dinner?" he asked when he returned, freshened his drink, and sat next to Liz.

"At least an hour," Liz said.

Collin kissed Liz on the cheek and took her hand. before addressing LouLou. "Do you feel well enough for this?”

“I have to say it all now. With the stronger medication, I may sleep for the next two days. Mom and I have a long story.”

Over appetizers, LouLou's mother started to tell Liz and Collin about the adoption because she considered it her story to tell. She and LouLou's father had deceived the family for thirty years.

Collin waved his drink as if he were swatting a fly. “You don't have to do this. Dr. Baldwin told me enough about why this Dan Ramsay is interested in LouLou this afternoon.”

“You didn't tell me,” Liz said to her husband. She turned to her sister-in-law. “This is your story. If there's some information we should know, do you mind just giving us the basics?”

LouLou relaxed. Uncle Collin and Liz weren't going to quiz her mother. They just wanted to hear enough to understand what was going on.

Liz's words seemed to relax her mother as well. “Liz, we'd hoped to keep this private. LouLou was adopted from a beautiful, intelligent, gifted student at the Sorbonne. Her father and I took her home when she was two days old. We never told anyone. No one, including LouLou.”

“LouLou is your daughter and our niece. How she came to be is no one's concern,” Collin said. LouLou went to him and kissed his cheek. “Thank you, Uncle Collin. It's not important to me at all. Mom and Dad are my parents. Do you really not mind?”

“Of course not. I love you for you.”

“Do you mind, Liz?”

"Gracious no, dear." Liz hugged her as well.

Collin popped a fat olive in his mouth. "Liz, LouLou's biological father is causing a problem. He and LouLou were both in the same psych hospital when they were told of their relationship. This man, Dan Ramsay, may want more of LouLou than she can give. The feds are on it."

Liz looked puzzled. "What about the girl from the Sorbonne? The biological mother?"

"Dead." Collin popped another olive. "More than fifteen years ago. Suicide after 9/11. She's out of the picture. This Ramsay fellow can cause problems."

"Oh, I see." Liz drank half of her wine in about two sips. "This is quite sad, isn't it? For everyone."

Collin slapped his hands on his knees. "Shall we eat, then?"

"No, that's the tip of the story. Do you need an appetizer?" LouLou's mom snapped at her older brother.

"Well, yes, if this is going to be long. Liz, don't we have more of that Gouda and those thick biscuits? And some nuts? And pepper jelly?"

The tray must have been prepared because Liz was back in moments.

"Go on," Collin said as he made snacks for himself. He offered them to LouLou, who took a small plate, and her mom, who refused. Liz took two appetizers and finished her wine and poured another glass. "Uncle Collin, what did Dr. Baldwin tell you about Dan stalking me?"

He mother's hand flew to her throat. "He's really stalking you?"

LouLou touched her lightly on the arm so as not

to disturb Orchis's territory. "Followed. Remember, I told you Dan showed up at Vinyl on a flimsy pretense."

Her mother accepted the answer without responding. She sat quietly and stroked Orchid.

"Uncle Collin, what have you found out?" She hoped getting up-to-date information would ease her mother's mind—hers too.

"With your permission, Dr. Baldwin sent me an email with detailed information about your treatment and the impact stress caused by this man could have on you along with the sketch you made of him. I forwarded it to the proper authorities. I'm sorry you're going through this, but Ramsay will be arrested soon enough."

"Arrested?" said LouLou and her mother in unison.

"Of course." Collin took a handful of nuts and put them in his palm. "He's linked to the investigation of your father's murder. The murder of a diplomat. The feds don't mess around. They have a warrant for his arrest. They'll locate and arrest him. He'll be out of LouLou's life."

Collin brushed his hands together to remove any crumbs. "Let's eat."

# CHAPTER
# FIFTY-THREE

"Wait, please, "LouLou said. "I don't understand what this has to do with Dad's death."

Liz and LouLou's mom went outside for some air, leaving Collin and LouLou to discuss what the women already knew or chose not to hear.

"It's possible he may have killed your father."

"Dad?" LouLou asked. If she hadn't been so heavily medicated, she'd cry. "You think Dan killed Dad?"

Collin patted the sofa, and LouLou moved to sit next to him. Collin put his arm around her shoulders. She rested her head on his shoulder and started to cry. Being medicated didn't stop her tears. Collin let her cry for a bit before he spoke. He was his direct self, but his tone was kind.

"What I think doesn't matter. A federal investigation is underway. What investigators find, analyze, and decide is out of our hands. I know for a fact they're now following this line of investigation.

Ramsay has a psych history. He was awaiting a competency hearing on capital murder charges when you saw him in Petersburg. So, he's not unknown to the Virginia Bureau of Criminal Investigation.

"With distorted thinking, Ramsay may have believed with your father out of the way, he could step into that role. It's motive. A powerful one depending upon his mental state."

Dan couldn't possibly think that. She was thirty-one years old and in no need of parenting.

"Dad. I can't believe Dad died because of my adoption. I can't. Mom won't be able to stand it. She'll hate me. I'll lose them both." She was sobbing now like a child cradled in her uncle's embrace. She hiccupped.

Collin let her compose herself and then looked at his watch. "LouLou, it's time for some meds. Are they in your tote?"

She nodded. He handed her the tote, she took the meds she needed from her case that was marked with days of the week, AM and PM and hours. Collin poured her a glass of water with ice and refreshed his scotch. She gulped down three pills and held out her glass. Collin refilled it and sat next to her.

"Your mother will never love you less. Ever. Quiet yourself and let's stick to the facts. Becoming your parent would be a motive for Ramsay, according to investigators. He has a strong motive to get his love child back and plenty of time to follow a delivery or service-man into your parents' house, wait for the right moment, and wait again until he could leave. People have been arrested for less."

"But he lives with his mother." LouLou wiped tears aside with a cocktail napkin. "She'd worry if he disappeared. She'd call the police."

"True, but a man planning to commit murder would consider drugging or disabling his mother to buy himself time a mere detail."

LouLou shivered. Uncle Collin made sense. What's subduing his elderly mother when murder is his goal? She could see how Dan would appear to be a viable suspect to investigators.

Collin hugged her tightly. "The point for you is that evidence of stalking may turn up during the course of the murder investigation. That gets him arrested for starters and out of circulation. He has a tiger of a defense attorney, but no judge is going to give him bail. He'll either be tried and sentenced or at least sent to Petersburg pending a competency hearing. You'll be safe."

For a while.

"Uncle Collin, I loved Dad more than words can say. I hate whoever killed him. I just find it hard to believe it's Dan. He was so normal and clueless and sad when I met him. I don't know how or why he ended up in Petersburg, but he was pretty sick there. He might even have had a heart attack. No one ever said. Spending a couple of years at Petersburg had to have changed him. He was neglected at best except for..."

She'd been so stupid not to see it.

"At Petersburg, he saw me drawing every day and asked me to draw a symbol of running. I drew a winged foot on his arm with crayons as a fake tattoo. When I saw him at Ginter Gardens, he told me he still had the sketch and was thinking of getting it inked or matted and framed. He said it was a symbol that he could get well. Now, I realize he kept it because it was mine. Like an art project a child makes for her parents to put on the refrigerator."

"Okay. That's something for the investigators. He kept a talisman." Collin finished his drink and sat back. "What else? Is he smart? cunning? Anything else I should pass on?"

"No idea. He graduated from University of Virginia. He was a runner and has a dog."

LouLou started sobbing again. She stood and paced. "I don't want him or Bella in my life. I want them gone."

"Bella?" Collin put down his glass. "The girlfriend? Your biological mother?"

"Yes." LouLou exhaled. She was tired of this twosome and their story. "She's been haunting me."

She had Collin's full attention.

"Bella is dead. What do you mean?"

LouLou corrected herself. "She's made her presence known. If I hadn't found out about the adoption at Petersburg, Bella had arranged for me to learn of it on my thirtieth birthday. She lied to Mom and Dad. She broke their agreement." She told Collin about the blind trust and how her friend Quincy made it all go away.

"How much?" Collin asked. "How much was the trust account?"

"Just over ten million. I've no idea what the

actual transferred amount was after fees."

"And you turned that down?" Collin whistled.

"Of course. I want nothing to do with Dan or Bella."

"Did your parents know she'd betrayed them?"

"No, it happened just before Mom and I went to Paris. I told her after Dad died. She was stunned that the lovely young woman from the Sorbonne had lied."

Collin spoke as if he were the only one in the room. "So, Bella had big money if she was tossing off ten million to you. That means Dan didn't have to do it himself. He could've hired someone if he had money from her, too."

LouLou's stomach lurched. That's exactly what Big had said about Dan killing his wife. He didn't have to do it himself if he had money to pay someone. LouLou had stuck up for him, insisting Dan was too clueless to find a hitman. Now, Dan was a suspect in her dad's death. She sat and covered her face in her hands.

"LouLou, the feds are taking care of Dan. Quincy handled Bella's money. What's going on with you?"

"Uncle Collin, until he's in custody, I'm afraid of Dan. He's deteriorating. When I saw him at Vinyl, he hadn't had a haircut, he had the start of a beard, and his clothes looked like he'd slept in them. Not everyone is as vigilant as I am about beating, or at least standing up to, Sick.

"I'm even more afraid of myself. If he escapes the cops and pursues me past my breaking point, I could have an episode. They're increasingly violent.

Depending upon who's around, I could hurt or kill someone I love dearly. I don't want that to happen. I'd die if I hurt someone."

Collin pulled her to him and held her close.

"You and I have always been able to talk. I'm being straight with you. Dr. Baldwin told me you're on plenty of medication to prevent an episode. Dan's going to be caught. You're as safe as you can be. Don't push yourself into an episode by worrying about having one. It's a vicious cycle. Just keep taking your meds. We'll feed you healthy stuff, and there's plenty of exercise to be had around here. Rest, sleep, read. Do what you need to take care of yourself. Liz and I are here for you. Your mom couldn't bear to lose you. You're surrounded by people who love you. Remember that, okay?"

LouLou nodded.

"Now, for God's sake, can we eat dinner?"

# CHAPTER
# FIFTY-FOUR

After wolfing down a medium rare steak, steamed broccoli, and a baked potato loaded with butter, sour cream, and chives, Collin spent the evening behind the closed doors of his study. LouLou didn't know what he did before he retired. Investments was always the vague answer. She knew he had political connections. He also had a vengeful streak.

LouLou ate ravenously. Sometimes, medication did that. She could tell her mother was forcing herself to eat, but she, too, needed sustenance. Liz ate some broccoli and finished her wine.

Before he closeted himself in his study, Collin kissed LouLou goodnight. "I hope you do sleep for the next two days. You need rest. Do you have alarms for your medication times?"

LouLou nodded and started to cry. Again. That's all she did now.

Her mother tucked her in. She reminded LouLou

that she had a list of times for all the medications and would be sure LouLou got them. She left a pitcher of ice and water on her nightstand and LouLou's phone within reach in case she needed to call during the night. LouLou was loved and safe. For now.

***

LouLou's alarm went off at two in the morning for one of her meds. After taking it, she lay awake for a few minutes. Liz and Collin had a contemporary house with lots of light and wood beams. She lay under her white and blue comforter in a soft double bed and looked at the stars through two large skylights.

She wished she knew about constellations. Still, it was nice just to look at the blues, purples, and blacks that make up the night sky of the Virginia countryside. She counted stars, guessed which slice of moon showed, and watched landing lights of planes headed for Dulles.

Watching planes was a favorite pastime of hers at night. She loved creating back stories for the individuals on the flights—where they'd been, who'd be waiting for them, who they missed.

She wished Gregg could fly with her. He'd never done a lot of things because he'd been rounded up for being part of the undesirable population and tossed into Commonwealth Psych just after his eighteenth birthday. Outraged as she was, LouLou had to accept it. She had to fight the paranoia that was overcoming her, but her mind was full of terrible possibilities. Mostly, she was afraid Gregg would leave. She knew she should be grateful he lived with her now, in the twenty-first century, this decade, this year, this day.

He had so much music inside him. He told her he'd always felt it bubbling inside him. He couldn't write it fast enough. He had years of music pent up inside his head and his heart. He needed time to get it all down.

He told her she was his muse. Maybe she'd get that as her next tat. Gregg's muse. Written in an unusual language or code. Something just for the two of them. Like Bach.

She loved him. People with schizophrenia didn't have long life spans. Ghosts didn't either. Gregg would be the only man she would ever love.

# CHAPTER FIFTY-FIVE

LouLou slept for three days. She got up to eat, take her medications, and inject herself, but everything was a blur. Tux remained with her throughout. She felt good on the fourth morning of her stay.

"Let's have breakfast on the patio," her mom suggested. "It's good to see you looking rested and not so tense." She stroked LouLou's cheek. Over scrambled egg whites, homemade whole wheat toast, and berries, the two relaxed in each other's company.

"How are you, Mom?" LouLou asked.

"I'm still shell-shocked. I can't believe your dad is gone. Just gone and not coming back. Liz and Collin have been patient with me. They don't require anything of me. I walk one of the horses. Just walk alongside her on her halter every day. It gets me outside, and the horse is nice.

"I jolt awake every morning. He's gone. I want to

crawl under the covers and never come out. I don't, though. I get up, shower, and dress every day, but sometimes that's all I do."

LouLou held her mother's hand. "I can't imagine what it must be like for you. I'm sorry."

"I wish I'd had a chance to say goodbye. At our ages, we expected illness to take us. Not a killer. We thought we were past all that once he retired. I wished I'd had one more day with him."

LouLou let her cry. She hated when people told her not to cry. If you can't cry when your husband of almost forty years is murdered, when can you?

"Good morning, ladies." Uncle Collin, who was midway through his morning, stepped onto the patio. "LouLou, after breakfast, why don't you and I take a walk to the barn. Can you walk that far? Liz has a new filly I think you'll like."

LouLou dapped her mouth with her napkin. "I'm finished. Mom, will you be okay?"

"Yes. I'm going to finish my coffee and look at the magazines. Enjoy your walk."

"Let's go, then," Collin said.

Collin started off. When LouLou stood, Tux followed. LouLou and Tux almost trotted to keep up with Collin. He slowed as soon as they were out of hearing distance of the house. "I wish I could do more for your mom, but I can't. She's heartbroken and as far as I know, there's no cure for that. Maybe time. Maybe not."

LouLou nodded.

"You're safe now. The FBI executed a search warrant for Dan Ramsay's house, car, and computers. His phone records were subpoenaed. He was taken in for questioning. He didn't kill your father. He has a solid alibi.

"Ramsay's daughter was visiting from school when your father was killed. Her grandparents in Charleston have custody, and she boards at St. Margaret's. She's allowed to visit her father as long as her grandmother, aunt, or uncle is there too. She was visiting during the crucial period—the day of the murder as well as days before and after.

"The headmistress at St. Margaret's and the grandparents confirmed the visit. Entry and exit logs from the retirement community monitored gate confirm that the car only went in and out twice. Those trips are accounted for. Dinner. Movies. Soccer game."

LouLou sighed. She felt relief knowing with certainty Dan hadn't killed her father. That was too grotesque to consider.

"Why was the FBI involved?"

Collin gave her a strange look. "Your father was a federal official. That makes it federal wherever it happened."

LouLou nodded. She knew that. Little things like that slipped away from her all the time.

"That clears him for murder. Otherwise, Ramsay has gone off the rails. He missed his last three therapy appointments and his medication hasn't been refilled for two months. His laptop was essentially dedicated to you. His screensaver was a picture of you. He visited your website multiple times a day. He tracked your concert schedule. He downloaded all your music.

"He searched for your identity from one of those

internet information sites. He paid for the premium package, but no records came up for your name. He wrote long, and increasingly unintelligible, letters to you or Bella. I don't think he made a distinction."

LouLou lurched, and she stopped walking. Collin patted her on the back.

"Ramsay's attorney knows when to quit. She's been persuaded that the best interest of her client is a guilty plea for cyber-stalking and commitment to a forensic psychiatric facility. Petersburg. Given his unforgiveable experience at Petersburg with the aide exposing your adoption, the Commonwealth Attorney agreed that Ramsay may be transferred to a civil hospital at his expense after six months if he's not receiving appropriate psychiatric treatment at Petersburg. I don't know exactly how that works, but he may never be released. Proving his sanity seems to be a stretch.

"The point is, he won't be able to harm you or the other child. The maternal grandparents are especially protective of the only child of their late daughter. The threat of danger to either or both of you was a key consideration in his sentencing."

LouLou exhaled. Dan Ramsay would go back to Petersburg and because he'd get absolutely no treatment there, he'd go to a psych hospital for some undetermined amount of time. She'd be safe. She desperately hoped he could be dissuaded from the idea that contact with her wouldn't be anything but explosive. Funny, she no longer thought of him as High Life. He'd become Dan, and then Danger to her.

# CHAPTER
# FIFTY-SIX

That woman simply couldn't be her child. Surely, there was another blonde-haired, blue-eyed baby born in the American Hospital of Paris around that date in April. Surely, there'd been a terrible mistake and the Flemings received some inferior infant. There was no other explanation. Her child with Daniel couldn't be that daft.

Wishful thinking. Bella had no choice. She had to work with who she had—LouLou. The woman couldn't grasp the simple concept that sweet, dear Daniel was her father and naturally, wanted to spend time with her. A crumb. Bella knew Daniel's interest stemmed from his desire to be close to Bella until they could be reunited, no matter how poor a substitute LouLou was for her. Daniel wanted to get to know, or at least see, his child. The fact that she was an adult was a plus. He wanted a dinner companion, or someone to go with him to the museum and get him out of that claustrophobic house with Selma for a few hours. LouLou denied him even that.

Worse, she sicced the feds on him for cyber-stalking. Wanting to know his daughter wasn't a crime, yet LouLou flung him back into the filthy hole of justice from which he'd barely climbed above. He was back in Petersburg serving a sentence.

The ridiculous woman had thrown away millions of dollars that could have changed her life. In Bella's experience as a living person, no one except the über-rich tossed more than $10 million aside. For all LouLou knew, that money could cure schizophrenia. Bella didn't appreciate her gift being considered tainted and untouchable.

Twice Bella had wished LouLou love. Maybe the first time, LouLou rejected it without thinking. Bella gave her a second chance. She'd written a duplicate note, placed it in LouLou's loft, and again, the foolish woman shredded her note. Bella wasn't going to wish love for LouLou a third time. LouLou wasn't going to have love.

# CHAPTER FIFTY-SEVEN

They reached the barn. Liz and Collin had four horses, but they boarded horses for friends in DC who came out on weekends. The facilities were top notch. Collin greeted the grooms and exercise riders by name as he and LouLou made their way to the filly's stall.

"Here she is. Ridiculous long name. We call her Buttercup. She's so jaunty and fresh. Her conformation is a bit off for a Thoroughbred, and her owner didn't want to keep her. Liz fell in love with her and brought her home from Lexington. Rented and drove the horse trailer herself. She's a determined one, my Liz."

Buttercup nuzzled Collin's shoulder. He pulled out a carrot, placed it flat in his hand, and offered it to her. She took it immediately. "Feel how soft her muzzle is."

LouLou reached up and touched the young horse. Her nose was softer than a feather. "She's sweet. I like her."

"Liz has got your mother taking her for walks on a lead. I think they'll become fast friends." Someone caught Collin's eye. "Excuse me. I'll be right back." He handed LouLou another carrot for Buttercup.

Stroking the horse's face and ears was soothing. Just touching Buttercup, who felt like a combination of silk and fur, made LouLou feel calmer.

Tux had just settled down for a nap by the time Collin returned. "Ready to head back?" He reached down to scratch Tux's ears. "He's a sad fellow. I'm a poor substitute for your dad. He's getting old too. We'll walk slower back to the house."

LouLou took a last look at Buttercup and the barn.

"You have an extra stall. Another horse coming soon?"

"No, that's the ghost stall."

LouLou stopped. "The what?"

"Liz believes ghosts can be horses. She always keeps an extra stall. I think she's mentioned that it's been used at least twice."

Interesting. Entirely credible now that she knew Gregg.

"Thank you, Uncle Collin. Thank you for not minding that I'm adopted. Truly, I could have lived my life without knowing or caring. I felt awful for Mom and Dad. They were wonderful parents. They gave me so many opportunities growing up and never smothered or stifled my interests. They did everything to get me the best treatment when I was diagnosed with schizophrenia. They could easily have put me in an institution, but they went through what I can imagine were unbearable times. Still, they encouraged me to live normally. I'd do anything for them."

Collin hugged LouLou. "We all love you. I've never been one for pedigrees. Liz doesn't even care about horse pedigrees. Your cousins, I'm sure, will take the news in stride."

LouLou smiled. "If they can accept the fact that cousin LouLou has schizophrenia and could be off on a psychotic episode if she doesn't take her meds, I don't think knowing I'm adopted will register."

Collin looked off in the distance towards the house. "I must admit, we did become more vigilant about looking for signs of illness in them after you were diagnosed. Genetics was said to be a component of the disease."

"It's supposed to be, but Deirdre told me that her aunt had schizophrenia and her dad, my paternal grandfather, had what now seems to her to be clinical depression or even bi-polar episodes. She seemed depressed to me when she was here after Dad died. I know I'm not genetically related to her, but I thought it was interesting that mental illness wasn't a stranger to the family."

Collin looked thoughtful. "I can't think of anyone in our family who had a diagnosis. Your mother and I come from a long line of eccentrics and alcoholics, but that could just be code for mental illness." He seemed to think about that for a bit and then snapped back with rapid-fire questions.

"Tell me how you are. Other than this scare. Really."

"Good. I'm strict about taking my meds, seeing

my new psychiatrist, and recording new music. It's nice not to have to prepare for a tour. I have more time to create. I'm preparing for a November recital at the Terrace Theatre. I miss Dad, but I cherish my memories. He's not far."

"Why do you have a new psychiatrist?" Collin slowed his stride to match hers.

"Dr. Youzny classified my reaction to the news I was adopted as aberrant because I didn't care. I wasn't angry or hurt or betrayed. I thought he had less interest in treating me than using me as a case study for a journal article or presentation."

"Your instincts are good, LouLou. You spot BS quickly."

"Uncle Collin, I've spent half my life with psychiatrists and people with mental illnesses. I had to develop a BS radar to survive."

"A shame. Truly." LouLou could almost see him switching gears. "How's your business? Accounting, in particular. Still using that firm started by two young women?"

"Yes. Everything is in order."

"Must say you did a ballsy thing in refusing the trust money. That sum would turn many heads."

"I'm not impressed by the amount. It could have been one-hundred million or ten dollars. My answer would have been the same. I felt like Bella was trying to control me from the grave."

"Again, good instincts." He stopped to pick up a branch that had fallen on the dirt path. "LouLou, in my opinion, it's time for you to change lawyers. Brooks is out of his league with music contracts, royalties, and blurred producer/artist/songwriter credits these days.

"There's a boutique firm in New York that's just right for you. Sharp woman in her thirties. Worked in different aspects of the business. Well-respected. You should transfer your business there. By next Wednesday." He handed her a small piece of paper from a notepad. "Her name and number. No reason to dirty the waters with Brooks. You're free to change attorneys any time. He was fine when you were younger and working as a local DJ. The offers you're getting now need a more experienced hand, someone who knows the players. "

LouLou deciphered Uncle Collin's words. Hire the new attorney as the next step in expanding her business. Do it fast before telling Brooks. Make sure she was no longer on his client roster by Wednesday. Something unpleasant was going to happen to Brooks because he or his colleague had failed to spot the obvious possibility of Dan Ramsay as a suspect in his liaison with the murder investigators. The DNA connection was plain.

"I suspect Dr. Youzny won't be practicing much longer. Medical malpractice insurance premiums have increased to the point that doctors choose retirement over continued practice of medicine. Dr. Youzny's insurer is one of the most cautious."

No tears for him. He'd helped LouLou through dark periods, but he turned on her when he had the opportunity for self-aggrandizement. She needed to check herself. She was becoming as vengeful as Collin.

"Any news on that horrid woman who blackmailed Mom and Dad about my adoption?"

"Nothing," Collin said. "No one other than you and the man who usually walked with you saw her. Your descriptions match. It's as though she vanished."

# CHAPTER FIFTY-EIGHT

### June

"Vegetarian lasagna, arugula salad, and sautéed spinach." Roy presented the boxed meal to LouLou in her loft. "Where's your luggage?"

LouLou held up her tote. "I went without notice. I borrowed clothes. It's not like I needed anything more than pants and tee shirts. I missed you and Sara. How are you? Have the kids worn you down yet about a cruise?"

"Sara did. She convinced me our lives would be easier without the battle. The kids can do something called age appropriate activities, Sara can spend time reading on deck, and I can dine in ports. We're going to the western Mediterranean in late August. I'll make sure you're supplied with plenty of meals."

"Roy, don't worry about me. I can cook, you know. It just isn't very tasty. You're the spice king."

"I read where that guy in the sketch you gave me

was arrested for stalking you," he said with trepidation. He was always sensitive to her feelings.

LouLou nodded. She didn't want to think, much less talk, about it.

"Ah, LouLou. What a siege you've had."

"It's over. Thanks for keeping a lookout for him. Now I plan to do nothing for the rest of the summer."

Roy hugged her and left. LouLou counted ten beats before Gregg threw his arms around her and kissed her. "Hate to be an eavesdropper, but it saves you from rehashing the trip."

"Being invisible has its perks," she said as she buried her face in his chest.

He held her and kissed her hair. When he stepped back, he appraised her and asked, "Are you well?"

"Yes. With Dan Ramsay at Petersburg, I'm safe."

Gregg kissed her again and held her close. She put her head on his chest so she could feel his heart beat. "I thought of what you said to me before I left Dr. Baldwin's office, that you didn't want Dan or Bella to take me away from you. It gave me courage every day. I don't want to let anything come between us."

"You're brave, LouLou. You've survived a lot," he said.

She kissed him. "By the way, do you know anything about horse ghosts?"

"No. Why do you ask?"

"My aunt and uncle keep a stall vacant in case a ghost horse needs it. My aunt says it's been used at least twice."

"That's good. Your family is hospitable to ghosts. Nice to feel welcome."

***

LouLou dutifully ate the meal Roy had provided. "This is really good. I had breakfast and a quick lunch. I didn't realize how hungry I was."

She finished, washed her plate, and grabbed an apple for dessert. She stretched and sat on the striped sofa.

"Are you really going to take the rest of the summer off?" Gregg asked.

"Absolutely. I'll practice to be ready for the recital. Beyond that, I'm not taking any gigs. We have from now until the end of October to relax. What do you want to do?"

"Anything. Everything."

"We'll go to the park, outdoor concerts, the symphony's July fourth concert with fireworks. There's baseball. The Richmond Flying Squirrels. They're the minor league team for the San Francisco Giants."

"The Flying Squirrels? They don't sound like a team to be feared." Gregg laughed. "I like baseball, so I'd love to do that no matter how bad they are."

"Movies. There are always movies," LouLou said. "We could do double features. What else would you like to do? What have you missed?"

"An amusement park, if we skip the roller coasters. I'm afraid that might do me in. There are other rides, aren't there?"

"I don't know. I've never been to an amusement

park. I think there's one a little north of here and one south, near Williamsburg." She thought more. "Oh, and swimming. There are some private swim clubs with outdoor pools that don't require your genealogy to become a member."

"I like swimming, but I'll cause ripples in the water."

"Not if you're any good." LouLou winked.

# CHAPTER FIFTY-NINE

### October

Bella was thrilled with her plan to deny LouLou love. She'd stage a scene so wondrous it would become a shrine. People from all over the world would make pilgrimages to see where an angel held the baby Jesus in her arms on the day after Christmas. The stunt required nothing of her except to acquire costumes.

The weeks before Halloween were the best time for that. Even so, the color assortment of adult-size angel or fairy wings wasn't the best. Lots of pinks, blues, and whites. Gold or red feathered wings were hard to find. At the fourth costume shop she perused, there was a perfect pair of metallic gold wings made from rows and rows of feathers that created a cascading effect. They weren't as wide as she needed, but a ten-foot wingspan could work, especially once they were raised to imitate flying. A golden halo fit for a queen was also a solid choice.

A red XXL satin choir robe was just a Baptist church away. The other denominations were less colorful. Most church choristers wore a combination of black and white, even during the holiday season.

A long trumpet prop wasn't too hard to find at one of those Christmas-is-365-days-a-year shops, but they all were flimsy and obviously fake. A wooden recurve bow would be better—traditional, ornate, and Flemish. She'd have to make a trip to a specialty archery store because most sporting goods stores carried pricey junk in flashy colors. Only a serious archer would have a recurve bow.

One brown wig with long curly ringlets later, Bella had completed ninety-nine percent of her shopping. She'd rented a keyless entry storage unit because she had no place to hide anything. The few remaining items could wait until the last minute. Her to-buy list included a brown-haired baby doll that cried and a blue blanket.

# CHAPTER SIXTY

LouLou and Gregg solved their PDA problem by walking arm in arm when they walked together. She kept her arm close to her body so she wouldn't look like she was holding her arm away from her body at an abnormal distance, no matter how slight. The feel of Gregg sent signals of love and courage throughout her body.

"Got the shipment," Skylar said when LouLou and Gregg arrived at Vinyl. "Two perfect CDs of LouLou Fleming playing the lost compositions of Gregg Waites, Parts One and Two. Gregg, you're a musical genius and LouLou, your playing is awesome. Not bad for a DJ who says she never practices serious music."

LouLou bowed and motioned to Gregg to do the same.

"They look great, too, don't they? Straightforward covers without any old-fashioned watercolors of nineteenth century English castles." LouLou had been fierce with the producer about the cover.

"You're a knock-out. The photographer got a full headshot and the lid of the piano. Looks great."

"I hope you can keep up with the orders. They're available by download, but I think CDs will sell too. They'll be on sale at the recital."

"You're selling CDs at the recital?" Gregg's eyes registered his surprise. "Isn't that kind of crass?"

"Of course it is, but it's standard procedure now for any kind of concert. Classical. Rock. Rap. My DJ stuff is going to be all downloaded from now on. No CDs. My audience has lost patience with actually having to pick up a CD, hand it to a cashier, and wait for the sale to be authorized."

"Blasphemy. Don't talk like that in front of my vinyl children."

"Sorry, Skylar. I love hard copy, too, but I have to make a living."

"How are ticket sales?" he asked.

"Sold out."

"You're a star," Gregg said. She hadn't told him about the sales.

"No, the theatre only has a five hundred-seat capacity. It's not too hard to fill. I'm sure most of the sales are to Kennedy Center patrons. The concert hall at Georgetown University is only two hundred and fifty seats. That will be filled with musicologists, if no one else. Anytime a new composer is discovered, they all want to pretend they heard him first."

"Watch it, LouLou. Your inner snob is showing."

"Can't help it, Skylar. I just don't think music and academia are a good match. I think conservatories are the only place to study performance. Everything else is music history. Makes the ones who are accepted at Juilliard true artists." She winked at Gregg, who looked down at his feet.

"Do we know anyone who went there?" Skylar asked. He was absent-mindedly rubbing Robert's head.

"Didn't you read the liner notes? *Mr. Waites, a student at The Juilliard School of Music,* blah blah blah."

"No, I didn't. I didn't have my glasses. Gregg, you went to Juilliard? Aren't you a modest one."

"Well, I actually…."

LouLou interrupted. "The point is, the man knows his stuff. When are you driving up, Skylar?"

"I don't know yet. It's weeks away. I assume I'll be chauffeuring the composer?" He looked at Gregg.

"If you don't mind."

"It's an honor. We'll work it out. What about you, LouLou?"

"I'm going that Wednesday and staying in a hotel. Mom might join me. I'll do the recital at one o'clock on Friday afternoon at Georgetown and then the recital on Sunday afternoon at four."

"I meant to ask you. Four o'clock on a Sunday afternoon seems an odd time for a recital," Gregg said.

"The absolute only time for one according to the great pianist Vladimir Horowitz. He said his mind was at its best then and audiences were more content, alert, and relaxed. He thought concerts that started at eight o'clock on a weeknight were futile.

Having worked all day, the last thing people wanted to do was listen closely. He thought most were asleep."

"Don't listen to Horowitz or her, Gregg. No one will sleep through this music no matter what time it's played. It's fantastic," Skylar declared. "By the way, I've sent some promo copies out to people who'll spread the word."

"Thanks, Skylar. That's really nice." Gregg seemed uncomfortable with adulation and the willingness of people to promote him.

"Oh, complete self-interest, young man. I want to sell lots of CDs."

LouLou leaned over the counter and kissed Skylar on the cheek, gave Robert a few extra kisses, and took Gregg's hand. "We're off to the movies. Later."

***

"How does it feel to see your name on the cover of a CD?" LouLou asked Gregg while they were alone in the theatre.

"Awesome."

"I'm glad you let me work something out with my new attorney that allowed me to legally own the copyright. There won't be any problem if your parents, siblings, nieces and nephews or other relatives are alive and claim ownership. You wanted to avoid causing any fissures in what's left of your family, and you have."

"It's best for you too, isn't it?" Gregg looked at her with those entreating brown eyes. She loved that his feelings showed through his eyes, but she sometimes felt he depended on her answers too easily.

As the screen curtain parted, she realized what she saw was trust. Complete faith and trust is what he had in her. She'd never felt that, and the feeling gave her goosebumps.

"A little bit. Any problems would be handled by lawyers. You gifting the compositions to me just makes me feel closer to you. We're a team."

# CHAPTER SIXTY-ONE

"What happened to your mom?" Gregg asked when he arrived at LouLou's hotel suite late Friday morning. He kissed her neck, and she leaned into him.

"She didn't feel up to coming. She'll definitely be at the recital, but she has a serious aversion to DC now. She's pained by it. Everything and everyone she sees is a reminder of her loss. She says it feels like a nightmare and she can't wake up."

Gregg took her hands. "I can't imagine." He didn't stay solemn long. "How are you? Nervous?"

"Never. I'm never nervous. I know the music, I love to perform, and I want the world to hear your work. I can't wait to get there and play."

He pulled her to him and held her close. "LouLou, even if they hate the music, I thank you for everything you've done to make it known. You're a great pianist. My stuff is in the best of hands."

He leaned in to kiss her. She responded easily. Their kiss was long and delicious and a preliminary for more expression.

"I'm going to be late if we don't stop."

Still holding her long, delicate hands, he turned to go. "I'm meeting Skylar downstairs. Break a leg. People say that still, right?"

"Yes," she smiled, "they do. Thank you." She reluctantly let their fingertips release.

***

Polite applause greeted LouLou when she walked onstage in her backless orange mini dress. Her phoenix tattoo was on full display. She bowed deeply and sat at the keyboard. She launched herself into Gregg's piano suite and directly into the sonata. Although she had intended to have an intermission, she kept playing—the dances and the rhapsodic, fingers flying ballades.

The audience was on its feet after the first piece. Many remained standing throughout. Some moved to the left side of the auditorium to watch her hands better. Some moved to the back in order to get the full effect of the air and gusts and whirlwinds of sound coming from the stage.

LouLou flung her head back and smiled, thoroughly exhilarated after playing seventy-five minutes of solo piano. She stood, bowed, and left the stage. She walked quickly to the green room and locked the door. Gregg was waiting. He was sobbing as he pulled her to him and hugged her tightly.

"LouLou, you're fantastic. The crowd got it. They got my music. This is the second best day of my life."

LouLou pulled back from him but stayed in his arms. "What's the first? Nothing could be better than this. Don't you feel like you're on the best high of your life?"

"Nothing compares to the day I met you, LouLou."

"You're too perfect, Gregg." She kissed him with a promise of more. Then she shooed him out of the room, unlocked the door, and received visitors. "Never heard anything like it." "A phenom." "Where are the CDs?" "Where can I get the scores?" "Who did you study with?" "Where is the composer?" "People were recording with their phones."

"I hope they did record the music," LouLou said in response to the last question from a visitor. "It needs to be out there. Normally, I don't condone piracy, but for this I give permission to record everything."

LouLou deflected all questions about herself. She reminded everyone that information about accessing the written scores and CDs was on the paper recital program. She also told the story she and Gregg had agreed upon about his history. He was a bass player on his way to Juilliard who switched to composition. Tragically, he drowned at a young age. He willed all his compositions to LouLou. She crossed her fingers behind her back. The dates were close, but she'd been born before he died.

Gregg had made a holographic will on a yellow legal pad sheet to back up the story. Virginia accepted such hand-written documents as legal wills. It was in her safe deposit box along with the original scores.

Skylar, Robert, and Gregg were her last visitors. Skylar bounced into the room full of gossip and anecdotes and accolades. "LouLou, I've never heard you play live. You've got the goods. You could be a concert pianist."

She kissed him on the check. "Yes, I could, but I don't want to be. Thank you for the compliment."

"What's the plan?" Skylar asked. He held Robert, who wore his Emotional Support Animal vest.

"Gregg, it might be best if Skylar dropped you off at my hotel. The university provided a car service for me. I don't want to be rude and not use it. Skylar, you're welcome to celebrate with us."

Skylar snorted. "I highly doubt that. Besides, Robert and I have friends to visit. I'll see you Sunday."

# CHAPTER SIXTY-TWO

Night came while LouLou napped.

"Ah, you're up." Gregg walked over to LouLou's side of the bed and kissed her.

She pulled him to her for a long, delicious kiss. "What time is it?"

"About eight."

"I'll call room service for dinner." She got out of bed, put on one of the giant navy fluffy robes provided by the hotel, and placed her dinner order. She stretched and wound herself around Gregg on the sofa. "Wasn't it fantastic? Can you imagine what Sunday will be like?"

"The whole thing was surreal, but the response to my music made me feel like my life has been worth something."

"Of course it has. There's more brewing. I can tell." She pointed to the music composition book on the table. Gregg had been writing while she slept.

"There is. Plenty. I've got five pieces written and

two that need to go through my head, down my arm, and onto paper." He shifted so he could look directly at LouLou. "I was awed by the whole thing. The last time I went to a recital, it was at night, men wore dark suits, and women wore fancy dresses. The performers wore tuxes and the women soloists wore floor length gowns that covered their arms and bust."

LouLou smiled. She liked that Gregg used quaint words like bust.

LouLou got up and grabbed a club soda from the mini-fridge. "My dress must've been a shock. The change occurred as part of the movement to get younger people into orchestral audiences. The first time I heard the New York Philharmonic at an afternoon concert, I thought they all looked like accountants—navy blue suits for men and women—but the trend took off.

"Soloists, particularly women violinists, started wearing strapless and then short dresses that called attention to themselves. I can't imagine playing in a long dress. It would interfere with pedaling." She resumed her position on the sofa.

"And people milled around during the concert. What was that?"

"That was academicians showing off. On a university campus, there are no rules. I think it's a good thing that the audience wanted to see, hear, and feel the music and didn't stay in their seats to do so."

"I was surprised."

"Well," LouLou patted his cheek, "that's the Virginian gentleman in you. Did Robert enjoy it?"

"Hate to say this, but he slept through the recital."

LouLou laughed. "He hears music all the time. Maybe he'll be alert Sunday."

Gregg took LouLou's hands in his. "Do you feel okay? Tired? Off schedule?"

"I'm taking care of myself. I was exhausted after the recital, but as you know, I slept after our tryst. I'm on schedule with my meds. I'll give myself an injection after dinner." There was a knock at the door, and the room service cart was rolled in. "And now I'll eat."

She arranged her plates and glasses on a small table next to a comfortable chair and ate dinner. "Sorry for eating while talking. I carefully planned this event. I wanted an afternoon recital today with an evening, all day tomorrow, and Sunday morning off so I'll be rested. I'm spending Sunday night and possibly a few more nights here before going home. I'm being extra careful."

"You're brave and awesome to live according to the clock."

"I've no choice. The first time I had a psychotic episode, I knew I wouldn't survive another. My brain was still developing at sixteen, so meds that worked for three months had to be refined for the next two months, three months, six months. That was hard. I had two serious episodes, but my parents were right there getting me treatment ASAP.

"What about you, Gregg? You look wistful."

"I sound ungrateful for everything you've done, but I wish I could've been alive to hear my works. I felt like there was a glass wall between me and the stage. I was outside looking in. I wanted to applaud, to cheer, and to feel the audience's response. I feel selfish."

"Hold that thought." LouLou excused herself, got her rig, and went in the bathroom to inject herself. When she returned, she drank a full glass of water before sitting next to Gregg and leaning into him.

"That's not greedy. That's human. I don't care if you're a ghost. You have a human heart. It must be unbearable and exhilarating. I'm sorry."

She looked at him.

"Gregg, you look tired. Is that possible?"

"I don't know. I haven't felt one hundred percent for the last two weeks. I think it's the excitement of the recording, recitals, and all the things I never experienced as a musician."

"You don't have to stay with me if you need to go to your Ghost Place and rest."

"You know I don't have a Ghost Place or at least haven't found it yet. I only control visibility slightly more than I used to. I'll try to calm down. I'm glad there's a day in-between performances. I didn't think I, as a ghost, would need it. Seems like I do."

"As long as you come back."

"For as long as I can."

# CHAPTER
# SIXTY-THREE

Sunday's audience was even more enthusiastic. They insisted on an encore, and LouLou played Gregg's longing, yearning, sensuous "Elegy." Silence filled the room until the vibration of the last note dissolved into air particles.

When LouLou rose to take her bow, the crowd erupted into wild applause and shouts of *Brava*. Collin walked on stage and presented her with two dozen red roses. "Not nearly enough," he said and kissed her cheek.

In the green room afterwards, LouLou closed and locked the door, leaned against it, and exhaled. She needed to compose herself before seeing anyone. She drank a full glass of water over ice in a crystal glass.

"May the composer steal you for a minute?"

LouLou turned to see Gregg looking very handsome in a dark suit, white shirt, and grey tie. He was holding a small white box. He offered it to her. "What's this?" she asked.

LouLou opened the box. Inside was a single maroon orchid with errant strands of greenery made into a wrist corsage. "It's beautiful. So delicate."

"And rare, according to the florist," Gregg said. She held out her left hand for him to tie it on her wrist. She felt chills run up her arm. The effect with her red silk dress was stunning. She wasn't going to cry.

"I love it. Thank you. I feel cherished. I don't have to be envious of Mary Lynn Bailey anymore."

"I wanted you to have a corsage. You said you'd never had one." He kissed her softly. "I love you," he said before disappearing. "Your public awaits."

LouLou opened the door, and soon she was surrounded by family. LouLou first went to her mother, who was sobbing. "Darling, that was exquisite. The compositions and the performer were exceptional. Thank you for opening with the Bach and dedicating the recital to your father."

LouLou held her mother. For the first time, LouLou felt like the nurturer. Her mother had lost weight and had a sadness that was palpable. "None of this would have happened if you and dad hadn't surrounded me with music and given me piano lessons. It's my life. I'm forever grateful. Mom, I love you."

Her mother dabbed at her tears and spoiled makeup. "I'm sorry I couldn't come earlier and stay with you at the hotel. I just couldn't force myself to come to Washington. I couldn't have done it alone today. Thankfully, Collin and Liz were supportive, got me here, and protected me from well-meaning friends."

She hugged LouLou again. "Please forgive me, but I have to leave. I can't see people. So many of them knew your father. I just can't see them."

"Do what you need."

She caught Collin's eye. He gave her one of his bear hugs. "Exceptional. You know how to pick music and put on a show. Damn, you're good."

Liz joined him. "Wonderful. It was our pleasure to be here."

"Thank you for coming and for taking care of Mom. Do you want me to call security to help her leave quietly? She can leave via the performers' elevator."

"The elevator's enough. Just point me in the right direction."

Justice Bergen and her husband were next. She greeted LouLou warmly. "Music is truly a great mystery. What complex thoughts to create such works and an equally astute mind to interpret them. I know you've heard it before, but your dad would have been very proud of you today. Lovely of you to dedicate the performance to him. I miss him. I'm sure it's nothing compared to what you and your mother feel." She took a step back. "*Brava*, LouLou."

Her husband kissed LouLou on the cheek. "*Bravissima*," he whispered.

When LouLou made her way onto the terrace, she was mobbed. Everyone wanted to congratulate her, pepper her with questions, or get pictures with her. She usually didn't intermingle with those in the audience, but she wanted to be as gracious and open as possible for Gregg's works. Rumor had it that all five hundred copies of each CD had sold out before intermission. LouLou recognized a lot of friends of her parents, all of whom complimented her performance. Quincy had come down from New York.

"Oh, this is such a surprise." LouLou hugged her. "Thank you for coming."

"I don't think I've heard you play since junior year of high school. You've improved. And that dress is pure hotness." She nodded at the red silk satin backless mini dress LouLou wore. Quincy introduced her husband and said they had to rush to get the Acela back to New York.

After twenty minutes with the audience, LouLou signaled she wanted her car and driver. She could have flown on air to the hotel, but thought motor transportation would be more discrete.

Gregg, Skylar, and Robert met her at the curb. The driver held her door open, but she stopped to speak to them before gliding in. Gregg was completely overcome. "LouLou, I just can't speak."

She took his hand that was hidden from the driver. "They loved you, Gregg. I love you."

Skylar stepped between them. "I'll see that he gets back safely. He's in quite a state. He said he felt tired so I think it's best to leave now." LouLou nodded. "Thank you, Skylar, for everything."

She took Robert out of his arms and hugged him. "Robert, thank you for coming. Please look out for my two men."

Robert settled himself under her chin and purred.

# CHAPTER SIXTY-FOUR

Knowing she had to keep episodes at bay, LouLou stayed three extra days in Washington to rest. She'd underestimated the toll two recitals, interaction with audiences, and the desire to give Gregg's compositions the best possible launch would take. There was nothing to do other than accept the exhaustion, stay on her strict routine and medication, and rest before driving back to Richmond.

Skylar had sent an email that they had arrived safely and that Gregg had disappeared for a few days. Skylar was certain he'd be back. LouLou believed him.

LouLou had programmed her phone to allow only the ringtones for her mother, Skylar, and Roy. She didn't need to hear from anyone else. She wore her corsage until she went to bed Sunday night and placed it in a glass of water on the nightstand. Gregg. So thoughtful. To remember she'd never had one. She'd make potpourri with this too, even though it didn't seem to have a scent.

Monday, she called Roy to tell him she was staying a few more days.

"You're a star, LouLou. *The Washington Post*, *The New York Times*, and the *Wall Street Journal* all gave you and the composer excellent reviews. I saved them for you. Are you eating enough?"

"Yes, I'm choking down four-star restaurant food, but honestly, it has nothing on yours."

"Nice to hear."

"Talk to me. Tell me about Sara and the kids."

He did. For about fifteen minutes, LouLou listened to Roy's narration of normalcy at home. It was comforting. Before hanging up, LouLou assured Roy she was swimming in the hotel's indoor pool and taking her meds.

"Stay as long as you need," Roy said. "I'll keep holding down the fort."

She had great friends. Not a lot, but the ones she had were as loving and loyal as she hoped she was to them.

*** 

Gregg returned to the loft the day after LouLou arrived. He was carrying a contra bass, so Skylar walked behind him and pretended he was carrying the bass so as not to raise suspicion.

"You're full of surprises," LouLou said. She and Gregg exchanged a heartfelt kiss and deep hug. "What's this about?"

"Skylar rented it for me. One of my pieces is a

duet for contra bass and piano. I need to hear precisely how they work together. I hope you don't mind." He suddenly looked worried. LouLou was cautious about having too much furniture or sharp edges around.

"Not at all. As long as it goes in the closet when it's not being played."

"Skylar, how are you, aside from the back strain of hefting that bass?"

"Busy. My shipment of CDs sold out in one day. I've had walk-ins looking for it. I saved a copy of each for my library so people are listening to them in the booths. One man drove up from Raleigh to purchase them. I was sorry to tell him I was out. He did stay to browse and bought several nice LPs. He's a good, intelligent customer."

LouLou poured a root beer into a glass. "Have a seat before you go back."

Skylar took the glass and downed it. "Thanks. Can't sit or I'll never get up. Later."

As soon as the door closed behind Skylar, LouLou demanded a real welcome from Gregg. He agreed without hesitation. Their lovemaking was slow with a sweetness about it that LouLou enjoyed.

Afterward, LouLou and Gregg had their first conversation about the recitals as they snuggled on the striped sofa.

"I guess you heard about the reviews. Roy saved them for me."

"I'm still in disbelief. My compositions have been published, performed, recorded, and praised by the best critics. It was the thought of one day having an opportunity to get my music on paper that kept me going at Petersburg."

Gregg had never mentioned his time at Petersburg after he told her he'd been a patient there. LouLou assessed his mood and decided not to pursue it.

"What are the new pieces?"

"A piano concerto. Don't look at me like that," he said when she frowned. "You'll learn to love playing with an orchestra occasionally. The duet is just for us playing our favorite instruments. We're *simpatico*, as one reviewer called us."

"I love that idea. I do. You'll play contra bass again. Each of us playing our best instruments. That's romantic." She kissed him lightly. "I suppose most of my part will be high octaves."

He nodded. "Of course. I want the bass to shine, but I want it to be a blend that's rarely heard. At least as far as I know."

LouLou didn't know. "Check with Skylar. If he doesn't know, he'll ask one of his musicologist friends. They're all his absolutely best buddies now, hoping to get extra copies of CDs and gossip about what's in the pipeline."

She checked the time. "It's later than I thought. I'm having dinner with Roy, Sara, and the kids tonight. Will you be okay alone?"

"Sure. I've got loads of work to do. I feel like I'm racing time."

What did that mean? It was too soon for him to leave.

Gregg continued. "I felt the same agitation, I guess is the word, at the recital as I did at the university. It was wonderful and painful at the same time. I watched in a bubble. There's a part of me that thinks if I keep composing as fast as I can, maybe I'll become visible. We can be an almost normal couple. It keeps me going."

"Do you feel more energized?" One look in his eyes told her the answer.

"Sadly, no. I feel my energy is being drained. I have pieces to finish and I want to celebrate the holidays with you and your family, if only as a spectator."

"I'll know you're there. Your presence will brighten what will be a difficult holiday. Christmas Eve was always the most special when I was growing up. I know it's going to be hard for Mom. Maybe Dad will come to her like you did to me."

"That's a happy thought."

Gregg leaned in and kissed LouLou. Softly, at first, and the kiss grew more intense until LouLou felt her heart racing.

"I love you, LouLou, with all my heart."

She curled next to him. "I love you more than I knew was possible."

# CHAPTER SIXTY-FIVE

## December

*"Dort, dort, dort le petit fils, Mille anges divins, mille séraphins, Volent à l'entour de ce grand Dieu d'amour. Volent à l'entour de ce grand Dieu d'amour."*

LouLou sang with the instrumental ancient French carol as she drove south on I-95 the day after Christmas. Having Gregg with her had made this first Christmas without her father less painful. Her mother hid her feelings well, but she did have tearful moments. Orchid rarely left her lap. LouLou hated to see her mother in such unrelenting pain. The only bright spot was that her mother and Buttercup had become fast friends. Liz said they needed each other.

The best part of the holiday was snuggling in the double bed with Gregg as they looked at the snowy nights through the skylight. It was as peaceful and happy as LouLou had imagined. Tux snored at the end of the bed. He sniffed Gregg, decided he could stay, and fell sound asleep. Gregg was the best present she'd ever been given.

"You become a soprano when you sing that," Gregg chided.

"Because I learned it as a child. It's probably more falsetto now." She increased the speed of the windshield wipers. "The snow is coming faster, don't you think?"

"We were supposed to drive out of it by Springfield. The storm must be wider than forecasted. Are you okay driving?"

"Not if it gets worse. See if there's a news station that has a weather update."

Traffic was heavier and slower than when they left Collin's home in Middleburg. LouLou deliberately took the highways with salted roads that would make the trip longer, but she wanted to avoid snow-covered, two-lane roads. They passed a Miata that had skidded off onto the shoulder. The radio buzzed and fussed, but no distinguishable traffic news was broadcast.

"Nothing. I'll check the storm app." Gregg pulled LouLou's phone from her tote and pressed the weather icon. "No reception."

"That does it," she said. "I think we're near Stafford. I'll get off at the next exit. There's probably a motel there." LouLou crept up the left lane to switch to the far right lane. "Keep an eye out for exit signs."

Suddenly, everything before her was a mass of white. Two white tractor-trailers had collided, followed by a few cars. Snow was a barrier to seeing anything else clearly.

"Slow, slow," she said. "I've got room to stop."

She was talking more to herself than to Gregg. She gripped the wheel, sat up straighter, and took her foot off the accelerator.

Gregg rolled the passenger window down and up to shake off the sticking snow and gain a little extra vision.

"You've got it. We'll be good." Just as he spoke, the car behind them spun out of control and clipped the right rear end of LouLou's car, sending it off the road, and onto the median. It stopped, rammed into a row of pine trees.

"LouLou, are you okay?"

She could hear Gregg through layers and layers of consciousness. She floated above them. She watched Gregg immediately reach out to her. She saw herself slumped over the steering wheel. The airbag hadn't deployed. Gregg turned off the ignition.

She felt his fingers on her wrist—right where she had one of the suicidal razor tattoos—and muttered, "Good, not great."

She'd hit her head on the steering wheel. She vaguely felt Gregg touching her body. Not in a sexy way. He was checking for injuries. She was fine. He shouldn't bother. He gently lifted her head off the steering wheel and slid her seat back. He stuffed what felt like his plump knitted hat behind her head. He tried the cell again.

She could hear him get out of the car. No, he shouldn't do that. You're supposed to stay in the car when stranded. Where was he going?

When Gregg returned, he tucked a blanket around her. He held her gloved hands in his and rubbed them.

"LouLou, LouLou, wake up. Please wake up." He was almost crying. She wanted to wake up. She tried. He kept talking to her. Something about a Christmas angel on the highway, a pile-up, a red flag on the roof of the car.

She could feel it getting darker and colder outside. Why weren't they being helped? Gregg kept getting in and out of the car and running the heater for a few minutes. "Exhaust pipe," he'd said. She felt something soft covering her window. Her calves were being rubbed. She heard distant sirens.

"Gregg." She kept saying his name, but he didn't respond. Slowly, she opened her eyes and said it louder. "Gregg."

"LouLou, you're awake." He gave her a clumsy hug. "How do you feel? Are you hurt anywhere? Do you need anything?"

"Thirsty," she whispered. He put a bottle of water to her mouth and tilted it so she could have a few sips.

"Can you move your arms and legs?" She tried to move her legs, but felt there was too much heavy stuff on them. She'd have to take her boots off. She moved her hands and arms, bent her wrists, and wiggled her fingers.

"Good. You'll be okay. The important thing is to keep warm. Help is coming, but there are a lot of cars. Fifteen, maybe. Or twenty. I think we're near the back. It's snowing harder. Are you warm enough? We can only run the heat for ten minutes every half hour if there's no snow in the exhaust pipe."

LouLou smiled. "Boy Scout?"

"Navy family. Same thing."

"Seat belt?"

"I think you should keep it on in case someone else hits us from behind. Visibility is zero. We could be pushed deeper into the trees. Your seat is back as far as it can go."

She smelled acrid smoke. "Fire?"

"About half-mile ahead. Two trucks. One leaked fuel, but I heard it was contained. We're okay back here."

"What happened?" She was sleepy.

"People said a barefoot angel with enormous golden wings appeared in the middle southbound lane of the highway serenely holding the baby Jesus in a long blue wrap. Cars crashed trying to avoid hitting her, and the trucks crashed into everything in front of them. It sounds crazy, but that's what the drivers say they saw. They tried to stop."

"An angel. That's nice. Where is she?" she wondered.

"Disappeared. LouLou, are you sure you're warm enough?"

"Yes. Thank you for taking such good care of me." She reached her hand up to stroke his face. He pressed his face against her palm. She felt tears.

"What's wrong?"

"LouLou, it's almost time for me to leave you. I'll try to stay until EMS reaches us."

"Now? Why?" Suddenly, she was alert. She

wasn't drifty anymore.

"We knew it couldn't be forever. Now's the time. Promise me something."

He was fading. She couldn't make out his features and started to cry. "Anything, but please don't go. I love you. I love us."

"I love you. You're in my heart, but I can't control my being. It's time." He kissed her forehead. His voice was now a whisper. "Promise me whenever you feel like you're sinking under Sick, you'll go to a doctor. Don't stop taking your meds. You need them to live as much as you need air and music. Please."

She cried. "I'll try. I can barely see you."

"Promise me you won't just stop. Think of me."

"I promise." She looked toward the sound of his voice with longing. She was frightened because she couldn't see him.

Voices of rescue personnel were coming closer. Shouts. Orders. Screams.

She felt Gregg kiss her as deeply and passionately as she could remember. "I love you, LouLou. Always." His face, his voice, his body were gone.

"Gregg!"

The driver's side door jerked open, revealing the dark night. A reassuring and authoritative voice said, "Ma'am, are you okay? Looks like someone took really good care of you. You're warm, hydrated, and awake."

She looked at herself. She was covered by Gregg's parka and two blankets. Her feet were warmed by Gregg's blue sweater. She had two pairs of gloves on her hands. Another sweater insulated her window; a blanket curtained the passenger window.

Hands unbuckled her seat belt and encircled her bracelet. "Medic Alert. She needs meds. Check for a bag." Other hands helped her onto a gurney. "Ma'am. Ma'am, was there anyone with you? Did you have a passenger?"

Tears flowed and mixed with the still falling snow on her cheeks.

"Ma'am, is the person who helped you missing?"

She whispered, "No."

"Ma'am, are you sure? Should we be looking for someone?"

The falling snow felt like soft kisses on her eyes and lashes. Gregg's kisses.

"Ma'am?" She was being loaded into an ambulance. "Are you sure?"

"No one. I'm alone." LouLou closed her eyes.

Inside the ambulance, there was muted activity. She shared the bay with another patient. The shouts, noises, and lights outside seemed far away. They started moving. She kept her eyes closed and thought of Gregg.

She'd almost drifted into sleep when she heard a woman's voice. A beautiful, mellifluous soprano.

"LouLou, *ma petite fille*, you're not alone. I'm here. I'll take care of everything."

LouLou opened one eye. A stunning blonde woman about her age was sitting on the bench next to her, away from the EMS workers. She smelled like flowers. Amaryllis. Magnolia. A hint of boronia. Soft and serene. Her white blonde hair was swept to one side in a chignon. Her hands were powerfully delicate with long, graceful fingers. Her blue eyes were riveting. LouLou had never seen anything like them. They were mesmerizing. Hypnotic.

"Who are you?" she whispered.

The woman laughed a delicate bell-like lyric soprano that was lovely to hear.

"LouLou, *Je suis ta mère.*"

LouLou wondered what the woman meant. She spoke, or thought she did. "You don't look like anyone's mother."

That laugh again. "I consider that to be a compliment, but *c'est vrai*. I am your mother."

Bella was dead, but she could be a ghost, like Gregg. Someone who no longer lived in human form. And wanted something. Someone who wouldn't stop being a ghost until she got what she wanted.

"Bella?" LouLou asked. No, she had to get away from Bella. LouLou felt the ambulance stop. The doors to the ambulance swung open, and the antiseptic smells of a hospital invaded the bay. The other patient was unloaded first. Then LouLou.

"Bella?" she asked again and again as she was being gently unloaded.

"This one must have hit her head harder than we thought. She's pretty agitated. Take her straight for a CT scan," someone said about her.

"*Oui, ma petite fille.*"

"*Bella.*"

# About the Author

Born in Venice, Italy, Adam Zorzi is the author of Blind Spot, Blind Trust, and Blind Rage that comprise the Blind Justice Trilogy. He lives in New York.

**Facebook:**
https://www.facebook.com/profile.php?id=1000122
63627516&fref=ts

**Blind Justice Trilogy Facebook Page:**
https://www.facebook.com/BlindJusticeTrilogyAda
mZorzi/?fref=ts

**Twitter:**
https://twitter.com/adamzorzi

**Website:**
http://www.adamzorzi.com/

www.ingramcontent.com/pod-product-compliance
Lightning Source LLC
Chambersburg PA
CBHW031954130726
47904CB00013B/1478